Have Gender — Will Exchange

The Federation put the masculine mind of their greatest operative into the female body of Qwin Zhang. His/her job was to find the Lord who was working with enemy aliens and take control of the whole planet. And, of course, report back to the alter ego of his mind——by some means unknown to Zhang.

Being female and naked on a planet where utter ruthlessness was the major survival factor was a problem at first. But then he learned that on Cerberus, exchanging bodies was made routine by the symbiont bug——consciously or unconsciously. He could become male again——so long as he kept control.

He could also become immortal through such bodily exchange. And what kind of a damned fool would put duty to the Federation above a change to gain lordship of a planet——and immortality!

D0963780

Also by Jack L. Chalker
Published by Ballantine Books:

AND THE DEVIL WILL DRAG YOU UNDER

A JUNGLE OF STARS

THE SAGA OF THE WELL WORLD

THE FOUR LORDS OF THE DIAMOND

CERBERUS:
A Wolf in the Fold

Book Two of
THE FOUR LORDS OF THE DIAMOND

JACK L. CHALKER

A Del Rey Book

BALLANTINE BOOKS • NEW YORK

A Del Rey Book
Published by Ballantine Books

Library of Congress Catalog Card Number: 81-67840
ISBN 0-345-29371-1

Printed in Canada

First Edition: January 1982

Cover art by David B. Mattingly

For Richard Witter,
another unsung living
legend to whom the SF
community owes a great
deal

Contents

THE WARDEN DIAMOND

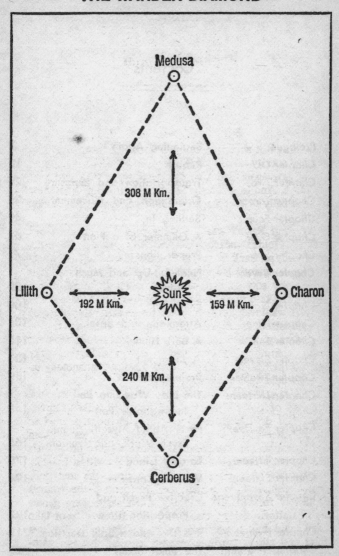

Beginning Again

═══════════

I

There was not supposed to be fear in the structured and ordered society of the civilized worlds; there was some sort of law against it. Clearly, there was nothing *to* fear any more. And in a society like that, somebody who knew the true folly of complacency could get away with almost anything.

Tonowah Resort was the standard for a standardized society. Golden beaches washed by warm, sparkling water and, set back from the ocean, a line of high-rise luxury hotels surrounded by exotic tropical plants and containing any sort of diversion that anybody might desire —from the traditional swimming, fishing, gambling, dancing, and whatever to the most exotic pleasure machines of a mechanized society. Leisure was big business in the Confederacy, where the basic manual-labor jobs were all totally computerized and human beings held jobs only because their leaders limited their absolute technology so people would have something to do.

Genetic and social engineering, of course, had reached the state of the art. People did not look alike. Experiments had demonstrated that such a direction tended to kill self-esteem in identical-looking people and cause them to strive, somehow, for the most bizarre ways to prove their uniqueness. Nonetheless, variety was kept within bounds. Still, people were all physically beautiful, the men uniformly trim, lean, muscular, and handsome, the women exquisitely formed and stunning. Both sexes were generally of uniform height, about 180 centimeters give or take a few, and had a uniform bronzed skin tone. Previous racial and ethnic features merged into an average with-

out extremes. Their family was the State, the all-powerful
Confederacy that controlled some seven thousand six
hundred and forty-two worlds over a third of the Milky
Way Galaxy; the worlds themselves had been terra-
formed to conform as much as possible one to another.
Medical science had progressed to the point that much
of what ailed people could be easily repaired, replaced,
or cured. An individual could remain young and beautiful until he died, quickly, quietly, at an age approaching
a hundred.

Children were unknown on the civilized worlds. Engineers did all the work and maintained the population stability at all times. Children were born in Confederacy labs
and raised in Confederacy group families in which they
were carefully monitored, carefully raised and controlled,
so that they thought as the Confederacy wished them to
think and behaved, as the Confederacy wished them to behave. Needed proclivities could be genetically programmed, and the child then raised with all he or she needed
to become the scientist, the engineer, the artist, the enter-
tainer, or, perhaps, the soldier the Confederacy required.
All were not equal, of course, but living in the civilized
worlds required only average intelligence, and only the
specialized jobs required geniuses. Besides, overly bright
people might become bored or question the values and
way of life of the civilized worlds.

There were worlds beyond the civilized worlds—the
and far between; in fact, the society of the civilized
worlds was the most egalitarian society ever known to
Man. Places were found outside the structure for obvious
aberrations. For those few who weren't detected until too
late, a small, specialized group known as Assassins fer-
reted out the rotten apples and eliminated the threat.

There were worlds beyond the civilized worlds—the
frontier, where nothing had yet been standardized. The
best Confederacy analyses had predicted early on that a
society such as the civilized worlds bred stagnancy and
loss of creativity and drive, thus ending innovation and
racial growth and eventually leading to the destruction of
the human race from internal rot. To prevent all that, a
small percentage of humanity was permitted to keep
pushing outward, discovering and conquering new worlds

and living in a more primitive style. Still subject to random gene mixing in the old tried and true ways, people out on the frontier were still very different-looking. Tight control was not exercised, for the Confederacy was not looking to make things easy out there. Hardship, deprivation, fierce competition, and aggression—all forced innovation, which was the safety valve for humanity, the system had worked for nine centuries because none were left to oppose the Confederacy—no alien races that could not be subjugated or eliminated easily, no competing empires that could threaten Man and his own empire.

Until now.

Until the nightmare theoreticians had warned about came to pass. Until there had come an enemy that so exploited the complacent egotism of the Confederacy that it could penetrate almost at will.

Juna Rhae 137 Decorator knew nothing of this. She was merely one of the products of the civilized worlds, a person whose job it was to meet with citizens wishing to alter their dwelling's appearance. She would sit down and discuss new layouts with them, run them and their psych profiles through her computers, and come up with new and different interior designs that would please her clients. As her name implied, she had been raised for this job, and since the Confederacy made few mistakes, she loved it and could think of no other citizen she would rather be. She was at Tonowah Resort just relaxing for a week, since she knew she would be busy for some time thereafter. She was about to face the greatest challenge of her career, a redesign of a Children's Family Center on Kuro that was switching its function from raising engineers to raising botanists, who, Confederacy computers projected, would be in short supply in about twenty years. Interior decorating was extremely important to career-based Family Centers, so she was looking forward to the challenge and was gratified by the confidence placed in her. Still, it would be a long time between vacations.

She had been swimming in the golden surf of Tonowah and just lying relaxed on the sand. Finally feeling relaxed and refreshed, she headed back to her luxury suite to shower and order a meal before deciding on the evening's activity. Once back in her room, she washed quickly and phoned for a meal—a real gourmet-type treat, she decided, at least for tonight. While waiting for her order, she was punching up clothing designs on the aptly named Fashion Plate, a device that contained over three million complete clothing elements with which to create personally designed outfits. Juna, like most people at resorts, dispensed with clothing during the day but wanted something stunning, complimentary, but casual for evening wear. In social situations she liked to be an object of attention, and it took clothes to accomplish that when everybody was gorgeous.

She completed the outfit, based upon a clinging evening dress of sparkling emerald green, and punched in the code knowing that it would be manufactured and would appear in her clothing delivery slot within half an hour.

The door buzzed, and she called for them to enter. A man dressed entirely in white stepped in, carring a covered golden tray. Resorts anachronistically retained human serving staffs, an extra touch of luxury; the men and women in the service industry loved what they were doing and would never do anything else.

He entered, not even glancing at her nakedness, put the tray down for a moment on a table, then picked it up again with both hands and triggered little switches on both sides. She heard a short buzz, and from under the tray dropped thin, strong supports. The man deftly triggered what he alone knew was there, and the tray became the centerpiece on an elegant, modern dining table. He then lifted the cover, and she gasped and smiled at the delights thus revealed.

Though much meal preparation was roboticized, the chefs were top creative artists, designing new food delicacies all the time, and certain parts of such meals were even supervised and partly created by hand. Top hotels and resorts provided real food, not the synthetics and simulations of day-to-day life. She tasted the first dish, smiled as if enraptured, and nodded to the waiter that all was excellent. He returned her smile, bowed, then turned and left.

When he returned more than half an hour later, she was out cold on the sofa. He went over to her, checked her physical condition, nodded absently to himself, then went back out and wheeled in a large laundry cart. He picked up her limp, naked body and placed it in the cart, covering her with some linen. Looking around, he spotted the lighted Fashion Plate and walked over to it and punched *Cancel,* then went to the master control panel and punched the *Clean-and-make-up room* button, which lit up. Satisfied, he pushed the cart easily out the sliding door and down the broad corridor toward the service entrance.

She awoke slowly, groggily, not comprehending what had happened to her. The last she remembered she had been eating that wonderful meal when suddenly she'd felt incredibly tired and dizzy. She had wondered if she'd been overdoing things and had leaned back on the couch to get hold of herself for a moment—and now, suddenly, she was . . .

Where?

It was a featureless plastic room of some kind—very small, walls and ceiling glowing for illumination, and furnished only with the tiny, primitive cot on which she lay. A section of the wall shimmered slightly, and she stared, curious but naively unfearful, as a man stepped into the room. Her eyes widened in surprise at his chunky build and primitive dress, and particularly at his long, curly hair and bushy beard, both flecked with gray. He was certainly not from the civilized worlds, she knew, and wondered what on earth was going on.

She started to get up but he motioned against it. "Just relax," he urged in a voice low and rough and yet somehow clinically detached, like a doctor's. "You are Juna Rhae 137 Decorator?"

She nodded, growing more and more curious.

He nodded, more to himself than to her. "Okay, then, you're the right one."

"The right one for what?" she wanted to know, feeling much better now. "Who are you? And where is this?"

"I'm Hurl Bogen, although that means nothing to you. As to where you are, you're in a space station in the Warden Diamond."

She sat up and frowned. "The Warden Diamond? Isn't

that some sort of . . . penal colony or something for frontier folk?"

He grinned. "Sort of, you might say. In which case you know what that makes me."

She stared at him. "How did I get here?"

"We kidnapped you," he responded matter-of-factly. "You'd be surprised how handy it is to have an agent in the resort service union. Everybody goes to a resort sooner or later. We drugged your food and our agent smuggled you out and offworld to a waiting ship, which brought you here. You've been here almost a day."

She had to chuckle. "This is some sort of resort game, right? A live-in thriller show? Things like this don't happen in real life."

The grin widened. "Oh, they happen, all right. We just make sure nobody much knows about it, and even if the Confederacy does find out, *they* make sure you never hear about it, either. No use panicking everybody."

"But *why?*"

"A fair question," he admitted. "Think of it this way. The Warden planets are a good prison because when you go there you catch a kind of disease that won't live outside the system. If you leave, you die. This—disease—it changes you, too. Makes you not quite human any more. Now, figure only the best of the worst get sent here. The rest get zapped or mindwiped or something. So what you have are four worlds full of folks with no love for humanity, being not quite human themselves. Now, figure some nonhuman race stumbles on humans and knows the two—them and the humans—will never get along. But the humans don't know yet that these aliens are around. You following me?"

She nodded, still not taking all this very seriously. She tried to remember if she'd ordered an experience program like this, but gave up. If she had, she wouldn't recognize what was going on as part of the program anyway.

"All right, so these aliens gotta know as much about humans as possible before they're discovered. They're much too nonhuman to go at it direct, and the Confederacy's much too regimented for raising human agents. So what do they do? They find out about the Warden

Diamond; they contact us and kinda hire us to do their dirty work for 'em. We're the best at that sort of thing—and down the road the payoff can be pretty good. Maybe getting rid of this Warden curse. You get it now?"

"Assuming for a moment I believe all this, which I most definitely do not," she responded, "where does that leave me? You just said yourself that none of your people can leave your worlds. And why a decorator, anyway? Why not a general or a security tech?"

"Oh, we got those too, of course. But you're right—we can't leave, not yet. But our friends, they got some real nice technology, they do. You'll see one of their robots in a minute. So human it's scary. That waiter who got you was a robot, too. A perfect replacement for the real person who once held that job."

"Robots," she scoffed. "They wouldn't fool anybody very long. Too many people know them."

The grin returned. "Sure—if they were just programmed and dropped in cold. But they're not. Duplicated in their nasty little minds will be every memory, every personality trait, every like and dislike, every good and bad thought you ever had. They'll be *you*, but they'll also take orders from us, and they'll be able to think and compute at many thousands of times the speed of you or me. They scare me sometimes because they could become us and replace us entirely. Lucky their makers aren't interested in that sort of thing."

She was beginning to fell uneasy now for the first time. Not only was this show very real—she would expect that —but it was passive, talky, not the kind of thriller show anybody would make up. But the alternative, that it *was* real, was too horrible to consider.

"So you can replace people with perfect robots," she managed. "So why a decorator?"

"One of our clerical agents spotted your entry in the routine contracts a few weeks ago. Consider, Juna Rhae, that your next job is to redo a child factory. A place where they're reprogramming to raise little botanists instead of little engineers, I think. Now, suppose *we* could do a little extra reprogramming there while you were going around replanning the place?"

She shuddered. This was too horrible for a horror script.

"Now," he continued, "we're set up. The moment you entered the Warden Diamond you were infected. Given a massive overdose of the pure stuff. Saturated with the Cerberan brand of the Warden bug. It'll take a while before you'll notice anything, several days or more, but it's already there, settling into every cell in your body."

The door shimmered again and through it stepped a woman, a woman of the civilized worlds, a woman more than vaguely familiar to her although she appeared blank, stiff, almost zombielike.

Bogen turned and nodded to the newcomer, then turned back to her. "Recognize this woman?"

She stared, feeling fear for the first time now. "It—it's *me*," she breathed.

Her other self reached out and pulled her to her feet with an iron grip. The strength in that one hand was beyond any human. The robot Juna Rhae took the human's hands and held them in a viselike grip with one hand while the other arm held her firmly around her waist. This hurt too much to be a show. She would never have ordered something like this!

"We Cerberans," Bogen said softly, "swap minds, you see."

2

The man reclined on a soft bedlike couch before an instrument-laden cluster in a small inner chamber of the space vehicle; he was wired, through some sort of helmet device, to the instruments around him. He looked tired, disturbed, and anxious.

"Hold it!" he called out.

The massive computer all around him seemed to pause for a brief moment. "Something wrong?" the computer asked, sounding genuinely concerned.

He sat up on the recliner. "Let me take a break before starting this next one. I don't think I can take two right on top of one another right now. Let me walk around, talk to a few people, generally relax, maybe even get some sleep. Then I'll be ready. The Confederacy is not going to fall if I wait ten or twelve hours."

"As you wish," the computer responded. "However, I do think that time is of the essence. This might be the one that tells us what we need to know."

"Maybe," the man sighed, taking off the helmet. "But we've been rotting here the better part of a year with nothing much to do. Another few hours won't mean anything. We'll probably need all four anyway, and nobody knows when the next two will come in."

"All that you say is logical and true," the computer admitted. "Still, I cannot help but wonder if your hesitancy is less governed by such practical matters."

"Huh? What do you mean?"

"The Lilith account has disturbed you a great deal. I can tell it by your body-function monitors."

He sighed. "You're right. Hell, that was *me*, remember. Me when I went down, and somebody I hardly knew at all when he reported. It's kind of a shock to discover that you don't know yourself at all."

"Still, the work must continue," the computer noted. "You are putting off the Cerberus report because you fear it. That is not a healthy situation."

"I'll *take* it!" he snapped. "Just give me a little breathing room!"

"As you wish. Shutting down module."

The man rose and walked back to his living quarters. He needed some depressant, he told himself. The pills were there, but he rejected them as not what he wanted. Human company. Civilized company from the civilized worlds, from the culture in which he'd been raised. A drink in the picket-ship bar, perhaps. Or two. Or more. And human beings . . .

In a system based on perfect order, uniformity, and harmony, the Warden Diamond was an insane asylum. Halden Warden, a Confederacy scout, had discovered the system well over two centuries earlier. Warden himself was a legend for the number of planets he had discovered, but was considered something of a nut, even for the sort of men and women who preferred to spend most of their time alone among uncharted stars. He loved his work, but he considered discovery his function, leaving just about everything else for those who would follow. He paused only long enough to take positions and beam back the information in as terse a form as possible. The trouble was, he was usually so terse people couldn't figure out what he meant until they got there—and for the Warden Diamond he was in top form.

His initial signal was a seemingly simple "4AW." The meaning of this signal was far from simple—it was impossible. It meant a single solar system with four inhabitable worlds, a statistical near impossibility in a galaxy in which only one out of four thousand solar systems contained anything remotely of use. It was Warden, though, who had found the impossible and named them. His entire report was pretty characteristic of his worst.

Charon—looks like Hell.

Lilith—anything that pretty's got to have a snake in it.

Cerberus—looks like a real dog.

Medusa—anybody who lives here would have to have rocks in his head.

And that was it. That, the coordinates, and the caution "ZZ," which meant that there was something about the place he didn't like but that he couldn't put his finger on. Dangerous—proceed with extreme caution.

When the first party, armed to the teeth, reached it, they immediately perceived what spooked Warden beyond the existence of the incredible four planets. They seemed to be at right angles to each other around their F-type star.

It turned out, of course, that this configuration was a freak occurrence—nobody since has seen the Diamond form as perfectly as Warden when he discovered it, and there was really nothing unnatural about such once-in-a-lifetime configurations, but the early name stuck. The Warden Diamond.

An enormous amount of space junk was in the system —asteroids, comets, you name it, as well as the usual gas giants—but the second through fifth planets were what held everyone spellbound. Each was within the life zone for temperature; all had atmospheres of nitrogen and oxygen, all had water.

Charon, at 158.551 million kilometers from its sun, was

a hot, steamy jungle world with bubbling mud and horrible heat and humidity. The dominant life form seemed to be large reptilian creatures that resembled the smaller dinosaurs. Indeed, the planet did look like some visions of hell.

Lilith, at 192.355 million kilometers, was an Eden, a warm paradise all over. Heavily forested, and rich in a variety of plant life, the planet was inhabited by insects from very small to tremendous. The fruit proved edible, the grasses versatile, and even the insects were sources of protein. It was a paradise, all right, with nary a snake in sight. Yet.

Cerberus, at 240.161 million kilometers, was colder, harsher, and the strangest of the four. It appeared to be covered by an enormous deep ocean without any land masses. However, the ocean was covered by a dense growth of plants so gigantic they rose more than two or three kilometers from the seabed to the surface and beyond, forming a riot of colors and supporting a surface plant ecosystem growing on the tops of the great plants themselves. You could build cities in those treetops, and, in the temperate zones, live very comfortably from a climate point of view. But with natural resources other than wood so far out of sight as to be unreachable if available at all and with such an odd place for living, the planet was something of a dog as far as possible settlement was concerned.

Finally there was Medusa, at 307.768 million kilometers, a cold, frozen world dotted with a few forests but covered mostly with tundra and polar ice. The only one of the four with obvious signs of volcanism, it was a hard, harsh land whose only inhabitants seemed to be a mammalian assembly of wandering herbivores preyed upon by some particularly nasty-looking carnivores. Medusa was ugly, bitter cold, and stark, compared not just to Lilith but to any of the others; the early explorers had to agree that anybody who voluntarily went to such a world to live and work would most likely have rocks in his head.

The Exploiter Team had chosen Lilith for its main base, naturally, and settled in. Nothing happened for about six months, as they lived and worked and studied under a rigid quarantine, although with their shuttlecraft

they had established preliminary camps on the other three
worlds as well. They were just beginning to relax when
Lilith's snake struck.

By the time all their machinery had ceased to function
it was already too late. They watched first as the power
drained out of all their equipment, then, frantically, as that
same equipment and all other offworld artifacts started to
break up into so much junk, rotting before their eyes.
Within a week there was simply no sign that anything
alien to Lilith had ever been there; everything was gone,
even their clearings being overgrown with astonishing
speed. Soon nothing at all was left—nothing but sixty-two
stunned, stark-naked scientists, bewildered and scared half
to death but without even the most elementary equipment
to explain to them that they hadn't all just gone stark staring mad.

The other worlds, too, had not escaped. All at one
point had been on Lilith, and they'd taken the snake back
home with them to the other three planets. Finally, using
remote probes, the combined scientific studies of a major
lab cruiser off the planets found the culprit—an alien organism like nothing else ever seen.

Submicroscopic, it lived in colonies within the cells.
Though not intelligent in any human sense, it did seem to
be able to enforce an amazing set of rules on an entire
planet, given an incredible capacity for evolving to meet
any threat to the ecosystem and subdue it. Living an entire life span in only three to five minutes, its ability to
evolve into whatever was necessary to obey its genetic
coding—to keep things as they were—was strong. Within
six months the organism had evolved enough to take care
of the human interlopers, attacking and corroding all non-
native materials and permeating and establishing a sym-
biotic relationship with the humans.

The other planets, however, held different fates for in-
truders. Different atmospheric balances, gravitational
forces, radiation intensities—all sorts of differences existed
on each, so this bug, this submicroscopic life form, could
not change those worlds into Lilith. Instead, the organism
changed. On Medusa it adapted the host organism to the
new environment, striking a balance that way. On Charon
and Cerberus it struck a balance within its hosts that was

to its liking but which caused bizarre side effects in those
hosts.

Worse, the Warden organism seemed to have some sort
of link to the solar system of its origin. Remove someone
infected by it and the Warden organism died—and sadly,
since the organism had modified every cell of the body to
to its own convenience, the host also died, horribly and
painfully. Humans could live in the Warden Diamond,
even travel in-system, but they could never ever leave.

Many scientists devoted their lives and careers to the
problem, deliberately trapping themselves on the Warden
worlds and establishing scientific colonies still run by descendants. But the solution, in the main, defied them—
which of course only infuriated them and spurred them on
all the more.

But it was not to be the scientists who would settle the
bulk of the Diamond; it was the criminal class. A utopian
system sophisticated enough to maintain a frontier did not
want to waste those people who had somehow found and
exploited flaws in their system. The cream of the criminal
class in a technological society was often the most brilliant
and innovative, but such deviates could hardly be allowed
in the civilized worlds or even tolerated for long on the
frontier. Until the discovery of the Warden Diamond,
these people had to be eliminated for the good of the
social order. Now it was possible to transport this criminal
elite, along with assorted political prisoners and other
social undesirables, to a place where they would be free
to be their immoral or amoral selves and still retain the
inventiveness necessary to come up with something the
Confederacy could use.

The perfect prison. Only, of course, what that accomplished was to place the most brilliant sociopathic—and
psychopathic—minds together in one place, in contact
with one another. They and their descendants built empires. Each world had unique attributes, held attractions
for those the Confederacy and its Assassins had not yet
caught. Cash could be shunted away to Cerberan and
Medusan banks; loot of all kinds could be hidden forever
on Charon or Cerberus until needed. Even Lilith, which
would tolerate nothing alien, was a true repository for
secrets channeled in and out of its protected orbital sat-

ellites to trusted members of the Lilith hierarchy. The
strongest, cleverest, and nastiest reached the top and
held power over planet-wide criminal syndicates whose
influence reached into the heart of the Confederacy. The
heads of these syndicates called themselves the Four Lords
of the Diamond, and they were doing a nice job getting
even with the society that sent them there. Now they were
working for an alien enemy that had the potential to
destroy the entire system, a fact the Confederacy discovered very late in the aliens' game—and almost by accident.

The humans had little defense, as the aliens surely had
realized. Agents sent to the Warden worlds faced almost
certain death if discovered. If not, they were stuck there
along with the criminal lords and their descendants and
subject people. The situation tended to make keeping an
agent loyal a big problem, since there was nothing he or
she could be offered as a reward and it was a lifetime job.
One such agent, a volunteer, became one of the Four
Lords himself.

Yet the Confederacy's only link to the alien menace
that might attack and destroy them at any time was the
Warden Diamond. They had to put not just agents down
there but their best—and they finally figured out a way to
do it, more or less. They took their best agent, an Assassin First Class of absolutely impeccable loyalty and devotion, and then introduced him to the Merton Process, by
which the personality and memories of someone could be
stored in a computer and then fed into other bodies.

The original minds in those surrogate bodies were of
course destroyed. Twenty or thirty individuals died before
a personality graft "took," but that was all right—they
were all antisocials anyway. Thus was their best agent
"placed" into four totally different bodies and dispatched
to the four Warden worlds. Once there, each had to act
alone to find out what he could of the alien menace and,
in any case, to accomplish a true Assassin's task—kill
each of the Four Lords of the Diamond, causing at least
a disruption in leadership that might buy the Confederacy
some time.

All the while the original Assassin sat in orbit off the
Warden worlds on the picket ship that enforced the quarantine and waited for his four alter egos to report so that

he could correlate what they found with his analytical computer.

Three of the four had within them a tiny organic transmitter that the computer and special satellites could pick up signals from and amplify, making them walking communicators on the surface. Raw data would be fed constantly to the analytical computer, then through a process called integration the computer and original agent could be linked, his own mind sorting the raw data bits into a subjective report that could be used to evaluate the raw data. The transmitter gave them what the alter ego on the planets said and did; the integration process gave what he thought.

The same man could thus be four different places at once while he also evaluated the information as an objective observer. Each agent would try to assassinate the Lord of his particular world; the original would try and take their experiences to solve the riddle of the alien menace.

But on Lilith things had gone both right and wrong. Right because the job had been done, but wrong in that the man had changed, or been changed, by his experiences, by his isolation, by his hatred of his other self up in space.

Two reports had come in almost at the same time. Lilith was taken first, and it shook the watcher's self-confidence and self-image. Nothing had happened the way it should have. The mission was on track, but in the process his own ego had somehow gotten derailed.

Cerberus would be the second report, and he was very nervous about facing it. He didn't fear for the mission—that was a different matter. He feared what he might find out about himself. But after a night in the ship's lounge and a fitful sleep that didn't help at all, he knew he would go back, knew he would undergo the process. He feared neither death nor any enemy, and in fact had only now found the one thing he *did* fear.

Himself.

And so he finally approached the reclining chair once again. Slowly, hesitantly, he relaxed, and the computer lowered the small probes which he placed around his head; the computer then administered the measured injections and began the master readout.

For a while he floated in a semihypnotic fog, but slowly the images began forming in his brain as they had before. Only now they seemed more definite, clearer, more like his own thoughts.

The drugs and small neural probes did their job. His own mind and personality receded, replaced by a similar, yet oddly different pattern.

"The agent is aware that no transmitter was possible with Cerberus," the computer reminded him. "It was necessary to land the needed equipment at predetermined points by remote and, at the time of cerebral imprinting, to place an absolute command to report at intervals. Subjectively, however, the process to you will be the same."

The agent didn't react, didn't think, just accepted the information. He was no longer himself, but someone else, someone like him and yet in many ways quite different.

"The agent is commanded to report," the computer ordered, sending the command deep into his own mind, a mind no longer his own. What would follow would be a sort of total recall from the mind of his counterpart down below, which his own mind would sort, classify, and edit into a coherent narrative, a narrative in the form of a report.

Recorders clicked on.

The man in the chair cleared his throat several times. It still took more than three hours to get him to do more than mumble some odd words or sounds, but computers are nothing if not patient, knowing that the man's mind was receiving a massive amount of data and struggling to cope with it.

Finally, though, as if in a dream, the man began to speak.

CHAPTER ONE

Rebirth

After being briefed by Commander Krega and a little preparation to put my own affairs in order—this would be a long assignment—I checked into the Confederacy Security Clinic. I'd been here many times before, of course, but not knowingly for this purpose. Mostly, this was where they programmed you with whatever information you'd need for a mission and where, too, you were "reintegrated." Naturally, the kind of work I did was often extralegal—a term I prefer to illegal, which implies criminal intent. All agents had their own experience of a mission wiped from their minds whenever it involved sensitive matters.

It may seem like a strange life, going about not knowing where you have been or what you've done, but it has its compensations. Because any potential enemy, military or political, knows you've been wiped, you can live a fairly normal, relaxed life outside of a mission structure. There's no purpose in coming after you—you have no knowledge of what you've done or why or for whom. In exchange for those blanks, an agent of the Confederacy lives a life of luxury and ease, with an almost unlimited supply of money and with all the comforts supplied. They have sensors in you that they constantly monitor and decide when you need a good refresher. I often wondered just how sophisticated those sensors were. The idea of having a whole security staff see all my debauchery and indiscretions used to worry me, but after a while I learned to ignore it. The life offered in exchange is just too nice. Besides, what could I do about it, anyway?

But when a mission came up it wasn't practical to forgo all the past experience you'd had. A wipe without storage simply wouldn't have been very practical, since a good agent gets better by not repeating his mistakes. So in the Security Clinic they kept everything you ever experienced on tap, and the first thing you did was go and get the rest of you put back so you would be whole for whatever they'd dreamed up this time.

It always amazed me when I got up from that chair with my past fully restored. Even the clear memories of the things I'd done always amazed me—*I* of all people had done this or that. The only difference this time, I knew, was that the process would be taken one step further. Not only would the complete me get up from that table, but the same memory pattern would be impressed on other minds, other bodies—as many as needed until a take was achieved.

I wondered what they'd be like, those four other versions of myself. Physically different, probably—the kind of offenders they got here weren't usually from the civilized worlds, where people had basically been standardized in the name of equality. No, these people would come from the frontier, from the traders and miners and freebooters that existed at the edge of expansion. They were certainly necessary in an expanding culture, since a high degree of individuality, self-reliance, originality, and creativity was required in the dangerous situations in which they lived.

The damned probe hurt like hell. Usually there was just some tingling, then a sensation much like sleep, and I woke up a few minutes later in the chair, myself once again. This time the tingling became a painful physical force that seemed to enter my skull, bounce around, then seize control of my head. It was as if a giant fist had grabbed my brain and squeezed, then released, then squeezed again in excruciating pulses. Instead of drifting off to sleep, I passed out.

I woke up and groaned slightly. The throbbing was gone, but the memory was still all too current and all too real. It was several minutes, I think, before I found enough strength to sit up.

The old memories flooded back as usual, and again I amazed myself by recalling my past exploits. I wondered if my surrogate selves would get similar treatment, considering they couldn't be wiped after this mission. That realization caused me to make a mental note that those surrogates would almost certainly have to be killed if they did receive my entire memory pattern. Otherwise, a lot of secrets would be loose on the Warden Diamond, many in the hands of people who'd know just what sort of use to make of them. No sooner had I had that thought than I had the odd feeling of *wrongness*. I looked around the small room in which I'd awakened and realized immediately the source of that feeling.

This wasn't the Security Clinic, wasn't anyplace I'd ever seen before. A tiny cubicle, about twelve cubic meters total, including the slightly higher than normal ceiling. In it was a small cot on which I'd awakened, a small basin and next to it a standard food port, and in the wall, a pull-down toilet. That was it. Nothing else—or was there?

I looked around and spotted the most obvious easily. Yes, I couldn't make a move without being visually and probably aurally monitored. The door was almost invisible and there was certainly no way to open it from inside. I knew immediately what sort of room I was in.

It was a prison cell.

Far worse than that, I could feel a faint vibration that had no single source. It wasn't irritating; in fact it was so dim as to be hardly noticeable, but I knew what it was. I was aboard a ship, moving somewhere through space. I stood up, reeling a bit from a slight bout of dizziness that soon passed, and looked down at my body. Looked down—and got what I think is the greatest shock of my life.

A woman's body. A Confederacy-standard woman at that. At that moment a tremendous shock and revulsion ran through me. First and foremost I was most solidly and assuredly male and liked things that way, but, worse, that body told me the most horrible of facts. I was not the original but a surrogate. *I'm one of them!* I thought in sheer panic. I sat back down on the cot, telling myself that it just wasn't possible. I knew who I was, remembered every bit, every detail of my life and work.

The shock gave way to anger and frustration. Not only was this female body foreign to me and my personality, but that very mind and personality wasn't real but a copy, an imitation of somebody else entirely, somebody still around, alive, possible monitoring my every move, perhaps my every thought. I hated him then, hated him with a pathological force beyond reason. He would sit there comfortable and safe, in his man's body, watching me work, watching me do it all—and, when the mission was over, he'd go home for debriefing, return to that easy life, while I—

They were going to dump me on a world of the Warden Diamond, trap me like some kind of master criminal, imprison me there, hold me there for the rest of my life— of this body's life, anyway. And then? When my job was done? I'd said it myself upon awakening—passed my own sentence. The things I knew! I would be monitored at all times, of course. Monitored and killed if I blew any of those secrets. Killed in any event at the completion of the assignment just for insurance's sake.

Well, I told myself, the system worked both ways. I knew how *he* thought, how *they* thought. This monitoring worked both ways. I was going to be a tough son of a bitch to kill. No, I thought, suddenly morose once more, not son. Did I in fact *want* to live the rest of my life in this body? I really didn't know. Not now, certainly—and not ever, deep down. And yet the tiniest of suspicions rested in the back of my mind that my attitude might be just what they had in mind. The perfect double trap for me. If that was the case, they were mistaken. If I began believing for one minute that they did this to me just so I wouldn't want to outlive my mission, I'd live a thousand years just to spite them. There was probably no such plot, though, I knew. Either they had an ulterior motive having to do with the mission that caused this, or they just didn't consider it one way or the other. I wished I knew.

But what about now, in any event? For now I'd bide my time, hold my peace, and adjust as best I could. Odd, in a way, how very *ordinary* and *normal* I felt. Arms, legs, head, all in the same places. A lot lighter in weight, yes, but that was relative; and being a little weaker in the arms wasn't anything you really noticed, particularly not in a barren prison cell. Only occasionally did I feel protrusions where none had been before, or the lack of something that had always been there. I knew here in an isolated cell I wouldn't be aware of the differences. Only later, down there, on whatever hellhole they dumped me, around lots of other people—*then* things would get rough.

I was very dry after waking and located a small water tap and cup in the wall just above the basin. I drank a good deal. Naturally, it went right through me, whereupon I discovered that having to piss was the same feeling only I now had to do it sitting down. I pulled down the toilet and sat and relieved myself—and got yet another shock.

The thing worked by skin contact—don't ask me how. I'm not one of the tech brains. It was not as good as a neural program, but it allowed them to talk to me in total privacy, even send me pictures only I could see and hear.

"I hope by now you are over the initial shock of who and what you are," Krega's voice came to me, so loud and clear it seemed impossible that none of the monitors could hear. "As you recall, the Merton Process of personality transfer is rather wasteful of bodies—roughly thirty die for one take, as it were—and of the first four that did take, one was this woman. We decided to use her for several reasons. She will put any Warden authorities off their guard if there's been any sort of leak about you, and Cerberus, the planet to which you are being sent, has unique properties that make your sex and age totally irrelevant. To calm you down, I suspect, I should tell you right off that Cerberans enjoy a natural form of the Merton Process—in fact we got the process partially by studies on Cerberus. In other words, you can expect to change bodies once or often down there, as well as sex, age, and all the rest."

I gave a half-startled cry at this thought and stood up, causing the toilet to flap back into the wall and flush. It worried me for a moment that I might have wiped the briefing; but because my old professional self was re-emerging, I knew that I would have to wait before finding out just to ward off any suspicion by my unseen jailers.

I walked back to the cot and sat down once again, but my mood had abruptly changed. Body switchers. That changed everything! I was suddenly *alive* again, alive and excited.

I'd had some nasty shocks, but the worst one was merely temporary. The other—the discovery that I wasn't who I thought I was but some artificial creation—was still there. The old life, the life I remembered even though I really hadn't personally experienced it, was gone forever. No more civilized worlds, no more casinos and beautiful women and all the money I could spend. And yet, as I sat there, I adjusted. That was why they'd picked me from the start. My ability to adjust and adapt to almost anything.

Memory, thought, personality—those were the individual, not the body that intelligence wore. *I was still me!* This was no different than a biological disguise of a particularly sophisticated sort. As to whom was really me—it seemed to me that this personality, these memories, were no more that other fellow's than my own. Until I got up from that chair back at the Security Clinic I'd really been somebody else anyway. A lot of me, my memories and training, had been missing. That old between-missions me was the artificial one, the created me. He, that nonentity playboy that presently did not exist, was the artificial personality. The real me was bottled up in storage in their psychosurgical computers and allowed to come out only when they needed it—and for good reason. Unlocked, I was as much a danger to the power structure as I was to whoever they set me against.

And I was good. The best, Krega had called me. That's why I was here, now, in this body, in this cell, on this ship. And I wouldn't be wiped this time—and now I was sure I would not permit them to kill me, either. Suddenly I no longer felt hatred toward that other me out there someplace. In fact I found I could no longer feel much of anything for him at all. When this was all over he'd be wiped once more—perhaps killed himself if my brother agents on the Diamond and I found out too much. At best he'd return to being that stagnant milquetoast. Not me. I'd still be here, still live on, the *real* one. A whole person. I would be more complete than he would.

I was under no illusions, though. Kill me they would, if they could, if I didn't do their bidding. They'd do it automatically, by robot satellite and without qualms. But my vulnerability would only last a short time—even less on Cerberus than elsewhere, since they would have to find out *who* I was as well and without the aid of biotracers or any other physiological gadget. I wondered how they were going to get me to report. I remembered Krega saying something about a thing implanted in the brain, but the moment I switched bodies that was useless. Probably there was some deep psychocommand to report, perhaps with the aid of agents or paid accomplices on Cerberus. I would get to that matter when I could. Until then, I'd do their dirty work for them. I had no choice, as they undoubtedly knew. During that vulnerable stage—who knew how long?—I was their property. After—well, we'd see.

The thrill of the challenge took over, as it always did. The puzzle to be solved, the objectives to be accomplished. I liked to win, and it was even easier when you felt nothing about the cause, just the challenge of the problem and the opponent and the physical and intellectual effort needed to meet that challenge. Find out about the alien menace. The outcome no longer concerned me directly, since I would be trapped on a Warden world from now on. If the aliens won the coming confrontation, the Wardens would survive as allies. If they lost—well, it would only maintain the status quo. This reduced the alien question to an abstract problem for me and made my situation perfect.

The other assignment created a similar situation. Seek out the Lord of Cerberus and kill him if I could. In a sense doing so would be more difficult, since I'd be operating on unfamiliar ground and would therefore require time and possibly allies. Another challenge. If I get him, I'd only increase my power and position on Cerberus. If he got me instead, then I wouldn't give a damn because I'd be dead. But the thought of losing is abhorrent to me. That set the contest in the best terms, from my point of view. Trackdown assassination was the ultimate game, since you won or you died and never had to live with the thought that you'd lost.

It suddenly occurred to me that the only real difference that probably existed between me and this Lord of the Diamond was that I was working *for* the law and he—or she—against it. But no, that wasn't right, either. On his world *he* was the law and I would be working against it. Perfect again. Dead heat on moral grounds.

The only thing that really bothered me was the disadvantage of not having a psychoprogram with everything I needed to know all neatly laid out for me in my mind. Probably, I thought, they hadn't done it this time because they'd had me on the table in four new bodies with four separate missions, and the transfer process to a new body was hard enough without trying to add anything afterward. Still, the omission put me in a deep pit. I sure hoped that the rest of that contact briefing recording hadn't wiped when I'd gotten up. It would be all I had.

Food came—a hot tray of tasteless muck with a thin plastic fork and knife that would dissolve into a sticky puddle in an hour or so, then dry up into a talclike powder. Standard for prisoners.

This being my first meal in some time, it wasn't long before I had to go once again, and so I faced convincingly my moment of truth with the toilet that talked.

"Now, as to this process"—Krega's voice, picking up right where we left off, gave me a tremendous feeling of relief—"we had to brief you this way because the transfer process is delicate enough as it is. Don't worry about it, though—it's permanent. We just prefer to allow as much time as possible for your brain patterns to fit in and adapt without subjecting the brain to further shock. Besides, we haven't the time to allow you to completely 'set in,' as it were. This will have to do, and I profoundly regret it, for I feel you have the trickiest task of the four."

I felt the old thrill creep in. The challenge . . . the challenge!

"As I said, your objective world is Cerberus. Like all the Diamond colonies, Cerberus is a madhouse. Third out from the Warden sun of the four Warden worlds, it is subject to seasons and ranges from a tropical equatorial zone to frozen polar caps. The most peculiar thing from a physical standpoint about the world is that it is a water world with no above-surface land masses. It is, however, a world abundant in life. The geological history is unknown, but apparently the sea covering was quite slow and the massive numbers of plants in its distant geological past kept their heads above water, so to speak. Thus almost half of the surface is covered with giant plants interwoven into complex networks, some with trunks tens of kilometers around—necessary support, since they are rooted in the seabed from a hundred meters to an impossible two to three kilometers below. The cities and towns of Cerberus are built atop these plants.

"No additional physical descriptions will be adequate, and you will be well briefed below by the governing officials upon landing. However, we feel a complete physical-political map would be useful and are thus going to imprint that map on your mind now."

I felt a sharp back pain, then a wave of dizziness and nausea that quickly cleared. Whereupon I found that I did in fact have a detailed map of the entirety of Cerberus in my head. It would be very handy. There followed a fast stream of facts on the place. It was roughly 40,000 kilometers around the equator, and its gravity was 1.02 norm, so close I'd hardly notice it. Equatorial and summer temperatures were a pleasant 26 to 27 degrees centigrade, mid-latitude spring and fall were between 12 and 13 degrees centigrade, chilly but not uncomfortable, and polar regions and mid-latitude winters could drop as low as 25 below, although the sea cover and the location of settlements along warm currents that the great plants also followed usually kept it well above that and relatively ice-free even in the worst of times.

A day was 23.65 standard hours, close enough to cause no major disruptions in my biological schedule, a pretty normal environment—if you liked water, anyway.

Cerberus was industrialized—I could hardly wait to see factories in the treetops—but lacked heavy metals or easily obtainable hard resources of any sort. Most of its ore and other needed industrial materials came from Medusa in exchange for finished goods, and from mines on the many moons of a gas giant much farther out. While technological, the Confederacy kept close tabs on what was built on Cerberus, and the industry, though good, was forcibly kept in obsolete channels. In effect this was the best of news, since there wouldn't be a machine on Cerberus I didn't know intimately or couldn't get complete details on from above. To ensure some technological retardation, there was the Warden organism, whose fancy name nobody used or remembered. It got into literally *everything*, right down to the molecules in a grain of sand, and it resisted "imported" materials—that is, materials that did not also have Warden organisms inside. Thanks to early exploration spreading the contagion from Lilith, this meant not only the four Warden worlds but, to my surprise, the seven barren but mineral-rich moons of the ringed giant Momrath, outside the zone of life. For some reason the Warden bug could still live were no others could, even way out there, but no further. Beyond Momrath the things died as they did going out-system.

"The Lord of Cerberus is Wagant Laroo," Krega's voice went on. "He was an important Confederacy politician until about thirty years ago, when he grew too ambitious and forgot his sacred oaths, taking his sector from the paths of civilization into his own private kingdom. As befitted his position and former contributions to the Confederacy, he was given the option of death or Warden exile; he chose the latter. He is a megalomaniac with delusions of godhood, but do not underestimate him. He has one of the most brilliant organizational minds the Confederacy ever produced, and it is coupled with total amorality and absolute ruthlessness. His power and rule extend far beyond Cerberus, for many antisocials within the Confederacy use Cerberus as a storehouse for hidden records, location of loot, and even the storage of blackmail. I fear I must warn you that, if the impossible happened and there was some sort of leak about you, he will know of it. No security is perfect, and this possibility must be considered."

I nodded to myself. Despite Krega's patriotic phrasing, few if any top Confederacy politicians were immune to scandal or blackmail on some level, and this guy was a master.

"Finding Laroo might well be impossible," Krega warned. "Cerberus has the Warden organism, but it is a mutated strain. More of this will be explained on orientation, but you must trust to the fact that bodies are as interchangeable as clothes on Cerberus. So even if you saw Laroo, had him pointed out to you and shook his hand, you could not be absolutely certain it was really he, and

even less certain that it would still be he days, hours, even
minutes later."

That didn't really bother me much. For one thing, if
Laroo had this kind of dictatorial control somebody always had to know who he was or he couldn't give the
orders and expect to be obeyed. Furthermore, a man like
that would love the actual trappings and exercise of
power. Then too, Laroo couldn't be at all certain who *I*
might be a few minutes, days, or weeks later, either.

"At last count there were approximately 18,700,000
people on Cerberus," Krega went on. "This is not a large
population, but it has a very high growth rate. There are
more jobs and space than people even now. Since the ad-
vent of Laroo's rule the population has been expanding at
a rate that almost doubles it every twenty years or so. We
believe that only part of this population push is economic,
though. Much of it, we think, is because, on a world of
body switchers, the potential for immortality exists if there
is a constant and available supply of young bodies. Laroo
seems to have some control over this process, which is the
ultimate political leverage. Naturally, this also means that,
short of being killed, Laroo could literally rule forever."

Immortality, I thought, and the idea sounded very
pleasant. How long will *you* live, my other original self? I,
sir, had an infinite answer to that one. Perhaps this was
not such a terrible assignment after all.

Krega had a lot more routine stuff for me, but finally
the lecture was over and I simply got off the john and
heard it flush. The next time I used it, I discovered that
this time the message had been flushed as well. Because it
had been a direct neural transmission, even with the interruption, it had taken only a minute or two for the whole
thing.

Efficient, the Security boys, I told myself. Even my
ever-vigilant jailers on the other end of those lenses and
mikes would have no idea I was anybody other than who
I was supposed to be.

As to who I was, that had come in a rush as well. I
was Qwin Zhang, forty-one, former freighter loadmaster
and expert smuggler, a virtuoso of the computerized load-
ing and inspection system. A technological crook—that
fit many of my own skills perfectly.

I lay back on the cot and put myself in a slight trance to better sort out the information I'd received. Qwin *did* bother me a bit. I could follow her life and career without ever really getting a handle on her. Born and bred to her job, normal Confederacy upbringing, no signs of any deviation from the normal path millions of others followed, the path set out for them from birth that they were not only *expected* to follow but *designed* to follow. I mentally followed the steps in her routine life and found nothing unusual, nothing to show what I was looking for.

And yet she stole. Stole expertly, methodically, and efficiently, even using the computer routing systems not only to shave cargo loads but actually to misdeliver them to waiting fencing operations out on the frontier. Stole almost from the start of her career, and so well she was caught only when a freak accident on a freighter with a bit more cargo than it was supposed to have caused a total inventory and alerted Security. She'd been probed and poked and studied, but there seemed little there. She'd stolen because she could, because the opportunity was there. She felt no guilt, no remorse for this "crime against civiliza--tion," and didn't seem to have any clear idea of what she would one day do with all that money had she gotten away with it.

Where was the corruption point? I couldn't find it, nor could the psych boys. What dreams had you had, Qwin Zhang? I mused. What event disillusioned you or turned you from the paths of righteousness? Some exotic love affair? If so, it wasn't anywhere to be found in what they gave me. Not much interest or history in sex of *any* sort. Perhaps the answer was there, somewhere in somebody's sexual theories of abnormal psychology, but it didn't really show.

Still, she'd been a nonetity. Her crimes depended on that, and such crimes were hidden, never publicized, lest others get ideas. Because she had had a norm body and looks and an average personality, it was unlikely anyone on Cerberus would ever have heard of her. That suited me just fine. The last thing I wanted was to bump into one of her old buddies down there. I wouldn't have the memories to match.

CHAPTER TWO

Transportation and Exposure

Except for regular meals there was no way to keep track of time, but it was a fairly long trip. They weren't wasting any money transporting prisoners by the fastest available routes, that was for sure.

Finally, though, we docked with the base ship a third of a light-year out from the Warden system. I knew it not so much by any sensation inside my cloister but by the lack of it—the vibration that had been my constant companion disappeared. Still, the routine wasn't varied. I suppose they were waiting for a large enough contingent from around the galaxy to make the final trip worthwhile.

All I could do was sit and go over the data again and again until I was comfortable with all of it. I reflected more than once that I probably wasn't very far from my old body (that's how I'd come to think of it). I wondered if he didn't occasionally come down to take a peek at me, at least from idle curiosity—me and the three others who were probably here also.

I had time to reflect on my knowledge of the Warden system, the reasons for its perfection as a prison. I had not, of course, swallowed that line whole—there was no such thing as a perfect prison, but this had to be close. Shortly after I was dropped on Cerberus I'd be infected with an oddball submicroscopic organism that would set up housekeeping in every cell of my body. There it would live, feeding off me, even earning its keep by keeping disease organisms, infections, and the like in check. The one thing that stuff had was a will to live, and it survived only if you did.

But it needed something, some trace element or some such that was only present in the Warden system. Nobody knew what and nobody had been able to do any real work to find out, but whatever it needed was found only in the Warden system. The element wasn't in the air, because in shuttles run between the worlds of the Diamond you could breathe the purified, mechanically produced stuff with no ill effects. Not in the food, either. They'd checked that. It was possible for one of the Warden people to live comfortably on synthetics in a totally isolated lab like a planetary space station. But get too far away, even with Warden food and Warden air, and the organism died. Since it had modified your cells to make itself at home, and those cells depended on the organism to keep working properly, you died, too—painfully and slowly, in horrible agony. That distance was roughly a quarter of a light-year out-system, which explained the location of the base ship.

All four worlds were more than climatologically different, too. The organism was consistent in what it did to you on each planet, but—possibly due to distance from the sun, since that seemed to be the determining factor in its life—it did different things to you depending on which world you were first exposed to it. Whatever it did stuck in just that fashion even if you later went to a different Warden world.

The organism seemed somehow to be vaguely telepathic in some way, although nobody could explain how. It certainly wasn't intelligent; at least it always behaved predictably. Still, most of the changes seemed to involve the colony in one person affecting the colony in another —or others. You provided the conscious control, if you could, and that determined your relative power over others and theirs over you. A pretty simple system, even if inexplicable.

I regretted not knowing more about Cerberus. This war far less briefing information than I was used to, although I understood their caution. It would cost me time, possibly a lot of it, to learn the ropes there and find out everything I needed to know to do my job.

About a day after I arrived—four meals' worth—there was a lurching and a lot of banging around that forced me to the cot and made me slightly seasick. Still, I wasn't disappointed; the activity meant they were making up consignments and readying for the in-system drop of these cells. I faced this idea with mixed emotions. On the one hand, I wanted desperately to be out of this little box, which provided nothing but endless, terrible boredom. On the other, when I next got out of the box it would be into a much larger and more attractive cell—the planet Cerberus itself, no less a jail for being an entire planet.

Shortly after all the banging started, it stopped. After a short, expectant pause, I felt again a more pronounced vibration than before, indicating movement. Either I was on a much smaller vessel or located nearer the drives.

Still, it took another four interminable days, twelve meals, to reach our destination. Long, certainly—but also fast for a sublight carrier, probably a modified and totally automated freighter.

The vibration stopped, and I knew we were in orbit. Again I had that dual feeling of trapped doom and exhilaration.

A crackling sound and a speaker I'd never known was there came to life. "Attention, all prisoners," it commanded, its voice a metallic parody of a man's baritone. "We have achieved orbit around the planet Cerberus in the Warden system." For the first time it occurred to me that others were also being sent down—logical, of course, but I'd never really considered it before. I knew what they all must be going through, considering my own feelings. Probably a hundred times mine, since at least I was going in with my eyes open, even if I was no more a volunteer than they had been. I wondered for a fleeting instant about Lord Laroo. Once he too sat here, naked in a common cell, feeling these same feelings and facing the same unknown future as we. He had started as low as I —lower, in fact, as a prisoner—and now he ran the place. Nobody had given the position to him on a platter, nobody had elected him. He'd gone in, naked and isolated as I was, and he'd conquered. And I certainly considered myself superior to such as Wagant Laroo.

That very line of thinking started me slightly. Was that *me,* aiming at becoming a criminal chief?

"In a moment," the voice continued, "the doors to your cells will slide open and you will be able to leave. We strongly recommend you do so, since thirty seconds after the doors open they will close again and a vacuum pump will begin sterilization operations within the cells, operations fatal to anyone who remains."

Nice touch, I reflected. Not only did it ensure against breakouts en route, but you moved or you died on their schedule. I couldn't help wondering if anyone had chosen death.

"Immediately after you enter the main corridor," the voice continued, "you will stand in place until the cell doors close once again. Do not attempt to move from in front of your cell door until it closes or automatic guard equipment will vaporize you. There will be no talking in the corridor. Anyone breaking silence or failing to obey orders precisely will be instantly dealt with. You will receive further instructions once the doors close. Ready to depart—*now!*"

The door slid open and I wasted no time in stepping out. A small white box, complete with marks for feet, showed you where to stand; I did as instructed, galling as all this was. There was something to being totally naked and isolated on a ship controlled only by computer that humbled you more than was right. It created a sense of total futility.

I could still look around and saw that I'd been right. The thing was basically a long sealed hall along the sides of which had been attached the little cells. I looked up and down and counted maybe a dozen, certainly no more than fifteen. The cream of the crop, I thought sourly. A dozen naked and bedraggled men and women—an equal number of each—beaten prisoners about to be dropped and left. I wondered why these had been chosen rather than wiped, considering the transportation expense alone. What had the computers and psych boys found in these dejected specimens that dictated they should live? *They* didn't know, that was for sure. I wondered who did.

The doors snapped shut. I waited expectantly, perhaps to hear the scream of somebody who didn't move fast enough as the air was pumped out, but there was no hint of melodrama. If anybody had taken that way out, the fact was not evident.

"At my command," the voice barked from speakers along the ceiling, "you will turn right and walk slowly, in single file, as far forward as you can. There you will find a special shuttle that will take you to the surface. You will take seats from the front first, leaving no empty seats between you. Strap yourselves in immediately."

I could hear some grumbling from the others, and suddenly small laser beams shot out, hitting the deck with an audibly nasty hiss down the line of people but hitting no one. The grumbling stopped.

The voice, pausing for this show of force, now took up its instructions with no reference to the demonstration. None was needed.

"Right turn *now!*" it commanded, and we did as instructed. "Walk slowly forward to the shuttle as instructed."

We walked silently, definitely in no hurry. The metal floor of the corridor was damned cold, though, and this made the shuttle at least preferable to this damned refrigerator.

The shuttle itself was surprisingly comfortable and modern, although the seats weren't made for naked bodies. I sat about six rows back and attached the safety straps, then waited until everyone had been seated and done the same. The shuttle itself could seat about twenty-four, but there were just thirteen of us, eight—no, *seven* males and six females. I kept forgetting who I was and what I was, and I scolded myself mentally for it. This was not the time for any lapses. The next day or two would be the most dangerous of all for me, since our new class would get a great deal of attention and they'd be particularly interested in any of those who didn't seem to be what they appeared.

The hatch closed automatically, followed by the hiss of pressurization. Then without further fanfare came a violent lurch and we were free of the transport and on our way down. The shuttle was much too modern and comfortable for mere prisoner transport, I told myself. This, then, was one of the interplanetary ships regularly used for transportation between worlds of the Warden Diamond.

The overhead speakers crackled, and a pleasant, human-sounding male voice came on. It was a great improvement. "Welcome to Cerberus," he said, sounding for all the world as if he meant it. "As has no doubt been explained to you, Cerberus is your final destination and new home. Although you will be unable to leave this solar system, once you get off below you will no longer be prisoners but citizens of the Warden Diamond. Confederacy rule ended when you entered this shuttle, one of many owned by the Warden worlds in common. The System Council is a corporate entity fully recognized as internally sovereign by the Confederacy and has its own seat in Congress. Each of the four worlds of our system is under its own sovereign and independent government."

The voice paused for a moment, and I reflected that it was odd not to hear anyone commenting, cheering, grumbling, or anything else. You could cut the tension with a knife, and I admit I felt it as much as the others.

"No matter who or what you've been in the past," the voice continued, "no matter what you've done or what your previous status was, you are now and forever citizens of Cerberus, nothing more—or less. You are no longer in any way prisoners and nothing you have done in the past will follow you here. You start with a clean slate and a clean record, and only what you do from this point on, as Cerberans, will matter."

Fair enough, I thought. The contrast in tone between this and the mechanical horror we'd first been exposed to was startling.

"We will be landing shortly," the voice continued, and I could feel the braking being applied and hear the whine as stabilizers deployed for in-atmosphere flight. "We would appreciate your getting off quickly after the hatch opens, as we must service this craft and return it to normal service. A government representative will meet you and take you to a place where you can get clothing, a good meal, and orientation. Please cooperate with this person and give no trouble. It wouldn't be a bright idea to start off on the wrong foot your first day on your new world."

Even a psycho could go along with them when the instructions were put that way, I told myself. They had such a *nice* way of making threats. Well, this was a world made up of and run by people just like those on the shuttle.

We made a long, slow approach, the pilot taking no chances, then finally settled into a berth of some sort. The caution warnings blinked out and the airlock hissed; when the hatches slid open, we undid our safety harnesses and got up, moving slowly and quietly toward the open area. This was it!

We filed slowly out into a long and modern passenger ramp, which was totally covered but not heated. It was chilly, and that sped us along. None of us could really think of the chill, though; all had been pushed out by a single, overriding fact.

The moment that chill had hit us, the moment that air reached our skin and nostrils and entered our bodies, we were systematically being invaded by a submicroscopic organism that was our new, and final, jailer. We were here, and free, but we were, from this moment on, also stuck.

CHAPTER THREE

Orientation and Placement

We entered a small lounge, and were greeted by two men and a woman, all dressed like soldiers in tight-fitting khaki uniforms and boots, although we quickly learned they were not military. We were given robes and sandals as a temporary measure; then our names were checked against a clipboard list and we were quickly ushered out of the terminal to a waiting air-bus. Robe or not, it was damned cold and the bus's heating system, though good, was hardly comfortable.

We lifted quickly and swung out away from the terminal, and with this maneuver we had our first look at our new world. It was a strange vista—the ocean gleaming in the sunlight to our right and the "shoreline" to our left, but shore it definitely was not. Rather, it was a dense-looking forest of reddish-brown and orange trees topped with huge, broad leaves of varying shapes and sizes. At many points the trees had been partially or completely cut into.

Clearly, people lived inside the trunks themselves—you could see sunlight reflected off windows. Here was a surrealist's vision, this great forest with trunks half resembling ancient, gnarled trees of tremendous size and half resembling a complex of modern office buildings. Often we could see where some of the great trunks branched, one had been cut off horizontally and then refinished or surfaced with some glossy material, providing landing platforms and entryways.

The woman in charge saw us gaping and smiled. Picking up a small PA mike, she became an impromptu tour guide. "Welcome to Cerberus. My name is Kerar, and my two associates are Monash and Silka. You are in the Borough of MaDell. We use boroughs here because the nature of the living space makes anything as dense as a big city nearly impossible. Fortunately, with efficient transit we are able to link up areas sufficient to make cities in economic terms, and that's what we call boroughs. As you can see, there is no land whatsoever on Cerberus. Biologists tell us that people were once tree-dwelling creatures. Here, of necessity, we have returned to our origins."

I kept looking out the window at the eerie tree-land. Somehow the whole place looked like a piece of furniture I once owned, with a support pole and several flat, cloverlike surfaces surrounding the stem as small shelves. Of course, this was much larger and rougher-looking, and not all the "shelves" were flat or barren, but it still had that look about it.

"You are seeing many different types of trees," Kerar continued. "There are over five thousand varieties of big trees on Cerberus, with about eighty different types in MaDell alone. As you can see, many types can be used extensively as dwellings, since much of the circulatory system goes around the outside of the trunk, allowing the trees to be hollowed out without killing them. A few are naturally hollow, although the outer bark in most parts is up to eight meters thick. They can support an enormous amount of weight because they get much thicker below the water's surface, and, over the millions of years they evolved, they also support each other. Master botanists have a special place here because they are responsible for telling us how many branches can be cut off for building and landing zones, and which ones, and also which architect's ideas for tree dwellings are practical and which are not. Mistakes can be costly. The death of one key tree might well undermine the support for a dozen, even hundreds more, in a mushroom effect that might kill our whole community."

I could see the point she was making—don't mess around with the trees. I wondered how many of the earliest pioneers had, and what sort of damage they'd wrought.

I looked out toward the ocean and caught sight of many boats, some quite large, others obviously pleasure craft— even some sailboats. Looking back into that fantastic jungle, I caught sight of a huge, imposing structure up ahead, a gleaming, modern building many stories tall sitting atop one of the cut-off sections, which, I was to learn, were called mesas on Cerberus.

"Up ahead is the government center for the borough," our guide informed us. "That is where we are heading."

We were ushered into the place and guided past curious onlookers to a tenth-floor room. There waiting for us was a hot buffet lunch. I frankly didn't recognize much of what was there, but after all that time on prison food it tasted just great. After we had eaten, while we were all just sitting around enjoying that stuffed feeling, an efficient little man came in and took our measurements. Within a hour he was back with some bundles, which turned out to be underwear, a pullover thick shirt, work pants, heavy socks, and low boots. Also included were belts and a full range of cosmetics and toiletries. In twos we were taken down the hall to a full lavatory complete with showers, which we all happily used; then we put on our clean, new clothes. I had little trouble with so simple an outfit despite the gender problem, but was thankful that my hair had been cut very short, prison-style. Come to think of it, though, Kerar's was short, too, although professionally cut and styled.

Finally, now that we were feeling human again, they decided we were ready for the full briefing. We sat in folding chairs while our guide gave us the basic stuff.

"The first world to be explored in the Warden system was Lilith," she began. "Lilith is a beautiful world, like a tropical garden. From their base camp, the first Exploiter Teams reached and set up bases on the other three Warden worlds, as well as examining the moons of Momrath, a huge gas giant further out. What they didn't know was that they were carrying an organism from Lilith, an alien thing like no other."

Briefly she recounted how the organism at last had struck Lilith, wiping out all manufactured things and reducing the population to primitive savages. Machines wouldn't work there, and the entire society was nontechnological. I couldn't help but think of my poor counterpart on Lilith. I was good, yes—the best. But I was born and raised and existed my entire life in a highly technological society. How would I be able to function in a nontechnological one? Would I be able to? I wondered, and felt more relieved that it wasn't my problem.

"The organism," Kerar went on, "was carried to the other places, where it thrived and mutated. There are many theories on this, the most logical being that it reacts to the sun's relative energy and perhaps the amount of solar wind itself, but nobody really knows. Here, as you can see, it did not destroy machines. On Lilith, its native world, it adapted men to the planet, made them a part of Lilith's ecosystem. Here *it* had to be the one to adapt, and it did. It's inside you now, moving in, making itself comfortable, settling down in every molecule of your body."

We all stirred at this unpleasant thought, which we'd managed to push to the back of our minds until now. It was funny—I didn't *feel* any different. No dizziness, no signs of anything out of the ordinary.

"Early scientists had the idea that the organism had some sort of collective intelligence," Kerar told us. "It became obvious that every single tiny subviral form was somehow in contact with every other one. We now know that they were only partly right. It *is* one organism, each one like a part of a cell to a huge body, but it doesn't *think*. Its behavior patterns are well known and quite consistent. Once you know how it acts, it will never surprise you.

"On Lilith, this intercommunication led to some people getting tremendous power, since the organism there exists in literally every molecule of solid matter. Some there can simply will a hole to be cut in rock, for example, or cause trees, fruit, even people to mutate. This works because some minds are so strong that they can transmit their will through the Warden organisms in their own body to others in people and things nearby. Here we have a different effect."

Again there were murmurs, and again I thought of my poor counterpart. Such a world would seem to be one of magic, and there magic alone worked.

"On Cerberus," our guide continued, "the organism is also in every molecule of solid matter. We've found it in tree samples taken by divers a full kilometer below the surface of the sea, and in the sea and air creatures themselves. As on Lilith, it doesn't like things that don't have Warden organisms inside them, and it will invade them as it has you. It seems to have a much easier time with organic molecules, though, particularly ones in living creatures, because it adapts to you with little trouble. Put a manufactured item from, say, the Confederacy here, though, and it will try and invade that, too—not very successfully. The stuff just doesn't work and usually falls apart. Fortunately, it doesn't care which kind of Warden creature is there, at least on Cerberus, so we can import raw materials, finished products, and food from our fraternal worlds, and with the exception of Lilith, export our goods to them. The Lilith original just won't take anything that upsets the primitive nature of the planet.

"Now, there are some good things about this invasion of your body. For one thing, since it depends on you to give it what it needs to live, it keeps you in tip-top shape. It purges your body of disease, so nobody gets sick. It cleans out the blood vessels and directs cellular repairs, so you don't get cancer, heart attacks, strokes, or whatever. Even things like drugs and alcohol, for the most part, will be purged before they can have any effect—with the exception of solids from the Warden system, and those are very rare and restricted. The worst you can do to yourself is get a little fat or out of condition. And of course the organism cannot retard the aging process, al-

though even there it keeps you in far better shape far
longer than normal."

That was an interesting benefit, I told myself. Still, no
more getting drunk or high or using any kind of recrea-
tional drugs. This was a *clean* world.

Kerar looked at us and smiled a bit, pausing before
dropping the other shoe, the one only she truly knew
about. "However, you are fortunate to have been sent to
Cerberus. Only the best are sent here. No murderers, no
persons with violent histories. This is not a violent world,
and for very good reason. You see, only we here on
Cerberus have the potential of living forever."

There it was—along with an interesting additional bit
of information. No violent criminals. I wondered why.

When the rest of the group had caught hold of itself,
she continued her orientation. "I told you that on Lilith
people could contact and command Warden organisms,
and control and change them. That does not happen here.
However, all the Warden organisms here are in constant
contact with others, with proximity being the guide. The
closer you are to somebody or something else, the more
contact the Warden organism has with the other. When
you are awake, your consciousness controls those within
your body and there is no problem and no effect. But if
you are tired, sleepy, or asleep, or in semiconscious or
unconscious state, the Warden organisms reach out to
others near them." She paused a moment, choosing her
words carefully. "I'll give you an example, with the understanding that we know *what* happens but we have
never discovered exactly *how* it happens.

"Let's say I go to sleep here next to you, and you fall
asleep too. Unlike those on Lilith, Warden organisms here
tend to communicate mostly with those in complementary
positions, so those inside you don't communicate with, or
link with, or whatever it is they do, those in rocks, trees,
and the like the same way they do to those in other people. Freed from conscious restraint, the Wardens in *your*
body would link with the Wardens in *my* body. This linkage would become strongest during the short periods of
sleep when we aren't dreaming. If two of those periods
match—mine and yours—the Warden organisms in your
brain and mine would link, and, for reasons we don't

understand, start to exchange information. Now, remember, I told you that the creatures are in every molecule and actually can cleanse, change, repair, or replace parts of your body to keep you healthy. In the same way, as a by-product of their very nature, they change the molecules in *your* cerebral cortex to *my* code and mine to yours, even adjusting the brain-wave pattern to match. It's done in a matter of minutes. Since memory is chemically stored and electrically retrieved, this means a total change of information within the brain. So you wake up with *my* memories and personality, and *I* wake up with yours. In effect, we have switched bodies."

"Then why don't they switch *all* the information?" a bearded young man to my left asked skeptically. "You should have hormonal imbalances, differentials in respiration and blood pressure—enough wrong commands tailored for the wrong body to cause it to be very wrong and very sick."

"Agreed," she responded. "Good question. The answer is simply that in the early days some of that happened, but it no longer does. The Warden organism is incredibly adaptable, and it exchanges information with other parts of itself, even with other organisms outside its physical form. It learned. As to *why* it wants to do so—well, we don't know. We're not even sure it does. The person may be a by-product of its unique life form. It may be some necessary adjustment to keep itself going in the Cerberan atmosphere. We don't know. I'm not sure we ever will. But it does happen, it has, and it almost certainly will continue."

"Have *you* ever switched bodies?" another skeptic asked.

She smiled. "Many times. I am a native, unlike you. The switching phenomenon comes with puberty—a rite of passage here, you might say. Adolescents here undergo many switches, particularly since that age is more highly emotional and so control is more difficult. Besides, what adolescent could resist the experimentation? Boys curious about what it's like to be a girl, vice versa—that sort of thing. I often wonder what it would be like to be trapped at birth in a particular gender and body. I, for example, was born male, but by the age of sixteen, having been in three male and two female bodies, I found myself more comfortable, somehow, as a female. I found a female who felt more comfortable as a male and we slept together and settled it. However, don't think we run around swapping bodies as often as we change clothes. We don't. Oh, some of us change often, and there are occasional marriages where the partners switch around constantly, but those cases are rare."

A thought had occurred to me early in her talk and I wanted to get the question out before it slipped away. "You said it takes several minutes to exchange minds during this sleep," I noted. "What happens if you're awakened in the middle of it?"

"Normally, once the exchange begins it can't be stopped—you remain comatose, as it were, even if the building's burning down," she replied. "However, there are cases—very rare—when this happens. You're right to bring it up, since it occurs only among people from Outside like yourselves. The odds, I should emphasize, are one in a million, even to you. The transfer is all at once, so to speak, so all of the molecules in your brain start their rearrangement together. If you are jolted awake early in the process, you'll have a dim remembrance of that other life which will usually fade. If this happens late in the transfer, you'll have a period of psychological problems, a sort of schizophrenia, but that too will pass and the dominant information will control. But if the process is just about exactly half over, then both of you will be in both bodies. There is a lot of extra space in the cerebrum and the new information will slowly shift to the unused parts, creating either a total split personality— two minds in one body, alternating—or a merger into a new personality that is a combination of both. And, understand, this will be the case for *both* bodies. But I wouldn't worry; there have been less than twenty such cases in the history of Cerberus. You almost have to do it deliberately, and nobody wants that."

I nodded. Those seemed like favorable odds. She returned to her basic briefing once more, with a new question from a woman on the end.

"What happens," she was asked, "when a switch occurs to someone in a critically skilled field? I mean, suppose your doctor now has the mind of your janitor? How can you tell?"

"That was an early problem," we were told. "In a non-technological age or setting, like Lilith's, it probably wouldn't have been solvable. Fortunately, tiny electrical patterns in the brain set up to handle our specific memories are unique to each individual. The new brain adjusts to the new pattern. We have sensitive devices able to read and record that distinctive electrical 'signature,' and you'll find them all over the place. Before you leave here today we'll take your imprint and this will open your account in the master planetary computer. Early imprint reading devices were quite bulky, but now it's a simple device quickly and easily used, and it is used for everything. There is no money here, for example. You are paid according to job and status directly into your computer account. Any time you wish to make a purchase, your imprint is read and compared to your identity card. As you can see, it is virtually impossible for anyone to masquerade as someone else, since it is a crime not to report a body change within eight hours of its occurrence." She paused for a moment, then added, "For a society founded by what the Confederacy calls criminals, Cerberus has probably the most crime-free civilization in man's history."

I could see that this thought disturbed some of the others, and it disturbed me to an extent, too. In the most literal sense of the word, this was probably the most totalitarian society ever built. Not that crime here was impossible—the society was computer-dependent, and anything computer-dependent could be manipulated. But the system had few weak spots, and the ultimate penalty of death for crimes was even more terrifying here, in a society where it might be possible to move from body to body and stay young—if there was a supply of bodies, and if the government let you.

Were there old people here? I wondered. And if not, where did all the new, fresh bodies come from?

After another meal, they interviewed each of us in turn and had us take some basic placement tests, a few of which were familiar. The interview went smoothly enough, since their file on Qwin Zhang was no better than the one

fed me and I could be creative where necessary with little
fear of tripping up. But the personality tests, both written
and by machine, were much, much more difficult. I had
spent many months in classes and exercises learning how
to get around such things, how to give the examiners the
picture I wanted them to have—it involved knowing
everything from the theory of testing to the exact nature
of the psych probe machines used, as well as self-
hypnotism and total body control—and I felt reasonably
certain that nothing thrown at me was not properly and
correctly countered.

Later still we were holographically photographed and
fingerprinted, had our retinal patterns taken, that sort of
thing, and were also hooked up to a large machine the
operative part of which looked like a test pilot's crash
helmet. This, then, was the imprint-taker. A bit later we
were taken in and a small headset with three fingerlike
probes was lowered on our foreheads and a check made
on a computer screen. Apparently the big apparatus was
used only for the recording of the imprint; the little device would be the familiar control mechanism for checking it. There was no sensation with either device, and
therefore no way to figure out how they operated, something I very much wanted to know. Unless you could fool
or defeat that system any authority could trace your life
exactly—where you were, whom you were with, what
you bought, literally everything.

In the evening they brought in cots for us. Apparently
we were to remain there several days—until the Warden
organism had "acclimated" itself to us—while they decided what to do with us. A book on the basic organization of the planet was provided, too. Dry but fascinating
reading, including a great deal of detail about the social
and economic structure.

Politically there were several hundred boroughs, each
with a central administration. Some were quite small, others huge, and seemed to be based on economic specialties
as much as anything. The Chief Administrator of each
borough was elected by the Chairmen of the Syndicate
Councils in each borough. The syndicates were also economic units, composed of corporations of similar types, all
apparently privately owned stock companies. The eco-

nomic system was, then, basic corporate syndicalism. It works rather simply, really: all the like companies—steel, say—get together to form a syndicate headed by a government specialist on steel. The needs of the government and the private sectors are spelled out, and each steel company is given a share of all that business based on its size and productivity, guaranteeing it business and a profit, that margin also set by the syndicate and government expert—the Steel Minister, let's call him. The only competitive factor is that a corporation within the syndicate which markedly increases productivity—does a better job, in other words, perhaps for less and thereby increasing its profits—will get a bigger share of the next quarter's business.

Extend this to every single raw materials and basic manufacturing business and you have a command economy, thoroughly under government control and management, that nonetheless rewards innovation and is profit-motivated. Only on the retail level would there be independent businesspeople, but even they would be under government control, since with profit margins fixed all wholesale prices would also be fixed. Then, using something as simple as borough zoning and business licenses, the government could apportion retail outlets where the people and need was. Because no money changed hands and the government handled even the simplest purchases electronically, there could be no hidden bank accounts, no stash of cash, nor even much barter—since all commodities would be allocated by and kept track of by the syndicates.

Nice and neat. No wonder there were so few crimes, even without the ultimate punishment angle.

From the individual's viewpoint, he or she was a free employee. But since the ultimate control was the governments, you'd better not make the syndicate mad or you might find yourself unemployed—and being unemployed for more than three months for reasons other than medical in this society was a crime punishable by forced labor. It seemed that those basic raw materials came mostly from mines and works on several moons of Momrath, and the mining syndicate was always eager for new workers.

To do anything you needed your identity card, which

contained all your physical data, including your photo, but no name or personal details. That was on a programmable little microchip in the card itself which could be changed automatically should someone else find himself or herself in your body. Not to report a change was a crime punishable by being locked in an undesirable body and packed off to a lifetime of meaningful labor under the shine of beautiful Momrath.

The next day I asked our hosts how it would be possible to lock someone into a body, and was told that some people, through sheer concentration and force of will, could essentially "cut off" your Warden beasties from sufficient contact to make a switch. These people, called judges, were on call to the government; they didn't judge but merely carried out sentences. Top judges working together could actually force a transfer, too.

And of course there it was. Older, undesirable bodies were always around, and you could reward the faithful with a young, new body while shipping the malefactor off to Momrath until he or she dropped dead.

Chief industries were light manufacturing in general, computers and computer design, weapons, tools, all manner of wood products, seafood protein, and fertilizer. They even exported some of this stuff beyond the Warden system, something I hadn't realized was possible. It was even possible to "sterilize" some types of things, mostly inorganic compounds, and keep them together and working. That led to an obvious connection. That very human robot that had broken into the defense computers, for example. Was it possible that somewhere here among the more primitive machines, at least one place was turning out these sophisticated robots to some alien-supplied design? And if so, was there here some sort of programming genius capable of turning out robots so real they would fool even close friends and family, as had the alien robot? It sounded and felt right. No violent criminals here, they said. Only technological ones. The best.

By our fourth day all of us were becoming bored and restless. As much as could be learned in any brief period had already been taught us, so obviously we were being kept here at this point only for reasons not yet revealed by our hosts. For me, the wait was getting dangerous, since several of the prisoners had formed casual liaisons and I'd been propositioned repeatedly. Pressure mounted as I became a "challenge" to a couple of the men. I had no desire for any such experience, not in *this* body, but the situation was causing a social gap to open between me and the others. I wanted this waiting over with and for us to be out in the world as soon as possible.

I also wanted classification, something they certainly should have been able to do long before now, considering all the tests. I'd tried to angle the aptitude parts heavily toward computers and math, since not only was that consistent with the individual I was supposed to be but also that was where the greatest potential for moving up and finding out things might be. Besides, I'd listed a high level of expertise on many of the older-type computers in use here.

Near the end of the fourth day it hit me just what we *were* waiting for. Obviously, if some measure of control was needed, they didn't want to throw us Cerberan virgins out before we knew just what the Warden facts of life would be. Close proximity, they'd said.

All those cots all close together.

Acclimation, they'd told us, took three or four days, so it was about right. They were waiting, then, until the morning when all or most of us woke up in different bodies.

That thought brought up a mental dilemma for me. If we had to switch to leave, I'd rather leave as a man—but because of the personal problem I noted, I'd been sleeping off in a corner nearest the other women but more or less to myself. How many days would it take? I wondered. And did I have the skill and the guts to get on with this? I finally decided I had to give it a try or be trapped on the wrong side. So I picked my man carefully with an eye to age, looks, physical condition, and the like. Fortunately, my candidate, Hull Bruska, was a shy, somewhat gentle-seeming man who had caused me the least problems. His crime was even more remote from people than Qwin's had been. Apparently he'd managed electronically to tap and shift small parts of planetary budgets into frontier accounts, all from a small repair service on one of the civilized worlds. He was somewhat proud of his accomplishment, and not at all hesitant to talk about it. The cause of his downfall, ironically, was that he was too successful. Too much money showed up in the accounts of several frontier banks, the kind that attracts security police just because of the size of the assets. Obviously he needed to use more than the four banks he did to spread it out. When a bank's assets quadruple in less than two years without apparent cause, you *know* somebody's going to ask how, but Bruska's forte was machines, not the fine points of getting away with the spoils.

Curiously, he had no real plans for the money. He'd done it, he told me, mostly out of boredom. After nine years of repair and redesign of financial computers he'd simply worked it out as a mental exercise, "more or less for fun." Then when he'd put his plan into action just to see if it would work, and it had, doing it again became sort of irresistible, almost to see how much he could get away with. "I wasn't really hurting anybody," he explained, "and there was a tiny bit of satisfaction in fooling the whole Confederacy, of putting one over on them. Kinda made them human."

I liked Bruska, who also enjoyed talking about himself enough that we never got through the hand-holding stage that night. He was shy enough as a man that maybe, I hoped, becoming a woman would open up a whole new social life for him.

We slept very close, my cot against a wall and his next to mine to minimize any risks on my part. I fell asleep that night hoping against hope I'd get lucky, and quickly.

DATA REPORT INTERRUPTION. END TRANSMISSION DIRECT TRANSCEIVER. AS SUBJECT LEFT ORIGINAL BODY, ORGANIC TRANSMITTER LINK BROKEN. SUBSEQUENT REPORTS VIA READOUT BY SUBCONSCIOUS DEEP-PROBE HYPNOTIC COMMAND INTO DEVICES SUPPLIED, CUED, NATIVE AGENTS IN OUR EMPLOY. RUN NEXT SEQUENCE READOUT. SUBJECT UNAWARE OF COMPULSION OR READOUT.

CHAPTER FOUR

Settling In

All but four of us changed bodies during that fourth night. Luck being with me, I was once again young, male, and Confederacy standard, although Bruska didn't really accept the swap with good grace. They separated all of us quickly to minimize the trauma, and I was assured that good psychs would help those who needed it to adjust.

They did a complete set of tests once again, mostly on the psych side, to determine if any of us not showing severe distress were actually hiding it. Naturally I passed with flying colors. I was overjoyed at my carefully planned result.

I also found that the two most objectionable men had changed with their female partners during that night, which I considered poetic justice. Let them find out how unpleasant men like them could be from the other side; then perhaps if they got to be men again they'd be better and more considerate.

The small ID card was simply placed in a slot. I was told it would work from *any* slot for it, in stores or even to unlock doors, if you first called the number of the Identity Placement Bureau and told them which slot you were using. Basically, Bruska's name and computer code were erased from the little chip and mine were placed there. They did a check with the brain-reading machine to make sure all worked okay, and it had, so at last I was given an assignment.

"Tooker Compucorp in Medlam needs programmers," I was told, "and your experience fits that bill. Two hundred units have been credited to your account compliments of the government, which will be enough

49

to get you there and get you settled. It's a good company and a good location if you like the tropics. Warm there most of the year."

And with little more than this and some instructions on how to buy things like clothes and tickets and who to see, I was off.

I found that the little three-pronged gadgets were literally everywhere. To get on the shuttle to Medlam you walked up, put your card in the slot, and put on the little device. If everything checked, the fare was deducted from your account and your card returned to you, and in this case a physical ticket was printed. Very efficient and very simple.

I also found that a number of small purchases worked just with the card—newspapers, confections, that sort of thing.

It was a long ride with a lot of stops and several times I had to keep myself from dozing off—the situation could get serious if somebody else was dozing, too. Fortunately the shuttle had a small food service dispensing system where you could get stimulant drinks, including a Cerberan version of coffee and another of tea, and snacks. I drank a lot of stimulant drinks along the way and needed all of them.

I arrived late in the afternoon, but got a robocab to the Tooker offices anyway on the off-chance that I wouldn't be too late for that day.

The place was imposing, that was for sure. Glassy windows lined towering tree trunks all around, and in between, cradled like some play treehouse for the impossibly rich, an imposing all-glass-fronted office building that connected to all the vast trunks. This, then, was Tooker.

The main offices had already closed for the day, but the night staff was very cordial and recommended a nearby hotel for the night. The hotel, entirely in a massive trunk, was modern and luxurious inside. Nervously, I called the Central Banking number to see how much I still had left after all this, and was surprised and relieved to find that I still had 168.72 units in my account.

The only unusual thing about the room was that there was a switch in the headboard of the bed with a sign that read: TURN BEFORE SLEEPING. I discovered that turning it raised plating around the bed from floor to ceiling, plates of some thin but firm plasticlike substance through which ran metal threads of some sort.

Claustrophobia, then, was a real problem on Cerberus. The shield was obviously there to ensure a good night's sleep with no unexpected exchanges. I wondered what sort of distance would be the maximum range for a sleep exchange and decided I'd have to know that. I asked one of the desk employees about it, and he, upon finding I was new, told me that the shields weren't necessary in the hotel and that almost nobody used them, but they were there because some big shots became paranoid. Although in some cases, an exchange could take place at up to twenty meters, the walls, floor, and ceiling of all rooms were treated to shield. That made me feel a little better, and I didn't use the shield again that evening.

The room vision monitors were no help, since they seemed composed of years-old bad programming from the civilized worlds and some really horrible and amateurish local programming, but I got a print-out of the local paper and looked it over. Not much there, either—not big-city scope at all; more like the vacuous weeklies produced in some rural areas. The only unique item was a small column back with the classifieds for personals and announcements called "switched," followed by a double column of names—maybe a dozen pairs. One way to know who your friends really were here, I reflected.

In fact, the ads were the only things of real interest. There was evidently a small but thriving competitive sector on consumer goods allowed between the corporations, assuring a variety of goods at less than totally uniform prices. On the civilized worlds, of course, there were few brands of anything. For example, the best tested and most recommended toothpaste was everybody's toothpaste, perhaps in three or four flavors, and there were no brands or competition. Here there was, for the first time since I'd been on the frontier, and I found I kind of liked it.

There were also banks, although they were not such full-service institutions as those with which I was familiar. Apparently you could take some of your units out of the

master account and place it with a bank at interest, and
also borrow money from such banks. There was therefore a semi-independent subeconomy here, and that too
was worth noting.

Judging from the want ads, Tooker was the big employer, but many other places also advertised, so some
movement was possible on one's own. The independent
merchants advertised a lot for part-time help, too, suggesting some economic disparity and also indicating that,
even if the executive offices closed in the late afternoon,
Tooker operated around the clock in many divisions.

To my surprise, some churches were listed—in fact, a
fair number of them for just about every belief under
the sun, including some new to me that sounded pretty
bizarre. Also part-time schools to better yourself or your
position, lots of the usual stuff like that.

That brought up a point, and I checked the local phone
directory. No schools for the young were listed anywhere,
nor were there any headings for day care or other services
for children or parents. Obviously I still had gaps to fill
in for this new culture.

Medlam, being subtropical, seemed to have a number of resorts and tourist-oriented stuff, including several
for "Thrilling Charter Bork Hunts!" whatever a bork
was.

Interestingly, nowhere, not in the briefing, not in the
guide book, nor anywhere else was there reference to
Wagant Laroo. The Lord of Cerberus certainly kept a
low profile.

The next day I checked out bright and early and
showed up at the Tooker personnel office. They were
expecting me and quickly processed me into the corporation. The job was thirty-eight hours a week at 2.75 units
per hour, although that could increase up to 9.00 units
with seniority in my assistant's position and even more
should I move up. I definitely intended on moving up. I
was told, too, that I was a Class I Individual, which was
reserved for those with special skills. Class I's kept the
same job regardless of body. Class II's kept the same *job*
regardless of who was inside the body. There was also
a Class III for unskilled workers who could switch jobs if
they and their employers agreed—a sort of safety valve,

I guessed. Idly I asked what happened if a I and II switched, and was told matter-of-factly that in that case the decision on who did what was made by the government, usually getting judges to switch them back forcibly.

"Take my advice if you're the kind that likes switching around," the personnel manager told me. "Switch only with other I's. It's simpler and causes no trouble."

"I doubt if I'll do much switching in the near future," I assured him. "Not voluntarily, anyway."

He nodded. "Just remember the possibilities and guard against them, and you never will switch unless you want to, and then only with *whom* you want. And when you're gettin' older and want a new start—well, that's up to you. Stay clean, work hard, and make youself indispensable or at least important—that is the best insurance. Make 'em *want* to give you a new body every thirty years or so. That's the best way."

I nodded soberly. "Thanks. I'll remember that." Of course I had no intention of settling into a regular routine for that long a time. But I *did* need some time like that, time to get to know people and get to know the world and the society. Patience is the greatest of virtues if you're going to subvert a society, and there's no substitute for preparation.

I would like to say that during the next four months I did all sorts of daring and exciting things, but the truth is that there are only brief moments like that in a job like mine—all the rest is boring, plodding stuff. The corporation provided me with subsidized housing—a comfortable tree-lined flat with full kitchen, air conditioning, and the rest that was quite pleasant. The job they started me at was anything but demanding, and the speed with which I "assisted" designers in improving new circuit designs marked me quickly for bigger and better things, particularly since I was careful to let my superiors take the credit while keeping evidence of who really did the work—evidence they knew about. This put them in my debt without my seeming threatening. I could have hogged full credit and had not. In a word, I was becoming indispensable, at least to the next level above

me, like the man said. It was child's play, actually, since
the designs used on Cerberus were a good ten or even
twenty years out of date and quite limited in one area.
No self-aware computers of any kind were allowed here.
That was really the key to retardation in the Warden Diamond, and a clever one on the part of the Confederacy,
which was very real, even here. You didn't have to land
or even enter the atmosphere to wipe an entire borough
off the face of the planet, and they'd do that as an object
lesson if they got wind of any bending of the rules.

In point of fact, that very primitiveness imposed on
the planet aided me over many other technological mas-
terminds, since most or all of them were trained and
developed on machines too advanced for here. There
were very few of us, really, who could do the utmost
with the older designs.

I made a number of friends and quickly became a
social gadfly. The corporation had a lot of teams competing against other corporate employee teams in just about
every sport I knew. After working out regularly and fine-
tuning this body I now wore, I excelled at them, as
usual, though I was never able to get myself up to the
physical peak of my original body.

Bork hunting, however, I passed on, at least for the
time. It seemed that bork were monstrous, nasty creatures that inhabited the oceans, seemed to be composed
entirely of teeth, and occasionally grew large enough to
swallow boats whole. They had a natural dislike of everything and everybody and were even known to attack
boats just for being there and sometimes even to snare
a low-flying shuttle. Hunting them just required too
many specialized skills, and that sport had no initial ap-
peal for me. Though bork were nasty, the oceans contained an enormous number of creatures that had some
commercial uses, from unicellular protein creatures that
linked together into floating beds kilometers long to
smaller sea creatures that provided edible meat, skins,
and other such things. Bork hunting might be a thrill for
some, but to the ocean harvesting corporations it was a
commercial necessity.

The flying creatures with such names as geeks and
gops, made me wonder just what sort of person first

named all these things. The flying things, mostly small, served the function of insects on other worlds, cross-pollinating this jungle from the top. In addition, there were a few predatory fliers that were monsters, too. One giant flier with a thick barrel-like body about a meter around had a neck more than three meters long and a wingspread of more than ten meters. Its head looked like a nightmare of blazing reptilian eyes and sharp teeth, but nobody much paid attention to them as long as they didn't come too close. These were carrion eaters mostly, and they remained aloft over the oceans much of the time.

Body switching was rare, although I was approached once or twice in a casual way. Every once in a while somebody new would show up who would turn out to be somebody old after all. Although few people switched—except for the occasional couple that switched almost nightly, always with each other—the subject was nonetheless a regular topic of conversation in lounges and at parties. The possibility was always there, around you, even if you didn't see it. You were reminded of it constantly when you went home or stayed at a hotel on a company trip, and you always slept shielded and alone, no matter how friendly or intimate you became with others.

There were some topics nobody really referred to, though. One was children—you just didn't discuss it—and second was advancing age. Few people you met looked any older than forty, and those who looked the oldest seemed much more jittery and under a lot more pressure than most.

Body switching ended any sort of sexual stereotypes, to a greater extent even than on the civilized worlds. When gender could so easily be exchanged, it seemed silly to think of separate sexual roles, particularly since it seemed that all the women I met had been sterilized. That, too, interested me—this was true of both sexes on the civilized worlds, where all breeding was done in bio breeding centers, but the actuality seemed particularly peculiar here. So when I saw the pregnant girl, I was drawn irresistibly to her.

* * *

I had taken to frequenting a small store near the docks which specialized in entertainment electronics and which seemed to have some sort of a remarkable underground connection stretching off-world at some point that got a lot of the latest performances from the civilized worlds. Here was a piece of home, a place where you might run into other former prisoners, now exiles like myself, there also to get a little taste and memory of what was lost.

She was there one day, looking over the latest selections. A tiny young woman—it was impossible to think of her other than as a girl. From her looks, she could hardly have been out of her mid-teens. She had extremely long reddish-brown hair, perhaps a meter or more in length, that was held loosely with a brightly sparkling headband.

Actually, I wouldn't have known she was pregnant except for Otah, the owner of the place. I happened to be talking gadgets with him, as usual, when I spotted her. "Hmmm. Cute. Never saw *her* around here before."

"You stay away from that one," Otah warned gravely. "She's with child."

I frowned. "First time I've heard *that* here. I was beginning to wonder how any of the natives came about. But what's the taboo?"

"Pregnant. Don't you know? It's not a condition, it's a Class II occupation."

Well, there it was at last. "It's a *job?* She makes a living having babies?"

He nodded. "Hell of a thing, ain't it? There's a whole colony of them down off Akeba. There's some that love it, but most of 'em would kill to switch bodies outta there. Once you're that, you're *that.* Best to keep 'em on a business basis only."

I had to chuckle. "What do they do? Steal your soul?"

He looked stricken. "Don't say that. Some of 'em's desperate enough to do most anything."

I couldn't help but chuckle at his caution and wonder just what could be so horrible. I *did* sort of wonder about the whole idea, though. Cloning was certainly within the allowable technology, if they wanted to spend the massive setup costs. Instead they seemed to have opted to take a percentage of young women, probably selected

I had to admit it was sounding less and less pleasant. I was beginning to see why Laroo's assumption of power had been accompanied by a population increase all out of proportion to the numbers. Although the system probably predated him, he would order stepped-up life quotas strictly out of paranoia. The top leadership's one nightmare would be a declining birthrate.

"Surely you can quit. A simple operation—"

She laughed derisively. "Sure. And forget all about being reborn into a new body. Because you lack any useful skills, there's only the dirtiest labor jobs to make any sort of a living, and that would be only if they let you. Most likely you'd just not find a job, be declared a vagrant, and then it's a one-way trip to the mines, or maybe they'd just knock you off. Those mines are mostly automated—most folks don't think too many people are really sent anywhere."

More information to file, but the subject was becoming increasingly unpleasant. "I don't know about that lack of useful skills, though," I told her. "You have a pretty good vocabulary."

She shrugged. "Mostly self-taught. You get bored and have to do something, A lot of girls are artists or try and write stuff or things like that. Me, I just read and watch Otah's bootlegs. Hell, I'm just twenty, bore four kids with another comin' in six months, and I'm already climbing the walls. I got fifteen, maybe twenty more years of this before they let me out. And you know what they'll do? Give me another fifteen-year-old girl's body and put me back at it again! After twenty years I'd be an expert at nothin' but motherhood."

The bitterness and frustration in her voice was very real, and for the first time I understood Otah's attitude and the attitude of most Cerberans toward both the mothers and the subject of children. Nobody liked to think of children, since they realized that was where their new bodies would come from. Having once been young themselves, they really didn't like to think they were robbing some kid of a lifetime, advancing him or her from fifteen or forty-five in one step, perhaps condemning him or her to death or forced labor on some airless moon. They knew—but they wanted to live, wanted *their* new bodies, and so they just didn't talk about it, tried not to think about it, on the grounds that facts ignored were not facts at all. Seeing those who bore those children brought up all the guilt, so they were treated in the same way as people with some horrible disease. And they *did* carry such a plague—it was called conscience.

What this told me was that they had already sold their souls. Sold them to Wagant Laroo. The population of Cerberus took on a whole new light for me that day, there in the bright sunshine and salt air. I remembered old horror stories of vampires—the living dead who drank the blood of the living to survive, to be immortal. And that's what Cerberus really was—a planet of vampires.

You're lucky to be sent to Cerberus. Here you might live forever!

Yeah, in absolute slavery to a government that could grant you eternal life—at the cost of an innocent child's life—or take it away.

"I don't understand why they don't just invest in cloning," I told her. "They would still control the bodies and thus the people."

"They can't," she told me. "The Warden organism can't cope with a clone in the early stages. The natural way's the only way on any of the Diamond worlds."

Well, so much for the easy way out, I told myself. Still, there had to be better ways than this. Better managed with less heartbreak. I took a fresh look at Sanda Tyne. Tragic figure, perhaps, but the ultimate vampire herself.

"I would think the lure of eternal life wouldn't be enough for some people," I noted. "Some might prefer death."

"Not outside the motherhood," she responded. "And inside, yes, you're right. But they monitor us *very* carefully for signs of depression and suicidal tendencies. Almost nobody really goes through with it—maybe two or three a year. The rest—well, I guess the will to live is too strong. And if you try it and don't make it, they can put you through the ringer. You don't have to have much of a brain to do what we do. They take you into a little room, point a little laser probe here"—she pointed to her forehead—"and *zap!* You walk around with this nice little smile on your face and you don't do or think of nothin', but you can still have babies." She shivered. "I think I'd rather die than that—but you see? The penalty for *not* dyin' is so much worse."

What a cheery afternoon I'm having, I thought sourly. Still, I truly understood and sympathized with Sanda and the others like her. There *were* better ways, I felt sure. Not less cruel, perhaps, to some of the children, for there would be a revolution here if the new bodies for old potential was destroyed, but at least for the people like Sanda. A technological world should allow mothers to be anything they wanted as well, and it should be able to meet its need not only to grow but also to replace. There was a simple system that would at least put the responsibility where it belonged.

Everyone could be forced to bear his own replacement. *Then* he alone would have the option of killing his offspring or himself in the normal way. And, with body switching, assuming sterility was ended, everyone *could* bear his own replacement. That it was the only fair way. It wouldn't end cruelty to the kids who got stuck as replacements, but far fewer would take that option—and nobody could sweep the responsibility under a mental rug.

This body-switching business sounded great at the beginning, but I was beginning now to see it for what it was —a disease. A disease that was population-wide and *required* a totalitarian system to maintain.

This realization made my assignment easier—and more urgent. I no longer had any thought whatsoever about *not* doing away with Wagant Laroo. And, at least for the period of time needed to create a real social revolution on Cerberus, I intended to be Lord myself.

CHAPTER FIVE

A Glimmer of a Plan

Over the next few weeks I continued to meet with Sanda, whom I not only felt sorry for but genuinely liked. She seemed to enjoy the company of someone from a place she would never see and a background she could hardly imagine—one who treated her as a person, not a pariah. I was, however, becoming restless and a little impatient. By this point I felt I had enough contacts and enough elements put together to get into action. But I lacked the proper starting point, the opening I needed to have any chance of success.

My long-range objective was clear: locate and kill Wagant Laroo, then somehow assume political control of the syndicalist machinery that would allow me to retailor this world for the better. The fact that my plan dovetailed with the wishes of the Confederacy was all to the good, since I didn't want any problems from that quarter and I knew that somehow they were keeping tabs on me, probably with the aid of blackmailable agents down here —exiles with family or something else to lose back home.

My experience at Tooker convinced me that computer and robotic science on Cerberus was too far behind the Confederacy to be directly linked to the alien robots, but I still had suspicions. At least a few really good minds in the organic computer field had wound up here. Though their names occasionally cropped up in shoptalk at parties and the like, they were nowhere in evidence. Of course Tooker wasn't the only or even the largest computer firm on Cerberus, but it was definitely a middleweight in the economic mainstream, unlikely to be left out of any major deals. Part of the trouble was I was still too low down in the hierarchical ranks to even hear the rumors of anything so secret.

Therefore, several steps had to be taken before I could even consider Laroo, one being I first had to make friends in high places who could be of help with such information as well as with favors. I also needed considerably more money than I had or could easily make—and some way to conceal it if I *could* figure out a way. Not that I couldn't steal money from banks—that was relatively easy with this computer system. The trouble was, money had to be put somewhere. In an all-electronic currency system it would show a conspicuous bulge. To disguise a stash properly would take a major operation with major resources. In other words, it would take a fortune to steal and hide a fortune.

Finally, after money and influence, I'd need somebody on the inside of Laroo's top operation. No mean trick. But that was the last of my problems and was contingent on the other two.

I traveled to Akeba one weekend mostly thinking these dark thoughts and hoping something would break my way. I had to go down there now to see Sanda, who was starting to show and so was generally restricted to her area, more by social custom than by any firm law.

Akeba House was a huge complex located on its own network. It resembled the hotel I'd stayed in my first night in town. I could see a swimming pool, various game courts, and other resortlike additions, and was told there were more such inside. But it was restricted territory, so I could get only to the gate.

Sanda had left a message for me at the gatehouse that she was down on the docks. I took the public elevator down. Just outside the compound was a small complex of commerical trawlers and bork-hunting boats, mostly the commercial type that protected the watermen rather than the sports charter type.

Sanda, out on a dock next to a formidable-looking hunter-killer boat, spotted me, called, and waved. I ambled over, wondering what she was doing down here.

"Qwin! Come on! I want you to meet Dylan Kohl!" she told me, and together we boarded the boat. It was sleek and functional with twenty-five centimeters or more of armor plate, a retractable hydrofoil, and a nasty-looking cannon. The vessel looked more like a warship than a commercial boat. I'd never been on one before, but found it fascinating.

Dylan Kohl turned out to be a tall, tanned, muscular-looking young woman wearing a sunshade, dark glasses, some very brief shorts and tennis shoes. Smoking a huge, fat Charon-import cigar, she was working on some sort of electronics console near the forward turret. At our approach, she dropped a small tool and turned to meet us.

"So you're Qwin," she said, her voice low and hard, putting out a hand. "I've heard a lot about you."

I shook the hand. A hell of a grip, I noted. "And you're Dylan Kohl, about whom I've never heard a word up to this moment," I responded.

She laughed. "Well, until you came along I was the only conversation Sanda had on a more than business basis outside the House."

"Dylan's a rare hope," Sanda added. "She's the only person I know who ever got out of the motherhood."

That raised my eyebrows. "Oh? And how'd you manage that? I've been hearing how impossible it was."

"Is," Dylan told me. "I cheated. I did it crooked, I admit, but I never regretted doing so. I drugged my way out."

"Drugged? Even caffeine and other stimulants usually get pushed out in an hour or less."

She nodded. "Some drugs work. Stuff distilled from Warden plants, particularly ones from Lilith. Strictly controlled, government use only—but I managed to get a little of a hypnotic. Let's not go into how. Swapped with a Class II dockworker."

We walked back to the aft section behind the pilot house, which had been set up as a sun deck while in port. I settled into a chair and so did Sanda. Dylan went below and returned with some refreshing-looking drinks laced with fruit. She then stretched out on a collapsible chaise longue. I tried the drink—a little too sweet for my taste, but not at all bad.

Dylan's hard, determined manner contrasted sharply with Sanda's. No matter what body she'd originally had, it was hard to imagine her as a professional mother.

"This dock down here did it," she began. "Watching the boats go in and out, hearing the stories, seeing the expressions on the faces of those who went out and came back every day. I don't know. Something in my head, I guess. I've had a lot of lovers, but I've been married to the sea ever since I can remember. It showed, I think— the water people would always talk to me. We had the same feelings. One of 'em finally took a risk and smuggled me out on a run. I was hooked. I knew that no matter what happened somehow I had to work the boats. Just shows that if you have enough smarts and you want something bad enough you can get it. I keep telling Sanda that when she's down."

I smiled and nodded. I was beginning to like Dylan Kohl quite a bit. Although I didn't share her love for the sea, in general attitudes her mind paralleled my own.

"This is your boat, I take it?"

She nodded "Every rivet and plate. Once I was out of the House I was determined to make myself a Class I secure, and to do it with boat work. I'd go out with 'em on my own from time to time, filling in where they needed help while doing my dock cleanup job. When openings came along, I got signed on as crew. There are usually openings in this business, but you gotta be crazy to be in it to begin with. On a world where everybody's trying to live forever I love a job where you get to be captain by surviving long enough. Eventually you either have your own boat or get swallowed whole or in little pieces. I wouldn't have it any other way."

"You're the captain, then?"

She nodded. "Shorter time than most, I'm told. Four years. I'm the sole survivor of her original crew of six. They were a pretty sloppy bunch, though—it's why I picked 'em."

Here was one tough woman, I told myself. And, I guess, you had to be in this kind of business. As she said, most Cerberans tried as hard as they could to stay away from any sort of danger, with death feared far more than any place where people died naturally and normally. But in her business you constantly courted danger. It was often fatal business.

"Ever been on a bork hunt?" she asked.

I shook my head slowly from side to side. "No, never really had the inclination after seeing the pictures."

"Aw, there's nothing like it," she enthused. "Going in and out against the thing at thirty to forty knots, your skill, knowledge, and reflexes against the monster's. You don't feel bad about killing them, either—they're so nasty and good-for-nothing. And you're saving the lives and livelihood of the salts who work the deeps. You feel good about it—and I am good at it. In seven months now as cap I haven't lost a crew member. Why, just the other day we were down off Laroo's Island and we—"

"What!" I exclaimed, almost rising to my feet. "Where?"

She stopped and appeared slightly annoyed at being interrupted. "Why, Laroo's Island. It's a little out of my territory, about a hundred and forty kilometers southeast of here, but we got to chasing a big one. A real challenge. You get like that."

"You mean Wagant Laroo?"

"There's two?"

Suddenly I was very interested in bork hunting.

Carefully, though, I steered the conversation away from Laroo and back into her tales of the hunt, which she obviously enjoyed repeating to a new audience. I could see Sanda with stars in her eyes at hearing all this. Even if she didn't feel like hunting borks, Dylan Kohl was the embodiment of her ideal. The hero-worship went really deep.

Inwardly, though, I felt some excitement and mentally checked my programmed map of Cerberus—nothing marked "Laroo's Island" on it. Taking a look to the southeast of Akeba, I detected only a couple of possibilities, isolated groves of great trees separated from the main body by perhaps thirty or more kilometers.

I began to see an unseen overhand in my current position and location. The Warden worlds weren't as free of some Confederacy machinations as they liked to think.

I saw more of Dylan after that, generally but not always accompanied by Sanda, and eventually eked out more information on Laroo's Island. The Lord of Cerberus was a secretive man, one who enjoyed power but not the celebrity that usually went with it. The island was neither the headquarters of the government nor his official residence, but he was there as often as possible.

The place was reputed to be truly grand, the ultimate in resorts. It was also constantly patrolled by air and ship, approaches monitored by just about every known surveillance system. If somehow you beat it, you then had to pass a brain scan to keep from getting creamed automatically. It was in fact as nearly impregnable a fortress as the Lord of the Diamond, Boss of all Bosses, Chairman of the Council of Syndicates, could design.

Like all absolute dictators, Wagant Laroo feared assassination the most—and more than any others, since that was the only way of getting rid of him or allowing his syndicate chiefs to move up to the top themselves. He himself had gotten the job by judicious and legally untraceable eliminations.

Well, I didn't want to wait twenty or thirty years to move up the ladder. Not only did I not have *that* much patience, but there was more of a chance that something would go wrong in such a slow rise than by the more direct route. But the challenge was becoming irresistible on its own merits. The little-seen political boss in his impregnable fortress! Just perfect.

All the elements were now in place for a break when it presented itself, and it did so a bit sooner than expected, judging by the worried expression on Turgan Sugal's face. Sugal was the Tooker plant manager, a pretty good one who took an extraordinary interest in every facet of the business. Even those of us on the lowest end of the seniority scale knew him, for he was always about, checking on us, making suggestions, socializing, playing on all the company teams. He was, in fact, a very popular boss, and highly accessible. He'd been around a while, too. Although his current body was barely thirty, he was said to be almost a hundred years old.

He looked the hundred, though, when he dropped down to my department to tell me he wouldn't be able to play in the company cordball game that evening. I was captain of the team.

"What's the matter?" I asked him, genuinely concerned. "You look like a man about to have his head chopped off."

"Not quite that bad," he responded glumly, "but bad enough. We just got the next quarter's production quota and allocations from the syndicate. They're sky-high. At the same time they're yanking several key people from me for some big project upstairs. Khamgirt's been out to get me for years, and he's dropped the whole load on my shoulders. I don't see how we can meet the quotas with a reduced force, and it's my neck if we don't."

"Can't you lay off some of the stuff to the other plants?" I asked. "Or get some help from them on personnel, anyway?"

He shook his head. "Normally, yeah, but Khamgirt really means business this time and he's refused. He's never liked my way of doing business, anyway, and canning me has always been a big goal." He paused and chuckled. "And you thought when you were the boss you didn't have to worry about this kind of shit any more, didn't you?"

I returned the chuckle. "No, I know the score very well. Remember, I had a long life and job before I ever got to this planet."

He nodded. "Yeah. That's right—you're from Outside. I keep forgetting. Maybe that's why you're easier to talk to, huh?"

"A damn sight cheaper than a psych, anyway," I joked, but my mind was already working. Here it was, I could *feel* it. Here was the break, the start in the chain that would eventually lead me to Wagant Laroo.

"Tell me, Mr. Sugal," I said slowly, choosing my pace with care, "how would things go next quarter if President Khamgirt wasn't president any more?"

He paused and looked at me quizzically. "What are you suggesting? That I kill him? That's damned hard and you know it."

That statement gave me an inward chuckle, since Khamgirt was a little enough fish that I could probably have taken him out effortlessly. But I hardly wanted to betray myself as a pro in that area. Not yet. Too many other nervous bosses would see me as a threat.

"Uh-uh," I answered him. "I'm talking about getting *him* canned."

Sugal snorted derisively. "Hell, Zhang, you'd have to prove gross incompetence, direct and prolonged mismanagement, or criminal intent against the state—and as much as I hate the son of a bitch, I don't think he's guilty of any of those things."

"Whether he is or isn't is beside the point," I told him. "Suppose I could hang one of those on him anyway?"

"Are you crazy? What you're saying is impossible!" he responded, but he sat down.

"Not only not impossible, but not even that hard if a little luck is riding with me—and it usually is. I'm pretty sure such a thing has been done before, many times. I studied the histories of a lot of our syndicate bosses and corporation presidents. This is a technological world founded by technological criminals, Mr. Sugal. Founded by them and run by them."

He shook his head in disbelief. "That's absurd. I would have heard about it."

"Would they tell you? So you could do it to them? Look, even Laroo has been on Cerberus less time than you've been around by far, and look what happened to him."

Sugal considered that. "How would you do it?"

"Given, say, a week and a little inside information. I'll know exactly. I have a rough plan in mind, but it'll need fine-tuning, the kind that can only come when it has a specific objective and target."

He looked at me somewhat uneasily. "And why would you do this? For me? Don't give me that bull."

"No, for me. What would happen to your position if I could do it? Where would that leave you?"

"Probably as a senior vice-president," he told me. "Higher up, certainly, particularly since I'd know it was coming when nobody else did and would be able to pave the way. I know how to do it, but the only opening to the top I had a chance at Khamgirt took. Still, as I said before, what's in it for you? I can hardly promote you to plant manager so suddenly."

"No, I don't want much of an advancement," I told him. "In fact, I'm thinking of a different direction for myself. One safe for you. Do you know Hroyasail?"

Again he was caught a little off-guard, which was fine. "Yeah, it's one of our subsidiaries. Harvests *skrit* off-shore. We use some of the chemicals from it in making insulators. Why?"

"I want it," I told him. "Right now the place doesn't even have a president. A company accountant comes down three or four times a year from the home office and that's about it."

"Sure. Something that small usually doesn't need one."

"I think it does. Me. And the position's already provided for, at least on the organizational chart. All it needs is certification by a senior official. *You* could do that as plant manager—but I'd prefer it coming from a senior vice-president, say."

"Now what in hell would you want that for?"

"My own reasons. But it's a nonthreatening position. The kind of job they'll give *you* if Khamgirt gets his way and you fail to meet quota. A pasture job. It pays well, has few responsibilities, has no experience prerequisites, and is still within the company. And of course as a company president I'd love to drop around occasionally and gossip with a senior vice-president of my parent corporation."

He thought it over. "Supposing—just supposing—you could pull it off. And, again just supposing, I could finagle that post for you. Would I have to watch my own back, then?"

"No, " I responded as sincerely as I could. "I'm not interested in your job, present or future. That kind of stuff would drive me nuts. This is a company world and I'm just not the company type. Believe me, Mr. Sugal, nothing in any of my plans would in any way harm you now or in the future. I like and admire you—but we're two different sorts with two different directions to follow."

"I think I believe you," he told me, still sounding uneasy, "but I'm still not sure if I shouldn't be afraid of you."

"What can you lose? They have you at their mercy now. *I'm* going to do something, not you. You alone will know that I did it—but neither of us will be able to ever use the information against the other because that's the only way both of us can ever be incriminated. If I fail, you're no worse off than you are now. If I succeed, we both get what we want. How about it?"

"I'll believe you can do it when I see it done," he said skeptically, "but I can't see anything against it, either."

I grinned. "You provide me with a few important bits of information, and I'll almost guarantee it. A deal's a deal." I looked at my watch. "And now, if you'll excuse me, I'm going down to change for the game. Sure you won't play?"

He shook his head. "Big meeting tonight with the area managers. But—good luck."

"I try and keep luck out of it, sir," I told him.

CHAPTER SIX

Preparations

Sanda Tyne, Dylan Kohl, Turgan Sugal, and, yes, even fat Otah. Especially him. The elements were all there.

The first thing I did was drop down to a store and buy an armload of electric slates. I needed a lot of plotting and planning with hard copy, but I wanted no trace whatsoever to remain after. No innocent slips of paper, no idle tracing to betray me. When the deed was accomplished, I'd have to stay well protected. The scam would be absolute and it would work, but those higher up, far beyond Khamgirt, would smell a rat somewhere, if only because they were variations of people like me and would have a nose for it. They'd know what had occurred was a frame, but even as they allowed Khamgirt to be led away to oblivion of some kind they'd be searching for the culprit. Khamgirt wouldn't be sacked because they believed him guilty, but for being so sloppy as to allow such a dirty trick to be played on him.

Dylan had exploited much the same weakness in the system when she had broken free of the motherhood by using a drug most people had never heard about or believed existed. I had no access to such substances, and even if I might get some that wasn't what I wanted. Any controlled substances, particularly those from offworld, could be traced by a determined group of investigators. The key to this plan as it developed was that, even if they figured it out, they would reject the explanation because of its very absurdity. I liked that touch.

Even as Sugal got me what I wanted to know—information on night shifts in certain parts of Tooker, various routine business transfer codes, and facts about certain basic computers supplied by Tooker to borough agencies—I started out to complete my subtle recruitment. This was not something that could be done alone, although I would have preferred to do it that way. But what had to be accomplished in very little time was too spread out and complex for any one person to manage. Furthermore, I wanted no chance of interruptions by third parties who might have to be dealt with, so I had to control everybody in the area for a stated period of time. That would be tough. However, I had some things to offer, and some interested parties to offer them to.

By now I had Dylan's measure pretty well and was certain of her ability to keep things quiet, including herself, and of her guts to pull off her assignment. Sanda was the problem. Now over seven months pregnant, she had little freedom of movement, and her life in that cloister was beyond my checking. She'd go along with my plan, of course, but I had to trust Dylan's judgment that she'd keep her mouth shut about it.

I decided on Dylan first, just because I needed her final evaluation on my pregnant potential weak link.

I had to wait for the weekend to get down there, though, because I needed the time with the information Sugal supplied to work things out. Also after a day chasing borks or at least patrolling for them and then cleaning and checking the boat, Dylan was not very lively company in the evenings. In one way we were incompatible: anybody who liked getting up at dawn to go to work was a bit strange and incomprehensible in my book.

I arranged to meet her at a small club in town to make sure that Sanda wouldn't be around. We'd met like this a couple of times before, just to be social—and we had gotten *very* social the last time—but this meeting would be slightly different. She was a very attractive woman, though, and even more so when she dressed for a night on the town rather than a day on the sea.

We ordered dinner and mostly exchanged small talk, then ate and went out to a small cabaret and did a little drinking and dancing. At the end of the evening, we went over to her apartment as we had before, but this time I had something additional in mind.

And at the right moment as I judged it, while we lay there, relaxed, I finally got to the point. In fact, she provided the opening. "You seemed distracted, far away tonight," she noted. "Something wrong with you? Or is it me?"

"No, nothing's wrong," I assured her, "but, yes, you're right. Dylan, it's time I came out in the open, I think, and I hope I know you well enough to trust you."

She sat up and looked at me, half puzzled, half expectant.

"Dylan, we've gotten to know each other quite well. I think we somehow complement each other. And we've talked freely about ourselves, I think. Still, what do you know about me?"

"You're Qwin Zhang, you're a computer programmer for Tooker, and you came from Outside," she replied. "And you've been an awful lot of places across the galaxy. You were loadmaster on a spaceship. And, according to some friends I know, your name is female on the civilized worlds. So? You trying to say you were once a woman? So what?"

"I came here as a woman, yes," I told her, taking the big gamble, "but I wasn't born in that body. It was Qwin Zhang's body—but I'm not Qwin Zhang. Not the original one, anyway."

"I thought only Cerberans could do that."

"It's a different process. A mechanical one, basically. But I wasn't a criminal and I wasn't a loadmaster."

She was staring at me, fascinated but not apprehensive. "So? Who *are* you, then, and what *did* you do?"

"I killed people the Confederacy wanted killed," I told her. "I tracked them down, found them out, and killed them."

There was a sharp intake of breath, but no other reaction. Finally she asked, "And they sent you here to kill someone?"

I nodded. "Yes. But it's someone who needs it, and since I'm stuck here the same as everybody else, that's important. They might try and kill me if I didn't, but that's beside the point. I'm confident enough they wouldn't succeed, and what they want is what I want, too."

"Who?" she asked.

"Wagant Laroo," I told her.

She whistled. "They don't think small, do they? And neither do you. Well, at least that explains why you were so interested in Laroo's Island."

I nodded. "I'm going to do it, Dylan. Nothing is more certain than that—although there are still a lot of steps in the way, and so a lot of time will pass before I can do it. Still it *will* happen. *Nobody* is invulnerable, not even me."

"Any particular reason why?"

"Problems. It seems Laroo and the other Lords of the Diamond made a deal with some aliens to help conquer the Confederacy. I don't have real affection one way or the other for the Confederacy, but I have a lot for the human race."

"These—aliens. What are they like?"

"We don't know," I told her. "All we do know is they're so nonhuman that there's no way they can do their own dirty work. That's why the Four Lords were hired. I'm sure they figure they'll get revenge and be on the winning side, but we don't know about these aliens. After they crack the Confederacy they might just decide they don't need *us* any more, either. They're trying to find out all they can about these creatures, whoever and whatever they are, but the only common link is the Warden Diamond. And one way of at least throwing a curve is to eliminate the Four Lords as currently constituted. A power struggle would disrupt things, buy time—and the new Lords might not be so thrilled about cooperating with and trusting these allies. I drew Laroo. But after seeing how he runs things here, I'd like a shot at him anyway. There are better, freer ways to run things than this, ones that don't cost people so much of their self-respect.

You only have to think of the motherhood to know what I mean."

"I'm not too sure I follow that last bit, but the rest I understand," she said. "I don't think anybody, not even the Four Lords, can commit people like me to help these aliens. All I keep thinking about is a race of sly, clever borks."

"Perhaps," I told her. "Or they might be a lot more appealing—it makes no difference. We don't know anything except that they're *very* nonhuman. Until I get a lot more assurances, that's all I need to know. We here in the Warden Diamond are sitting ducks when they don't need us any more. A civilization capable of crossing space and subtle enough to hire the Four Lords isn't one I could trust with my future."

She was silent for a moment, finally lighting one of those big cigars that took a fair share of her pay. Finally, in a haze of smoke, she asked softly, "Qwin? Why are you telling *me* this?"

"The first step is influence. I need influential friends in high places who can give me information. Dylan, who owns your boat?"

"Hroyasail, of course. Why?"

"Who's president of Hroyasail?"

"Nobody. I told you that."

I nodded. "Suppose *I* was president of Hroyasail? Set the salaries, got better parts, newer equipment—the best."

"What the hell are you talking about?"

"Suppose we *ran* Hroyasail, you and I. Not just a captain whose job can be cut by some bureaucrat, but really running the place. Boss. Sound interesting?"

"Go on."

"I need you to make that possible. You and one other. I'm talking about something criminal, but nobody gets killed or, I hope, even hurt. What I have in mind will take some guts, but I know you have that. Are you willing?"

"I don't know what the hell you're talking about."

"I'm going to get the president of Tooker fired. I'm going to totally discredit him. As a result, certain high-placed officials will move up and be grateful to me.

They'll give me Hroyasail and a big bank account and information when I need it. See?"

"You can *do* that?"

I smiled. "Easily. If they haven't changed the fire alarm system in the borough in the past three years."

"What!"

I spent the night with Dylan, and over breakfast we discussed the other problem. "Unless you can think of somebody quickly who I would trust, and you *could* trust, for an operation like this, we'll need Sanda as well," I told her. "She's got brains and spunk, and she can do the job, I think. But can we rely on her not to talk? I can't get into Akeba House to see what she's like away from the rest of us. You were there once. What do you think?"

"She'd be a good choice," she agreed. "She's got the biggest crush on you I've ever seen. But to do what you're proposing—I don't think the temptation is possible for her to resist. She'll blow it there."

"If I promise her a way out of the Motherhood free and clear at a later date? Right now I *need* her where she is. I need that expense account she has, and that anonymity as well. But when we're done, I can get her out."

"I don't know. The promise of something later versus something now isn't easy to handle when you're faced with it."

"I think *I* can handle that part," I assured her. "The question is, if I trick her back into her own body, will she blow the thing just for spite?"

"Nobody can say," she said honestly. "But my gut instinct is that she wouldn't. She's got it bad for you. For that matter, so do I, damn it. Qwin, is that all I am to you? Somebody to accomplish your mission, then be paid off?"

I took her hand and squeezed it. "No," I responded gently. "No, you're a lot more than that. And so is Sanda."

She smiled. "I wish I knew for sure. I really do. Somebody like you is a little out of my league, you know, and way out of Sanda's. You were born, bred, and trained for your job. People trust you and don't know why. People confide in you and don't know why. Women fall for you and don't know why. I wonder whether even you know what about you is real."

"In the past, in the old days, you'd be right," I responded honestly. "But not here now, and for the future on Cerberus. This is my home now. My permanent home, and my life. It's different now, Dylan, and so am I. Look, I've just put my life in your hands by what I've told you. You can see that, surely?"

"Well, there *is* that," she admitted, and finished her breakfast.

On Dylan's advice, I decided to talk to Sanda alone first, then let her go talk to Dylan afterward. I decided not to be as honest with her as I had been with Dylan, mostly because I was less sure of her abilities to keep things quiet.

"Dylan and I are going to try to do something very risky," I told her. "Basically, I've got a setup that could put me in control of Hroyasail if the law can be successfully bent, shall we say."

She was interested and fascinated. I could see the romance of it all catching on inside her. This was the kind of thing "real world" people did, not the mothers of Akeba House.

"Now," I continued carefully, "before I go any further, I have to warn you of something. This is no game. If I tell you more, you'll hold both my life and Dylan's in your hands because they'll kill us if there's any leak, if there's even the slightest *suspicion*. That means no talking to anyone except for the two of us—and no excitement, no betrayal of even the fact that you have secrets to keep, or you'll do us in. We need help, but not if you don't think you can handle it. Understand?"

She nodded. "You're afraid I can't keep it to myself?"

"There's nothing personal, but both you and Dylan have told me about life inside that harem, and it's sounds like harems throughout past history. You sit around, you talk, you gossip, you know each other so well you note when something's not right with somebody else and the

word gets spread all over. Be very honest—do you think
you could keep something like this to yourself?"

"I think I can," she responded.

"Not think. *Know!* Be absolutely sure of yourself or it
stops here and we find somebody else."

"I'm sure. I wouldn't—couldn't—do anything that
might hurt you or Dylan."

"All right, then. We really *do* need you on this for
what you can tell me even now. You had some nurse's
training?"

She nodded. "We all do. Some more than others, but I
got interested. Dylan knows more than me, though. She
was at it longer."

I nodded. "All I need is some basic information right
now. The first question is, have you ever been hypnotized?"

She nodded. "Sure. We do it all the time for deliveries,
since we can't use much in the way of anesthetics. Not
too many folks on Cerberus will come anywhere near
hypnotism, though."

That was certainly true. You put total control of what
body you wore and what body you would wear into
someone else's hands, and *that* was something you didn't
do lightly. Not here.

"All right," I told her, "now—Dylan told me that on
special occasions some of the mothers would switch so
those in the late stages of pregnancy could go out. Just a
temporary courtesy."

"That's right. It's not usual, but we've all done it."

"Good. Can you think of anybody you might be able
to switch with for a full day and night?"

She thought a moment. "Yeah. I guess so. Marga,
maybe, although I'd owe her one. When would this be?"

"Two weeks from now. Friday evening through Satur-
day evening or maybe Sunday morning."

"I'll work it out."

"Good. Talk it over with Dylan, too, all you want. I'm
going to be doing dry runs and setups all week. Next
weekend I'll work out a little test or two to see if there
are any kinks in company security. Now, two more
things." I fished a couple of papers from my pocket and
handed them to her. She looked at them quizzically.

"What are these?"

"Remember Otah?"

"Yeah?"

"Well, he does a lot of interesting bootlegs other than just entertainment," I told her. "If *I* came in with those, though, he might get suspicious, and the money would still be missing from my account. I want you—or somebody else who won't ask questions and can act for you—to go into Otah's place with those and ask for those specific parts. Tell him they are required spares for a surprise fire inspection at Akeba House. Tell him that they have to be exactly like those on the sheet because of special equipment in the House. If he presses further, act ignorant of any more, but insist he make those specific parts, without variations and without substitutions."

She looked at the diagrams, then turned them first one way, then upside down. "It won't be hard to pretend ignorance. What are they?"

"Computer memory chips," I told her. "I need 'em as soon as possible, but definitely within a week. Understand?"

She nodded. "He makes these things?"

"He can have them made."

"How much should I pay for them?"

"You have almost unlimited credit, you said. It's why I've let you buy me so many dinners. The price'll be high, since the transaction is under the counter. Probably two or three hundred units each."

She whistled. "Wow."

"Too steep for you?"

"No, but it's more than I'm ever used to paying."

"Will it show up in your personal account?"

"Oh, no. We don't have them. It's another way they keep us barefoot and pregnant. It's the House account."

I nodded to myself, then pulled her close and kissed her. "You know," I said, "I never realized before how sexy a pregnant woman can be to a man."

By God, I told myself, this crazy, insane, totally absurd plot was going to work!

"Tell me about nuraform," I asked them on the boat Friday night.

"It's an anesthetic, one of the few that works here," Dylan replied. "A couple of whiffs and you'll go out like a light for twenty minutes or so—but you won't be able to change bodies with it. That's why it's approved at all. Major operations and stuff like that, or on-the-job accidents where somebody's in great pain. But it's a controlled substance. Doctors and medical personnel only."

"That's no trouble," I replied. "The company dispensary keeps some around. I can steal it pretty easy."

"Why bother?" she asked me, and pulled a small magnakey from her pocket. "We always carry a small supply on the boats."

I not only could have kissed her, I did.

"But what good's nuraform?" Sanda asked. "I mean, you can't switch with it, and if somebody's knocked out with it they'll know."

"Not if they're asleep," I told her. "Look, let's go on to other phases of this operation. What about the chips?"

"He took the job," Sanda told me, "although it required some real haggling, and I had to do a lot of squirming. I also had to borrow Marga's body to get in there, so I'm really going to have to find something to get her."

"You figure that out and I'll get it," I assured her. "Now—when will you have them?"

"Tuesday. He was pretty firm about that, no matter what. I can send a messenger then, because it's prepaid."

"Okay. I'll need 'em Tuesday evening, and I'll drop down to pick them up. We're looking good—fewer hitches than I'd ever dreamed. You can do wonders when you're doing a dirty deed for the boss. The amount of information I've gotten would have taken a year of hard and risky work."

"I still say you're crazy and this plan's insane," Dylan said, shaking her head. "It's so crazy and so complicated it can't *possibly* work."

"You think they make this kind of operation easy? Look, every corporation president, every syndicate boss, got where he was by doing the insane and crooked thing at just the right time. Even with that, their investigators will know they've been had. Within two weeks they'll have figured out how it was done—although, hopefully, not who did it, since I'm not even the one getting rewarded at the end but pastured instead. No, they'll come up with the right solution, all right, but the scheme is so crazy they won't believe it themselves, and that'll stop that. As for its being complicated—yes, I don't like that. The more complicated something is, the more likely it is to go wrong. But at least there are provisions almost to the end to back out at any point, so if we do our jobs properly there's minimal risk of getting caught. Don't worry about that part—just worry about your own."

"I am," Dylan responded glumly.

"Look, let's go through the key rehearsal now. Just think about this, both of you. If it works, you, Dylan, will have your own boat under nobody's supervision and no real worries—independent and secure. And you, Sanda, I promise—if all goes as planned, we're going to liberate you from the motherhood and do it so slickly that nobody will bat an eyelash. If you can be patient and not jump the gun, the three of us might wind up running this damned world in a couple of years."

Neither of them believed that, but they believed in me and that was enough. It usually was. Only this time, for a change, I wasn't just pulling a con to set up a mission. I really meant business.

"Now, let's see what sort of hypnotic subjects you are," I said.

Sanda went under quickly and easily. Dylan resisted somewhat, and I could understand why and sympathize with her. After a long struggle she was who and what she wanted to be. Hypnosis was a threat to that. It took a good deal of smooth and soothing talk finally to get her to the point where she was willing.

Sanda had romance to gain and absolutely nothing to lose in this whole business—if we weren't caught on the spot. Dylan, on the other hand, had relatively little to gain but was risking all that she held dear in this business. She wasn't really doing this for herself, but for me, and I knew it.

I knew the routine well from past operations and had had a lot of practice. I'd also used Tooker's computers to do a lot of medical research on exactly how to handle this particular ticklish business, but actually doing so would not be easy.

Being there alone in a boat lounge with two attractive women in deep hypnosis was something of a kinky turn-on, but that feeling passed in a minute. This was business. In the Confederacy there were drugs and devices that could do this much better. But I was prevented from using the first by the Warden organism and didn't have access to the second. That's why we learned hypnosis from the start. You never had the right stuff around when you really needed it.

They both seemed to be asleep in their chairs, and I went over to Dylan first. "Dylan, you will listen to my voice and nothing else, listen and trust me and do exactly as I say. Do you understand?"

"Yes." Sleepily, faraway.

"Answer my questions truthfully, Dylan."

"I will."

"Would you ever betray me or my mission?"

"I don't think so."

"Dylan, why are you willing to do this?"

"Because you want it."

"But why is that so important? Why should you take risks for me?"

"Because I—"

"Yes?"

"I think I love you."

Love. A fascinating word and feeling. One I had used many times but still didn't quite understand myself. Certainly love was usually an abstract concept on Cerberus.

"You *do* love me, don't you?"

"Yes."

"Very much. Very deeply. More than you've ever loved anyone, more than you love yourself."

"Yes."

"You would trust me with your body, even your life."

"Yes."

"And I could trust you with my body, my life."

"You could."

I moved over to Sanda and repeated some of the process.

"Would you betray us or our mission?"

"No," she assured me. "Never."

"Have you told anyone in the House about this?"

"No."

"Has anyone there suspected you were up to something? Asked questions?"

"One or two."

"And what did you tell them?"

"I said I was in love with you and that you were in love with me."

"Did they believe you and press no more?"

"They were envious," she told me. "They ask me about you."

"And what do you tell them?"

"I tell them you came from Outside and you work for Tooker."

"And what else?"

The next segment was more than a little embarrassing to me personally. The romantic fantasies this lonely and bored young woman had concocted were graphic and hard to believe, and the image of me as someone approaching godhood was beyond any technique I'd ever studied. Still, it was satisfactory. They would understand those fantasies for what they were and put down a lot of her nervous excitement to meeting me.

Her emotional patterns were at once simpler and more complex than Dylan's or the average person's. She loved, truly loved, Dylan, but she worshiped me.

Confederacy agents are born and bred to their jobs and are as perfect as the biological and social sciences can make them for doing whatever needs to be done.

As a youngster in the game I'd been amazed at how easily people could be turned, how malleable they were in emotions and will if only the right words were said at the right times, the right buttons pushed. It was something I'd never really thought about, something that came almost instinctively. Even now it still amazed me. Two women were in love with me and were willing to risk their necks and who knew what else for me.

Even when they *knew*, as Dylan knew, they still went along. And yet standing there looking at the two women, I felt something that I had never really felt before, the stirrings of care, of concern, of real affection and appreciation for these two. Perhaps, I reflected, not quite understanding myself, I too could love.

But business came first.

I almost held my breath before this next one, since without it the whole thing would fall and have to be postponed. And time was running out on Turgan Sugal, and therefore on me.

I had them both open their eyes and rise, facing me. I instructed them to turn and face each other.

"Feel inside yourselves," I instructed. "Feel your mind. Feel the Wardens in your mind, calling out, connecting you one to the other, talking to each other mind to mind. Think of nothing else, concentrate on nothing else, but feel, hear, as they reach out, your mind to the other. Can you feel it?"

"Yes," they both answered in unison.

"Dylan, you wish to be in Sanda's body. You wish it more than anything else in the world. It is a beautiful body, not a mother's body, and it is the ideal body you have always dreamed of. You want to be in that body. Flow into it, Dylan. Become Sanda's body. Sanda, you will not resist. You *want* to exchange bodies with Dylan. You will flow into hers as she into yours. And when your bodies have changed, you will both go back and sit in your chairs, still in a deep hypnotic sleep."

Apparently when both were hypnotized and so instructed the exchange went more quickly and smoothly than in the "natural" way. Or so the computers had told me, although they also warned that, once complete, it would take another ten minutes or so to set in. Actually, although consciously the exchange was complete at that point, it took up to seventy-two hours for a true set, but that wasn't what I was after. All I wanted was a mental exchange, no more.

In less than ten minutes both women moved—and sat in each other's chairs. Dylan was now Sanda, and Sanda was now Dylan.

I went over to the new Dylan. "Dylan? Can you hear me?"

"Yes."

"Now, listen carefully. Soon I will awaken you, but you will still remain in a deep hypnotic sleep, even though awakened. And when you awaken, you will do the following exactly . . ."

Although I was a master of autohypnosis and had even gotten to the point of sensing the Wardens inside my own body, this was a bit too tricky to trust just to myself. So when she awakened, I allowed her to put *me* under, and the process was repeated, with me going into Dylan's old body and Sanda into mine. We were than all awakened, still under, and were able to compare notes, reactions, and the like. It looked like complete conscious control even in the short time allowed, and that satisfied me. We switched back again and Dylan brought me out, then I brought the two of them out, along with some handy posthypnotic suggestions. The suggestions wouldn't last more than a day or two, but tended to be of the self-reinforcing type, in which each of them would put herself under and repeat quite a lot over and over. It was an advanced form of hypnosis with limited use, but it was more than handy for memorizing things to do and to calm nerves.

All that afternoon we went over the plan again and again, until I was satisfied that all three of us had what we were to do down pat. Sanda had received permission to spend the night on the boat as long as she was in safe and enclosed quarters—their organization was run by a few incurable romantics, too—and we had a fancy dinner sent down from town which we ate on the aft deck.

"One thing puzzles me," Dylan remarked. "It seems to me you had all the elements to make this plan first. Which came first—the elements or the plan?"

I laughed. "The elements, of course. The plan was tailored for what I *could* do and what my friends, associates, and close partners—you two—could do. It was a matter of stating the problem when it came up—Sugal's subtle forced ouster—and then putting together all I had, all that I could have, and matching it up to the chinks I'd already found in this society's armor. So far it's all worked out—but if my research was wrong and something doesn't go right, well, I'll try a different plan. Plans are easy—this one took only a few minutes—but execution's the hard part, since you never really know what's possible until you try it. Like tonight."

Tonight would be yet another test, really, and it would depend on me more than anything. All those two had to do was go to sleep, shielded from each other. I'd have a more difficult task, and all my plans and theories depended on it. It was logical, my computers told me, but there wasn't much medical evidence to back it up—for obvious reasons, I knew.

Which is why I sat, in a deep but aware hypnotic trance, in the same room as Dylan but unshielded—yet a good five meters from her bed. Sat and reached out and felt the creatures in my mind. It was an eerie sensation, really. There was no sight, sound, or smell to betray the Warden organism, but when you were deeply under— and occasionally while you were in a really deep sleep— you could hear them, sense them, talking.

Not talking in any sense that we understand, but there was some sort of communication, some sort of linkage, as if one could sense the individual cells comparing information elsewhere. An energy network, intangible, invisible, yet very much there, creating a sense of linkage not only between minds but between literally *everything* solid around you.

Under hypnotic control I was able to tune out much of it, all but Dylan's sleeping form, which seemed almost to *burn* with the tiny tendrils of immeasurably small energy linking one Warden organism to another. I could feel myself being almost physically drawn to her, interconnecting with every part of her body, linking mind to mind, arms to arms, legs to legs, heart to heart. At this point, more deep than I'd ever been, I understood a bit more how those on Lilith must feel who could command, send messages through that network. One could also wonder, too, how such a creature as the Warden could have evolved, how it could possibly exist at all, on worlds otherwise not so different from many man had conquered, and far less alien than most. What are you? Who are you? Why do you exist?

And there seemed to be a faint answer somewhere, from all around.

We exist! We live! We are! That is enough!

Dylan had gone from lighter, dream-filled sleep to that period people went through several times a night. Rigid, deep, dreamless. Her Wardens burned bright, talking, singing along fields of invisible force—hers to mine and mine to hers. And for the first time conscious as it happened, we changed. It was a strange experience, but not a terrifying one. There was something eerily satisfying about it, my body building up a tension and then the core of my being flowing along those fields of force toward that sleeping body and the core of hers to mine, providing a wondrous feeling I could not then and can not now describe.

I arose in the body of Dylan Kohl, feeling somehow exhilarated, high, powerful. I went over to the dressing table, took the small bottle there and crept over to my old body, sleeping uneasily in the lounge chair. Carefully I placed it under his nose and pressed the stud, releasing a tiny whiff of vapor, which was quickly inhaled.

The body sagged slightly and the breathing became deeper, a bit labored but no real problem.

I shook him. "Dylan? Wake up." I shook harder. "Wake up, Dylan!" I almost shouted in his ear, and there was no reaction.

Satisfied, I clicked on the stopwatch, then tried moving the body. Though Dylan was a strong woman, she was still weaker than I was used to being as a man; I tried all sorts of ways to rouse the sleeper but got nowhere.

Finally I sat down on the bed to wait it out, going over every few minutes and trying again to rouse the unconscious form. About the fourth or fifth time I tried, the figure groaned a little and turned slightly. I reached over and clicked off the watch. Twenty-four minutes and a few odd seconds. Time enough.

Another minute or so, and I was able to shake Dylan awake. He shook his head and rubbed his eyes for a moment, seemingly unable to get his bearings, then sighed and looked at me. "So it *does* work."

I nodded. "Twenty-four minutes, with my additional body weight. I'll bet it's longer for your body. Any ill effects?"

"I feel dead tired but otherwise nothing much," Dylan replied.

"Now it's your turn," I said. "Hippogryph."

The posthypnotic command took effect, sending her under quickly. With only a minimal briefing—we'd been over this again and again earlier in the day—I went back over to the bed and stretched out. It was several minutes before I could relax enough to drift into sleep. The old excitement, the old fun of this sort of thing was rising fully in me once again.

We were able to get a reversal on me in under three hours, which was very good indeed, and then I tiptoed quietly into Sanda's partitioned and shielded side to do much the same thing. I was tired, yes, but the hypnotic state was somewhat restful in and of itself and this was far more important. I could call on mental reserves when necessary.

I didn't use the nuraform on Sanda, since I didn't need to—my body had already proven out—and I didn't want any risks in her condition to *her* body.

Sensorily, her body was also far different from Dylan's or my own. The fetus inside her was far enough along that even now it had its own unique Warden pattern, one that I could sense, although its own Wardens were out of reach to me, must as the Wardens in the molecules of the ship itself or the dock or the bed. It was a curious feeling.

Arising in her body was also something of a shock, as I was very much aware of the pregnancy and the vast differences in my new body, a body in a condition far stranger than merely the gender change from male to female and back again. My awakening on the prison ship that first time had almost been disappointing in that it felt so *little* different. Sanda was a far more startling experience.

But I had proved my theory and the heart of the scam. Proved it absolutely. I didn't know why someone else hadn't thought of it, too—but then again, maybe someone had. If so, it would take a rare sneaky mind like my own, since it required a knowledge of hypnotism and the body as well, and had involved an *awful* lot of homework that I would have found nearly impossible had I not worked at Tooker and had its vast computer system to play with.

Sanda's body was a marvel to me; I don't know how anybody can cope with it. It was awkward, and I felt bloated, and there were other sensations a bit too odd to describe. I began to get some appreciation of why she wanted out of this routine, although I couldn't believe it was like this most of the time. Still, I had to hang on for a bit, bring Sanda, now in my body, around and awake, and check out the one nagging doubt I had about my chosen personnel.

It was the first time she'd been in a man's body and awake and under control, unlike the hypnotic experiment earlier on the deck. She took some delight in the body, and in exploring it. I suspected the additional contrast between the body I was now in, in the condition it was—roughly eight months pregnant—and my own top physical form only added to her pleasure.

"Can't I stay like this a while?" he pleaded. "It feels so—*free!*"

I shook my head sadly. "No, not now. You have to learn how to exchange for next week, and it's already close to dawn."

"Oh, please! Just for one day? You don't know what it *means!*"

"I think I do," I sympathized, "but, no. Control, Sanda. We'll do this again tomorrow night if the House is willing to let you stay another night, as I suspect they will. We don't have much time, and we have a lot of practice to do."

He pouted. It was amusing to see the characteristics of Sanda in my body, as it had tickled me to see some legit switchers in similar circumstances. We learn our sexual and personality moves early on, and even on a body-switch world these come through—on people with a clear sexual identity, such as the three of us.

"I think we ought to get to this," I told him. "It's getting late, and you might get your wish by just keeping me up a little longer." I was somewhat concerned. The unfamiliar-feeling body would cause enough problems, but I was becoming more and more awake. Sanda, in this body, had had a lot more sleep than Dylan or I had had.

Sanda seemed to sense that, too, and seemed determined to keep the argument going until it would go his way by default. Realizing this, I snapped, "Will I have this problem again next week, when our lives depend on it?"

That brought him up short, and sounding a little apologetic, he replied, "Look. I'm sorry. I won't cross you up."

"I know you won't," I said softly, then said, "Hippogryph."

Thank heavens for posthypnotic suggestion, I thought with relief. That was my ace in the hole for the next weekend too, of course. I crossed my fingers on that one, lay down, and tried to get some sleep, which was a long time coming. The longer it took the more afraid I became of being trapped in this body, and the harder it was to get to sleep because of that fear. I finally managed, though, cheating a bit with some autohypnosis.

The sun was bright and it was late in the morning when Sanda, again herself, somewhat ruefully awakened me.

One more day of rehearsal, going over everything again and again, testing things out again and again, and one more night of testing, this time with Dylan doing the double switching, and we were as ready as we'd ever be. If Otah was as good as his word, I had one extra setup to accomplish on my own, and then a little sadistic fun, and we'd be ready for Friday afternoon.

CHAPTER SEVEN

Final Set-up and Much Prayer

Tuesday afternoon, while I was still at work, I got a call from Sanda telling me that a package had just been delivered to her at Akeba House. After I knocked off for the day, I went down there to get it.

I met her at the gatehouse, and we walked along the wood walk to the sea. We looked down on the Hroyasail fleet, already tied up below, but I wasn't about to disturb

Dylan at this point. She had her work to do and I had mine.

"I still can't believe there's a whole business in supplying special parts for computers and stuff like that," Sanda told me.

I grinned. "There's always some service like that, and people like Otah to provide it."

"But what would anyone use it for, except maybe to commit a crime?"

"Some of it's undoubtedly for that, but not much, or the authorities would shut 'em down," I told her. "A lot of it is for people making their own modifications in their own home or business equipment—modifications not approved by the manufacturer, who wants to control everything about his machines. Some of it is to modify stock security systems so somebody can't get the master keys and defeat them. And some of it, like our cover story, is due to people forgetting to fix stuff that's required by borough code, like fire and police alarms, because they were lazy or because they were too cheap to get a maintenance contract, only to be caught with their pants down when inspectors pull a surprise."

She shrugged and looked suspiciously at the unopened parcel. "How can you be sure it'll work? Or that Otah hasn't cheated you by supplying some standard part?"

"He wouldn't stay in business long if he did that, but if he has, then the plan won't work and we'll have to figure out something else, that's all."

"Why so many, then?"

I grinned wider. "Because the breakdown has to look natural. These are the same standard chips used in the old and venerable system this borough's had for years, only with slight changes. They're designed to react to different loads on the system. We can't just have something break once—they'll just come and fix it. We have to have a repeated series of breakdowns, and that means we have one go bad, get fixed, then another go, and so forth."

"But won't that attract suspicion, too?"

"You don't know machines. When one part goes, others often follow. No, the more failures they find, the more the blame will be laid to the antiquated system finally giving up under the strain of years. Trust me—it's my business."

She put her arm around me. "I *do* trust you, Quin. It's just all so—so *incredible*. I could never have come up with an idea as crazy as this."

"Yeah," I said. "That's why people like me—the good guys *and* the crooks—get away with so much. The average person, even the average law enforcer, just doesn't have the kind of mind to figure out things like this."

"You'd think they'd learn."

"They did," I told her. "They created a corps of specialists in the Confederacy for people who thought like this, to catch them."

"Sounds fascinating. But surely somebody by now would have designed a foolproof system."

I had to laugh. "The ultimate foolproof system is invented every year or two and has been since the dawn of time. It usually lasts only until the next genius figures out how to beat it."

Even you, Wagant Laroo, I thought, looking out across the ocean to the southeast. *No fortress has ever proven impregnable, nor is the best security without flaw. I'm coming for you, Wagant Laroo. One day, step by step, I'm coming. And not even your alien friends will be able to save you from me.*

Despite my glib assurances to Sanda, I didn't trust any bootlegger for anything. Wednesday I checked out the circuits in the lab. It was a fascinating business, a computer so small you could hardly see it with the naked eye, but it was naturally centuries out of date. What could be done with computers now was nothing short of awesome —but it hadn't been done, out of fear by power-loving, weak-kneed leaders who feared just who or what would be in control of humanity if they went too far. Here on Cerberus, where the system was even more retarded, I suspect that scientists from centuries earlier could probably have understood what I was doing.

Human history had always been like that—centuries, even millennia, of incredibly slow, creeping advance, followed by a few centuries of exponential multiplication of knowledge, followed by a collapse, a setback, and more lengthy periods of backwardness. We are hardly as backward as some, but the analogy still held. This was not an age of great advancement, if only for political reasons, nor the century for it. We were Neanderthals, primitives who could set the air conditioner on in our caves and drive comfortably down to the dinosaur pits.

The chips checked out perfectly. Otah's people had done a good job, and now it was up to me to be worthy.

Wednesday evening I checked out a company flier, which wasn't unusual, since I was due the next day in Comora, about a hundred and ten kilometers north, for a reorganizational meeting—standard stuff. What wasn't standard was where I went that evening after changing into a Tooker Service Systems uniform and, with a little easy sleight of hand, picking up an official repairman's tool kit.

My first stop was an apartment complex eight kilometers west of the main plant. My authentic Tooker ID badge got me easy entry—they didn't even take note of the name, just that its face and mine matched—and soon I was in the manager's office.

"The entire city master alarm system is undergoing an overhaul," I told her. "We've been having breakdowns all up and down the line. You can't really tell if the damn stuff goes bad until it does, but they want me to check the line anyway."

"Go ahead," she told me, not really concerned. "It's on level four, just above waterline."

I nodded, told her thanks, then added, "This system's so much of an antique maybe they'll get sick of these things and put in a new one."

"Ha!" she exclaimed. "Not until the Municipal Building itself burns down, or the fancy homes fill with water!"

I took the service elevator down and quickly found the master line that routed the fire alarm system to each floor and each room. One weakness of the system I'd spotted right away was the fact that people had to build in the trees—they couldn't kill the trees or replace them for lack of a foundation. And since the bulk of the plants were underwater, the tops were generally hollow and the circulatory systems were not extensive, as well as being exposed to the sun.

In other words, no matter how inert the materials used inside the tree buildings themselves, the outer bark was highly flammable, and was covered by a municipal alarm system. Although it was almost impossible to set fire to anything inside the man-made structures, you were always completely surrounded by the tree and had a fair way to go to exit. Fire would be a severe problem, with smoke potentially blocking all the exits.

The computer fire alarm system, then, was designed to detect any temperature rise anywhere in the exposed tree by the use of a selective monitoring system at all levels above the waterline. Other than this early warning system, the only real escape was by the chutes, which could shoot you from any hall to the waterline. These areas had special systems to keep them free of smoke and were for the most part in the center, where everything was man-made and insulated.

There were few fires, and even fewer than ever amounted to anything. Hence the alarm system as such had been mostly ignored for years, considering borough budgets.

I was not out to start any fires. I ran a systems check, stopping at predetermined points, and then replaced the tiny, almost microscopic chips with specific ones I'd brought with me, being careful even to spray a bit of dust and gunk on them so that there would be no evidence of replacement. Anyone removing one would probably complain about how dirty the area was and remark that it was no wonder the chips had gone bad.

I'd never done this with a fire alarm system before, but I'd done similar things countless times to security systems far more complex and technologically advanced than this. I'd never been found out once—even when they suspected what had been done.

It took less than half an hour to place all my key chips, but I had more stops to make, hitting the usual maintenance route mapped on the shop board. In the other places I did absolutely nothing, but anyone checking on the mysterious serviceman would find that he'd done nothing not routine and that in fact the servicing had been ordered and logged. I knew it had: I'd slipped the order in myself, then made sure it wouldn't come up on the assignment board so I could take it.

Modern man, I'm convinced, is vulnerable to any competent engineer. We depend on the computer to total our purchases, rarely checking each item for accuracy, and we rely on it for inventory, for security, for remembering to turn out the lights and remembering to keep the temperature in our homes at the same level no matter what. We trust them so much and take them so much for granted that most people can be had by simply nudging a computer to suggest what you want it.

By the time I'd reached the fire department I was well satisfied and had made about thirty stops on this particular system. According to service records at Tooker, false alarms were relatively common at almost every station, averaging two a week, so systems checks were routine—and pointless. At the fire station I removed and replaced the rest of my bootleg load in several places, and then left for the plant once again. Changing back to my normal clothes, I used my company pass to get back into inventory, where I replaced the tool kit and threw the uniform into the company laundry chute.

Then I went home.

The next morning I flew up to my conference, returned in the afternoon, and checked out early, going back down to maintenance and punching up their service record.

Two chips had gone bad at an apartment complex eight kilometers west of the plant, one around noon and the other not too long before I checked. The repair personnel were still on the job for that one. I smiled to myself, nodded, and went home for an early dinner.

By Friday there had been seven failures within the system, some at the apartment house, some through the system and apparently in the master control at the fire station, ringing every alarm on that particular string. There had also been one false alarm at another apartment—one I wasn't responsible for but had hoped for, considering the average two a week. It would keep my tampering from being obvious, although I couldn't imagine why any investigator or Tooker tech would even consider that somebody had gone to a lot of trouble and expense to ring false alarms.

I worked late on Thursday night, partly to catch up from the time lost at the meetings earlier in the week and partly because everybody was putting in at least one long day these days—we were *really* understaffed. Sugal had no idea where they went or what they were working on, but a rundown of the people pulled told me a little. All were junior staff like me, and every one of them had been involved in the field of organic computers, which were banned on Cerberus, before being sent here. It was only six, but they were all exiles, all experts in the same field, and all good minds. And, all of their forwarding addresses were care of the corporation headquarters building—a forwarding box service. Interesting. Obviously something was going on. Something I wanted to know about.

Late that evening, stretching my legs, I just happened to meet the night janitorial supervisory staff coming on. Most of the cleaning was automated, but the rules required a few human beings to make sure all was working right, since self-aware computers were banned on the planet. I looked at the men and women coming on, skilled technicians themselves, and noted that some of them looked tired.

During the day on Friday all hell broke loose in the fire control computer, with false alarms all over the place and the whole system going crazy. It took half of Tooker Service to track down the problem and replace the bad parts, but by early evening they had completed the job, fortunately—since most people worked regular days like me, and thus weren't there when all this happened.

Only the few night workers, most of whom lived in an apartment about eight kilometers west of the plant, went through hell. Few of them got any sleep at all, poor things.

According to the readouts, the system really *was* in awful shape. I hadn't caused nearly all that happened to that system on Friday afternoon. Apparently my defects triggered breakdowns in *real* defects within the system. I had hoped for that but hadn't planned on it. The system really *was* in dire need of replacement.

While all those people were having problems, I managed to finish early, thanks to my extra-long day the day before. At a little before four I walked down to the main entrance for a previously scheduled VIP tour. Like most, this VIP tour had no VIPs; many of us took friends on little demo tours to show off, and the company encouraged such things as good public relations.

Dylan had put in sick for the day, so she had plenty of sleep and was in fine shape for the evening. With her was a tiny, thin olive-skinned beauty with long jet-black hair and eyes I'd never seen before. I had to stop and shake my head in wonder. I'd *never* get used to this switching stuff.

"Sanda?" I ventured.

She smiled and nodded. "You wouldn't believe what this is going to cost you. I think you're going to have to wine, dine, and romance half of Akeba House."

I thought about it. "Doesn't sound too terrifying." I looked at both of them, sensing an inward nervousness in each that they were only partly successful in masking. I hugged both of them and whispered, "Don't worry so much. It's going great."

Beyond the public rooms, a scan was necessary to make certain that only authorized employees passed beyond certain points. Since I had prearranged the tour, which wasn't that unusual, entry caused no problems at all. Basically, you faced a door, put the headpiece on, then inserted your identicard in the slot. If all was okay, the door opened and you walked into a small antechamber, whereupon the door closed behind you. You then slotted the card again and the second door would open, admitting you—in the same way as an airlock did.

If the more than four thousand Tooker employees had to do this, they would be all day just getting to work, so the internal computers simply recognized your body features and all you did was put your card in the slot. Scanning took a couple of minutes, and since the system was tied to the master computer—which, I discovered, was in orbit and linked to the entire surface by a series of satellites—it was also advisable to discourage an expensive overload of any local system. Scans within Tooker were required only in high security areas.

That, of course, was a second flaw. Not only because they didn't use full scan everywhere, but also because you could walk right past all those security areas, outside, separated only by a floor-to-ceiling sheet of thick, unbreakable, and alarmed plastiglass. For extra security, you could see the whole of the security areas from this walk—although of course you couldn't get to anything going on inside or even get close enough to figure out what was going on. Computers monitored the inside of those areas to make certain that nobody except those properly scanned could enter, and the list of those so authorized was quite short.

We stood outside one such area while I acted the guide. Some of the staff were still huddled over consoles and transceivers, although they were thinning out as the end of the workday approached.

"This area controls the local banking system," I told them. "Eleven borough small banks keep all their transaction records here, and shift money and assets between them. Of course it's just a bank link to the master computer, where all our electronic money is stored, but that master computer holds only the total assets of every person and corporation. These machines hold where that money came from and where it's to go, and can effect a transfer of funds within the master accounts with a simple set of coded orders. The codes are pretty simple—so much so that anybody who could get to one of the register machines there could steal millions in moments."

"Then why aren't they made more complicated?" Sanda asked.

"Because, since everybody's money is in the master computer, any unusual bulge in it, or any pattern of smaller bulges, would flag the central banking authorities that something was funny and promote an investigation." We'd actually been over this material before, but with people still around we needed to complete the grand tour.

Her question, besides being a normal one, pointed up the second flaw in the system. It would be *damned* hard, beyond all but the best computer minds in the galaxy armed with unlimited resources, to get away with any sort of money theft on Cerberus. It *better* be—I was counting on everybody in the system being competent.

Down a long hall from the banking center was a small group of conference rooms. I selected one I knew wasn't scheduled for anything and opened the door. It was the usual small meeting room—rostrum, round table of nice, polished wood, and five comfortable executive chairs. You could lock the room from the inside for privacy, but not from the outside. There was no need.

We entered and locked the door, and in a matter of minutes I had put both of them under. Oddly, Sanda was the hardest to hypnotize—she was just too excited.

Dylan had brought two small bottles of nuraform from the ship medikit, and I gave one to Sanda. Under as she was, I had her repeat the procedure and everything she was to do exactly, then gave her all the added cautions. I also added a suggestion that she felt neither nervous nor excited and would calmly and coolly perform her duties.

We left her in the conference room and I took Dylan up two levels to the company accounting section, also a security area. Almost everybody was gone now which made it even easier.

The bosses were long gone for the weekend, so I used Sugal's office as Dylan's waiting area. Again I made her go through her own procedure exactly, then left her.

I returned to the main level and took out not one but three identicards and, one at a time, put them in the slot, allowing the equipment to act as if a person were going through each time. I used a rear exit to avoid any undue attention, although I had a cover story ready if I needed one. The third card was mine, of course, and I walked out with that one.

The computer not only didn't scan for exiting but didn't even look at you. Fire regulations required a fast exit, and the only reason for using the two women's cards was that there now would be a record of both of them leaving the building with me.

The nervous excitement was rising in me, too, and I considered a little autohypnosis to calm myself down. After all, I had a tough thing to do, too.

I had to go someplace and eat dinner.

CHAPTER EIGHT

Execution

Not only did I have a nice dinner, but I had it with two lovely women. Both were people I'd met socially off and on, and neither really looked like Dylan or the body Sanda was now using. That wasn't really important. If anybody wanted to check, they'd run my record for Friday night and see that I'd taken my two known close friends on a stock VIP tour, exited with them, then dined with them, on me. The restaurant used was a dark and unfamiliar one, and if anybody was to ask, the most anybody would remember was that I'd dined there in the company of two lovely ladies.

I had a tough time keeping my mind on their conversation, though. I knew what must be happening back at Tooker, and what would occur not too long from now. I realized that, despite my glib assertions, what was going to be happening was damned risky and by no means a sure thing. Now, sitting there at dinner, I could think of hundreds of things that could go wrong, and the more I considered them, the more certain I became that one or another of them *would* go wrong. Both Dylan and Sanda had been saying to me over and over how it was impossible, how absurd the whole idea was, how fraught with peril, but I'd talked, charmed, and hypnotized my way out of worrying about their warnings.

Unfortunately, they were right.

Still, that plan was in motion now. There was no way to stop it, nor would I if I could have at this point.

The best, Krega had called me. And how had I become the best? By taking insane risks, doing the absurd and the impossible, and getting away with it.

The trouble was, one of these days my luck was going to catch up with me. Tonight, perhaps?

What they had to do was damned tricky.

One of the women with me said something and I snapped out of my reverie. "Huh? Sorry. Just tired, I'm afraid."

"Poor darling! All I was saying was that Mural over in Accounting joined one of those body-swapping clubs. I mean, Jora and I swap a lot with each other because we contrast so well, but I'm not sure I could be somebody else every day without much control over what. I wonder what drives people to that?"

"Bored people, mostly," I told her, "and ones with real weird needs. I've heard some of those clubs are regular orgies."

"Hmmm! Who'd think *that* of somebody like Mural! I guess you can never tell . . ."

The janitorial staff for the executive floors of Tooker checked in for work. All were grumbling, yawning, and damned sleepy, but none had called in sick. Had it been midweek they might have, but as it was Friday, they would have the weekend to sleep off those damned false alarms. Besides, a supervisor for cleaning robots was rarely needed for anything anyway, and once their crew got to the security areas, not even a supervisor could catch them taking a little catnap.

"You've been working too hard lately," she said.

I nodded. "They've got us on double shifts some nights," I told the two of them. "Some big deal has taken some of our key people just when the quota's been upped. I've even got to go in tomorrow."

"Oh, you poor man! Well, we'll have to take you home and tuck you in early."

At a little after eleven, the janitorial supervisor finally reached the banking section. He was more than happy at the prospect; he'd been nodding off almost constantly. He went up to the entry doors, switched on the scanner, waited a couple of minutes, then put his card in the slot. Then he placed his special card, taken from the safety vault far below, in the slot as well, so the doors would admit the cleaning robots. Instructing the machines as to

what to do—and what not to do, particularly in the area
he was going to be—he drifted over to a large chair,
positioned it so that it was hidden from direct view of the
windows by some consoles, and settled in for a little
sleep.

Sanda, alerted by the noise, waited until he was clearly
inside, then pulled a wheeled chair out and down the
hall to the area near the door. From this point she could
see much of the room, although she could barely see the
form of the already sleeping supervisor. Relaxing, con-
centrating as only her hypnotized state would allow, she
felt the Wardens in her mind reach out. The distance between her and the sleeping man was more than eleven
meters, and she could feel some interference from the
Wardens in the machinery and even the plastiglass that
caused a bit of a focusing problem, but finally she had it.
It helped that there were no shields here, and no other
human beings on the floor. Slowly at first, then more pos-
itively, she felt the fields of force from her own Wardens
reach out, touch, and link with those of the sleeping man.

My mind is your mind, my arms are your arms, my
legs are your legs, my heart is your heart . . .

Twenty minutes later and several floors above Sanda,
another tired janitor entered another security area, first
by having herself scanned, then using the special card
that allowed seventy seconds for the cleaning robots to
enter. Since the floors were all sealed except to those in
the scanning computers, such as the janitor, the gap was
never considered a threat by security analysts.

"Home at last, Qwin! Thanks for a beautiful evening.
I'm only sorry you're so tired and have to work tomorrow. We could have an even more perfect evening."

I looked at both of them, then at my watch. "Well, I'm
not *that* tired."

Sanda was in the janitor's body. The cleaning equipment softly hummed, doing its business all around the
banking room, but that was it. Getting up, and knowing
exactly where to look, Sanda saw the form of her former
self still asleep in the chair outside the door. Now came
the most sensitive and riskiest part of the operation, and

the most discretionary. She could simply proceed with her job and risk the sleeper awakening, but the door had been relatively silent and its noise would probably be masked by the sounds of the cleaning equipment. She decided on a mild risk for more insurance, found the passkey for the robot equipment, went over to the door, and inserted the card. The door slid open, and she walked out. Taking the ten anxious paces to the sleeping form, she then picked up the nuraform in the small bottle next to the chair and, holding it under the sleeper's nose, saw its vapors inhaled and the figure slump.

She immediately put the bottle down and ran back into the banking room. Seven seconds later, the doors snapped shut once more. With an additional check of the sleeper and a check of the wall clock, she went over to a console and began performing instructions on it she did not understand but carried out just as she had been taught.

Above, in accounting, Dylan fretted nervously as the young woman inside the security area made no move to take a nap but went on checking the operation of all the machines. Five minutes passed, then ten. Finally, though, the woman picked a spot of floor behind the consoles and stretched out, using her jacket for a pillow. She did not go to sleep as easily or quickly as her counterpart below, but eventually she lapsed into it. Only then could Dylan set up as Sanda had below and begin the laborious process.

Sanda's part had been completed in only nine minutes, and she was satisfied. Now came the hard part—waiting. She placed herself in a deeper trance by a combination of autohypnosis reinforced by posthypnotic suggestion, and in full view of the sleeping form outside the plastiglass, waited in the chair for the nuraform to wear off and the sleeper to go into the characteristic deeper sleep of those who have just come out of nuraform.

Inside the sleeping, small form it took thirty-seven minutes for the nuraform to cycle out of the system, aided by Warden rejection, whereupon she began the process of switching bodies again.

*   *   *

Almost an hour had elapsed before Dylan could make her exchange. Once inside, she checked and saw that she'd positioned her body correctly and there had been no problems. The janitor still slept.

She decided, though, to take a chance on not using the nuraform. This was a light, troubled sleeper who might easily be awakened by the necessity of opening the doors. She went quickly to the consoles and, as Sanda had, followed instructions to the letter. It took less than five minutes to complete the job, and reconcile Sanda's alterations with those going on on a floor below.

Checking often her sleeping charge outside the room, she had several nervous moments when the figure shifted, but so far so good. She stretched back out on the floor, relaxed, and let her mind flow toward the other outside the plastiglass. Her own body was so tired and achy she feared she might accidentally go to sleep herself.

Sanda awoke back in the chair outside the plastiglass with a splitting headache and some double vision. It had been *her* body, after all, that had been nuraformed.

She looked into the glass—and froze, as the janitor's body shifted slightly and he awoke and looked around, a puzzled expression on his face. He stood up, looking not in her direction but rather at the cleaning equipment on the far side of the room.

He barked an order to it and it started to move toward him. Taking the noise as her only cue, Sanda slid out of the chair and pushed it away, down the hall, literally on her knees, one eye always on the janitor. It was a nervous time, but she was saved partly by his lack of suspicion and partly by the fact that the interior lights of the banking section reflected off the plastiglass, masking much of what went on in the darkened hallway. Once or twice he seemed to look in her direction and she froze, but then he'd just look away at something else or shake his head and yawn, and that was that.

Not until she was back in the conference room, though, and with the door closed and latched behind her, did she allow herself to relax and nurse her still aching head. She was just about to congratulate herself when she realized that she'd left the nuraform bottle right there, next to the door. Her nerves overcame her conditioning, but she had enough common sense to know there was nothing she could do about it now.

Back in the banking section, the janitor gathered up his machines, yawned, stretched once more, and wondered a bit about some strange feelings and after-impressions in his head. Putting them down to his exhaustion, he gathered his cleaning crew and brought them out the door once again.

The sweeping machine turned and started down the hall, sweeping up the tiny bottle and sucking it inside with the rest of the garbage.

It was more than two hours later before Dylan could make the switch, two anxious hours when it appeared that at any moment the sleeper would awake or, worse, Dylan would fall asleep herself. Still, she managed the switch, and back in the accounting room, thanks partly to the tiredness of the janitor's body and partly to the reclining form, there was no awakening. Dylan was able to return to her office hideaway and relax.

I in turn knew nothing of this at the time, but I finally kissed my two alibis off and settled down to a nervous wait. My greatest fear was that one or both couldn't make the original switch or the switch back without awakening the sleepers. I had never doubted that both janitors would take the snooze; they usually did anyway, and my false alarms just ensured that this night wouldn't be the exception.

I had also exempted, on the janitor's schedule, both the meeting room and Sugal's office. This wasn't unusual —those areas weren't to be used until Monday, anyway, and with a half crew on for the weekend they would be cleaned at that time.

I got a little sleep, but not much, and showed up at Tooker about 6:00 A.M. Very early, but not totally unusual in these hard-pressed days. You either worked really late or you worked early. I'd established an irregular enough pattern so that the records wouldn't show anything particularly odd.

Once in the still mostly deserted building, I headed for

my office and picked up the phone. No outside calls would be possible until eight, when the master building control computer came back on to normal, but the inter-office system worked regardless. I rang Sugal's office, letting it ring twice, then hanging up and dialing again.

"Qwin?" I heard Dylan's anxious voice and felt some relief.

"Yeah. Who else? How'd it go?"

"Hairy, you bastard. I'd much rather hunt borks."

I laughed. "But you did it?"

"Yeah, it's done, although I still don't believe it. Sanda?"

'I haven't called yet. I'll do that in a minute."

"Look, isn't somebody going to be coming in here shortly? When can I leave this mausoleum? I'm starving to death!"

"You know the routine. At seven-thirty the public function elevators will revert to normal, and you're on the office level. Just take the first car at seven-thirty down to the main level and use the emergency exit I told you about. No card needed."

That was true, for the fire code—but it *would* snap her picture along with day and time. That was no problem at all, though. As soon as they were both through, I'd use the handy little code Sugal supplied to erase the recording.

I gave her some encouraging words and rang the conference room with the same signal. The second time I called, Sanda answered, even more breathless than Dylan had been.

"How'd it go?"

She told me the whole story, of how the man had awakened and she had left the bottle there and, later, when the janitor had cleared the floor, it wasn't there any more. I calmed her, noting that he cleaned and polished the halls with that equipment, too.

Calmed of that particular fear, she was otherwise gushing. "It was," she told me, "the most exciting time of my whole life. More, even, than my first baby!"

I had to laugh at that, then reminded her of the exit procedures, and made certain that she, too, would be out of the building by seven forty-five. That was when I was going to take care of that little security record.

I sat back, feeling satisfied. They'd both been right: the plan had been absurd and certain to fail, so many variables beyond our control, all that. But it *had* worked. Worked perfectly. And the two women and I all had wonderful alibis.

I'd had all sorts of fallback positions in case something had gone wrong, including convincing cover stories for both of them to use about being locked in the building and all that. But that would have caused a lot of suspicion and might have blown the whole thing even if they were believed by the night janitors and security people. Nothing had to be used. Free and clear.

At seven forty-five I cleared the security recording.

At eight the Chief of Security checked, found a blank recording, and was satisfied that nobody had passed. By that time I was actually doing a little work, although I planned to knock off by ten. I was tired, damn it.

The whole plan looked crazy on paper, and it was; yet it was also tailor-made for the weaknesses inherent in the system. The conviction that nothing save orders from legal judges could change you against your will had made it possible to do just that with the janitors, under the circumstances of the deserted, familiar halls of the building.

But the final item that made it all possible was the certainty in every Cerberan mind that even if you could electronically steal money you couldn't get away with it, and that therefore nobody would bother to try. A few early and prominent examples sufficed.

The beauty of the plot was that nobody who did anything had any easily visible motive, and the man who did wouldn't have the slightest idea how the caper had been accomplished.

CHAPTER NINE

Aftermath and Reset

Sunday afternoon on the boat the three of us, with Sanda back in her own body, held something of a party to celebrate. I was particularly proud of Sanda, whose major reaction was that she wanted to do that kind of thing again. Dylan was more serious about it all; she knew the risks and the improbabilities of the thing as much as I did. We were a lot alike, Dylan and I, despite our very different backgrounds, except she was far more practical than I. Like those who would investigate this caper, she was fully capable of working out the details and dreaming it up, but she would never have gone through with it on her own. Had she not been in on it, she wouldn't have believed anybody would have. That, of course, was the ace in the hole for those invesigative types.

"Look," I told her. "The people who run this world—the corporation presidents, syndicate bosses, central administration—are the survivors. They are the ones who were audacious enough and smart enough to pull off their own operations and eliminate their competition—and lucky enough to get away wih it. There's a share of luck in all success stories, and only the unlucky ones make the headlines."

"Well, we were lucky this time," she responded, "and we did it. Your luck's bound to run out sometime, though. If it had last night, *your* mind wouldn't be going to the moons of Momrath—Sanda's and mine would. She can do what she wants, but is *it* for me. I'm not risking my neck on your harebrained schemes any more."

"You won't have to," I assured her as sincerely as possible. "Help, yes. We're all partners in this, we three. But this sort of thing you do once. From here on in it'll be something different—and only I can accomplish the final objective."

"You're still going after Wagant Laroo?"

I nodded. "I've got to, for many reasons."

"And if you get yourself blown away?"

I smiled. "Then I'll try again. They'll just send in another me, and another, until the job gets done."

That afternoon I also filled Sanda in on the rest of the truth about me. After what she'd gone through, I thought she had a right to know. I admit I was soothing Dylan with my promise of no more risk to her. I really didn't know what was going to happen next, and who or what I'd need, but it certainly would involve at least her boat. Concerning the promise that we three were partners as long as we were together, though, I was dead serious. I really did like and admire these two very different women, such a contrast to, say, those two I'd spent the evening with Friday night, with their shallow dreams and shallow fantasies about body-swapping clubs and office gossip.

The next few weeks were nerve-racking. I had depended on the system being efficiently and competently run by people who understood the criminal mind because they too each had one. But after the success of our mission I was beginning to fear that I had been too subtle.

However, late one afternoon Turgan Sugal came down to see me, looking like a man who had suddenly found eternal life and fortune. "They suspended Khamgirt today," he told me.

"Oh?" I tried to sound playfully ignorant, but inside I felt a rising sense of satisfaction.

"Seems he had a hidden gambling vice. He was in hock up to his ass and still owed, so he had been siphoning off corporation money and spreading it thin in a lot of small bank accounts. A banking securities check a few days ago turned up the account pattern in the banking records, and they traced it to him."

"Well, what do you know about that!" I replied sarcastically.

He stopped for a moment. "It *was* you, wasn't it?" he managed, as if struck by a sudden revelation. "You—*framed* him? How?"

"Me? I didn't do any such thing," I replied with mock seriousness. "Hell, do you realize what it would take to fake something like that? Impossible!" And then I broke into loud laughter.

He laughed along with me for a moment, then stopped and stared at me strangely. "Just what the hell did you *do* to get sent here, anyway?"

"The usual. Computer fraud."

"How the hell did they ever catch you?"

"The same way they caught Khamgirt," I told him. "That's what gave me the idea."

He whistled. "Well, I'll be damned. All right, I won't ask any more. Things are pretty turbulent right now, and there's an investigation of the whole thing, since Khamgirt has not only denied everything but has passed a truth scan."

"Sure. They *know* it's a frame. But that won't help him. Oh, don't worry—they won't kill him or send him to the mines or anything like that. They'll pasture him, with a slap on the wrist. Not for embezzlement. They'll know he was had. For getting framed. That means he is not only unable to protect himself and his secrets but vulnerable. The syndicates don't allow you to make mistakes. Just remember that when you get on the high and mighty side."

He nodded. "Makes sense. But what if they figure it out and trace the whole thing back to us?"

"What do you mean, *us?*" I shot back. "You weren't involved except in supplying some information they can't specifically trace to anybody in upper management. And I really wouldn't worry about it in any event. They'll have some grudging respect for whoever pulled this off. It was a risky operation that took a lot of luck, but it worked. They might figure out *how* it was done, but never who did it. Just relax and take advantage. I assume you'll be moving up?"

"That's what I came to see you about. They've asked me to fill in as corporate comptroller while the comptroller assumes the acting presidency. I'm finally leaving this place—and none too soon, either. We can't possibly make Khamgirt's artificially high quotas this quarter. Fortunately, as comptroller, I'll be able to adjust those to a more realistic figure on a temporary basis, maybe even show the board of directors that Khamgirt was conducting a vendetta against us. They'll be happy to believe anything of him now."

"And how soon am I paid?" I asked him slowly.

He paused a moment. "Give me a month to get a handle on the operation there. Then I can act—they won't find it surprising for me to reward several old associates. It's done all the time, to put our men into the underpositions. That's the earliest I dare move."

I nodded. "Fine with me. I have a lot of work to do here before I leave, anyway—*company* work, don't get that stricken look. But there are two other things."

He started looking uneasy again. "What do you mean? We had a deal."

I nodded. "And I'll stick to it. The other two are in the form of favors. One is simply that I be able to get an appointment, maybe a business lunch, with the acting corporate comptroller once in a while. Just to keep my hand in and find out the latest company gossip."

He relaxed a bit. "That's easy enough."

"The second's a very different favor, and it's not a requirement or condition. If necessary I can handle it in an underhanded manner, but it would be easier if you could do it normally."

"Go ahead."

"There's a young woman who did us both a real service, and she's stuck in the motherhood and doesn't want to be. That's bad enough, but she's extremely bright and talented and has a lot of guts. I'd like to get her out —I kind of owe it to her."

He thought for a moment. "I can see your reasons, but it's pretty tough, you know. I don't know of anybody with the power to do it unless you could force a judgment—catching somebody committing a crime against her. And that'd be pretty rough on her."

I nodded. "Just thought I'd ask in case there was some way out."

"Look, tell you what. Give me some time on this, a couple of months at least, and I'll see if anything can be done. Fair enough?"

I agreed. "It'll wait. She'll have sixty days' leave com-

ing soon, so it's not *that* pressing. Only if you can't, tell
me, won't you? And don't you want her name and
address?"

He grinned. "Don't need it. I keep very good track of
my employees."

That brought a little feeling of admiration from me.
Still, I felt compelled to nail him down a bit.

"As you can see, I'm a good friend—and a loyal one,
Mr. Sugal. I won't cross you now or in the future as
long as you don't cross me either. Just remember we have
a mutual stake in each other's protection. If you get in
trouble, a psych probe could smoke *me* out. If *I* do, the
reverse is true. So we have a stake in each other's wel-
fare."

"Funny," he replied. "I was about to give the same
speech to you."

Events proceeded in a slow, relaxed fashion after
that, but right on schedule. Sugal was promoted, and
within the month Tooker quotas were slashed and an
industrial investigation team from the government evaluated maximum production potential with the staff we
had against the quotas imposed and declared the quotas
unrealistic and false. That gave us a great deal of breathing space.

Also during this period a particular fire district had a
completely new alarm system installed, and our night janitorial supervisory staff was changed and its cleaning
methods modified. Several staff members, including me,
were discreetly questioned, known associates, that sort of
thing. The investigators found nothing, of course, and the
heat was off as quickly as it had appeared.

At the end of the month Sanda had her baby, a little
girl, and within a week after was looking and sounding
more like her old self again. I'd told her I was working
on her problem, but that it might take time, and she
seemed to accept that. After our little caper, she had the
utmost trust and confidence in my ability to deliver—
and of course that meant I felt honor-bound to do so.

Shortly afterward Tooker was reorganized, with a new
manager appointed and many of my colleagues and co-
workers promoted, moved around, and in a few cases,

canned—particularly if they had been known Khamgirt people. As for me, I was made president of Hroyasail Limited, a wholly owned Tooker subsidiary. The job paid extremely well, but as I knew, wasn't all that necessary, being one of those ornamental posts mostly used to pasture people like Khamgirt. My promotion raised no eyebrows, since it was explained as a personal decision based on my relationship with Dylan.

And so it was I had the upper offices of the Akeba marina cleaned and redecorated. There I was, a company president in less than a year—never mind that it was a dead-end job. Technically I was in charge of a fleet of four hunter-killer boats and sixty-two trawlers, plus assorted warehouses and processing centers for the catch.

The offices were a three-story affair overlooking the harbor and perched in the branches of a couple of huge trees. One branch had been cut and a deck put on it that extended, bridgelike, back to the offices, so there was a clear walk down to the boats themselves.

The lower floors contained basic administration and records processing and the initial holding tanks for the skrit, a reddish little creature somewhere between a plant and an animal whose internal body chemistry provided, among other things, chemicals that made superb electrical conductors. Once a week or so, more often if business was good, a big industrial flier would arrive, take the tank off to Tooker for processing, and then drop off a new, empty one.

The upper floor, however, had been closed off since the last president, at least eight years before. I spent Tooker's expense money lavishly, fixing up not only a comfortable office suite but also a huge luxury apartment with all the amenities. I moved in quickly. Shortly after, Dylan moved in as well, and we drew up and filed a marriage contract. Marriages were not usual nor necessary on Cerberus and existed mostly among people belonging to religious communities, but there were reasons for this one. On a practical level, it clearly defined joint and separate property and allowed us to establish a joint credit line. In that sense, it fulfilled my original promise of full partnership, and her position in Hroyasail sud-

denly became, as the boss's spouse, one of greatest among
equals.

And of course our relationship made my request for
the Hroyasail position all the more credible to any suspicious onlookers. But there was more to it than that. I felt
comfortable around Dylan, and not as comfortable
away from her. She was a close friend and absolute con-
fidante, and I'd never had that close a relationship. It
was more than that. Being with her felt *good*, somehow
—having her there, to know she was there even when we
were in different parts of the place doing different things.
However, this dependency bothered me, because up until
now I'd considered myself immune to such human emotional weaknesses.

We slept together as a couple, too, causing frequent
body switches that bothered neither of us. As Class I's we
did our regular job no matter who looked like who, and
the experience brought us closer than any couple I could
remember.

As for Dylan—well, all I can say is that I seemed to fit
into a hollow space in her life, possibly left over from
her previous career in the motherhood. She needed someone very close, and sleeping together without shields was
more important to her than to me.

The only two things that bothered me were her cigars,
which were pretty smelly even with the blower system on
full, and the fact that most mornings she'd go out on that
damned boat and risk her life. I wasn't on my post more
than a couple of weeks when they brought the first bodies
back, mangled and bleeding if the sailors had been
lucky, or in parts in body bags if they hadn't been. I
didn't want to see Dylan come home like that, but I
couldn't talk her out of it. It was her life, in her blood,
and no matter how she felt about me I knew I'd always
come second to the sea.

Sanda, of course, was the extra element in all this, but
it wasn't really so bad. Both Dylan and I were nearby
now, constantly within a quick elevator ride of Akeba
House. So Sanda couldn't have been happier, although
there was a wistful envy inside her that she could witness
this but was prohibited by virtue of the motherhood
from its paradoxical freedom and stability.

I had heard a few times from Sugal, who was digging into the comptroller's post so solidly that it looked like the "acting" titles for all of the board would soon be removed and the positions made permanent. Khamgirt, as I predicted, had been convicted of the charge, placed on probation, and pastured to president of a regional shipping line that was also a Tooker subsidiary.

Things were going well for me, but I resisted the temptation just to let things slide. There was still Wagant Laroo to catch, and all I could do was keep my eyes and ears open and wait for a new break.

CHAPTER TEN

A Bork Hunt

My worries over Dylan increased with each injury, and yet I understood her well enough to know that protesting was useless. Sanda, on the other hand, had gotten the bug bad from her exploit with me and was just dying for some more action.

We were sitting around the place one evening, just talking and relaxing, when Sanda brought the subject up after hearing a few new accounts from Dylan, who never tired of the subject.

"It sounds so thrilling," she told us. "I'd give almost anything to go out just once."

"You'd probably be bored stiff," Dylan told her. "After all, we don't have hunts and attacks every day—thank heaven."

"Still—just to be out there speeding across the waves, with the feeling that danger could come from anywhere —I've heard all your stories so often I can see it in my dreams. Instead, well, my leave's almost up. Next week it's back to the House and the hormones." The thought of that really depressed her.

"You know you can't go, though," I noted sympathetically. "You're certified valuable to the state. No risks allowed."

"I know, I know," she sighed and sank into depression.

Though this wasn't the first time the subject had come up, this had been the worst and most persistent round. I could see Sanda was getting to Dylan, partly out of friendship but also because she too had once been in the girl's position.

Later that evening, after Sanda was asleep in the guest room, we lay there, not saying much. Finally I said, "You're thinking about Sanda."

She nodded. "I can't help it. I look at her, listen to her, and all I can see and hear is me a few years ago. Anything on getting her out?"

"No, and you know it. Sugal's pulled every string he can find and it just isn't done. The only cases on record are ones in which a syndicate boss wants a private breeder, so to speak, to control his own kids—or for Laroo's own purposes. It's a dead end. Maybe I can come up with something of my own, but I've gone through all the possibilities and the system's just against me. Unless I can crack that master computer I can't do much, and to crack the computer I'd have to replace Laroo."

"What about the drug angle? It's the way I got out."

"And they closed that loophole after you," I noted. "After your switch they had a big debate and decided that there was nothing in the rules to use against you, so they let you go, but then they made some new rules. Any switch from the 'valuable to the state' category has to be voluntary on both sides now or either one can seek a judgment to reverse it."

"We could let her use one of our bodies now and then. That's something."

"Yeah, that's true, but not for the boats and you know it. If anything happened to either one of our bodies under those conditions we'd automatically wind up in the motherhood ourselves—permanently, regardless of our Class I status." I sighed in frustration. "That's the hell of this system. In some places, in human history and even out on the frontier, motherhood's not only voluntary but a normal and *respected* thing. Even on other Warden worlds, I hear. But the bosses are afraid that the birth-rate would decline low enough that it wouldn't sustain their need for new bodies as well as maintaining normal population growth. As long as *they* control and raise the babies they also control who lives forever and who dies—the ultimate control on this society."

"Hey! Don't forget, I was raised that way," she reminded me. "So was Sanda. They don't do a bad job."

"No, they don't," I had to admit. "And don't forget that my state raised me, too. It's going through and picking the kids who'll live and the kids who'll die that gets to me. Sure, sixty percent get a good upbringing, but it's that other forty percent that gets me. And as long as the system's as depersonalized to the average Cerberan as the birthing centers are in the civilized worlds, they'll never fully face up to what they're doing—killing kids for their bodies."

"Are *you* going to turn down a new body when your turn comes?"

I chuckled sourly. "Hell, no. That's the heart of this system. Even its opponents can't resist taking advantage of its benefits. Still, it probably won't matter to either of us, anyway. I'll probably get my fool head blown off in the next scam and you'll wind up lunch for a bork. What you said about me is also true for you—our luck can't last forever."

"I've been thinking along similar lines," she said. "I mean it—we're two of a kind. My luck's been astounding for the past few years, but it can't hold out forever. And I know that one of these days you're going to go off to do battle against Wagant Laroo, and one of these times it isn't going to work out. That's why I wanted this. Why I am, right now, having the time of my life. We're doomed, the both of us, doing the jobs we love, and every day might be the last. You feel that, too."

I nodded slowly. "I know."

"So you see, if we're professional risk-takers, why can't we take a risk with Sanda on the boat?"

"My instinct's just go against it," I told her honestly. "I can't explain why."

"Look, I'm going to tell you a story. It's about a girl genetically tested and selected while still very young.

One that the genetic experts said had all the right and none of the wrong genes. So when she was very young, she was taken out of the normal group and put in a special school composed entirely of other little girls and isolated from the mainstream of society. She received no more formal education, but instead was subjected to ceaseless propaganda on the wonderfulness of having babies, the duty to society and civilization to do so, and how to have them and give them prenatal and postnatal care. By thirteen she was capable of having them, but didn't yet, although she had been introduced to sex, sexual pleasures, and all the rest, while the mental conditioning reached such a fever pitch that she wanted desperately nothing but the life of the motherhood. She was also mentally and physically conditioned to a life of leisure and to the idea that she was in the most important class on all Cerberus."

She paused for a moment, a distant, wistful look on her face, and I said nothing. Finally she continued.

"So the girl finally passed her preliminary nursing and midwife exams and reached her fifteenth birthday, and they sent her to Akeba House. The next few months were an absolute heaven—anything and everything she wanted, plus the excitement of new people, trips into the cities, the resort and all that. And of course they arranged for her to become pregnant. That wasn't bad, either, although it's pretty dispassionate in the doctor's office. She felt herself change and marveled at the miracle within her. And finally the baby came—pretty rough the first time, but that didn't matter. And there was this beautiful baby boy, clinging, nursing, crying.

"And then one day, in about the second month, they came and took the baby away. They didn't"—she paused, her voice getting choked with emotion at the remembered pain—"they didn't even tell her. Just came and took him and that was that. And then they said go, take two months' leave and do anything you want—then come back. You have to have roughly a baby a year."

She sighed and I thought I saw the glimmer of a tear, the first time I'd ever seen Dylan cry.

"And so," she went on in that wavering, distant tone, "she ran to the others, her friends, for consolation, and got none. Either they were hardened to the system or they'd given up and were reconciled to it. The House staff also was very little consolation, finally offering to send me to a psych center so I'd adjust and be happy doing nothing but having babies. I couldn't accept that, either, so I sort of gave up. Gave up and gave in, like they all do. But Akeba House was located on an outcrop, and there was a small harbor on one side. I used to watch the hunters go out, and my mind went with them every time, as Sanda's does now. I became their friend, except for the times when I was obviously pregnant and they shunned me like a disease. Finally, during my leave time—after my fifth child—one of them, a very compassionate man I'll never forget, said much what you did just now—hell, you and he were a lot alike, really. He could be killed tomorrow and probably would be someday, so if risks were his business, well, he'd smuggle me aboard—and he did.

"And you know—nothing much happened. We sighted a bork, yes, but another boat took it and chased it out of view. The whole thing was pretty dull, really—but to me it was everything. It made me *alive* again, Qwin. I determined to get out of the motherhood, and I worked and schemed and plotted and took my opportunities just like you—and it worked. If it hadn't been for that joyride, though, I'd still be up there at the House, still having babies and gazing out at the sea, as Sanda is now. Wasting—just like she is. Do you understand now?"

I turned over and hugged her and held her close. "Yes, Dylan, I understand." I sighed. "So when are you going to take her?"

"Day after tomorrow. I wouldn't want it on my conscience that I killed a baby, too."

"All right. If your mind's made up. But please consider the matter again before you do. You're risking that sea, you know."

"Yeah, I know. Call me dumb or a softie or whatever. But I risked it for you, too. Maybe the luck'll hold one more time. The chances of getting caught are a lot slimmer this time. I've got a good crew. They won't talk, because it'd mark them as disloyals and they'd never get another berth."

"Your mind's made up, then?"

She nodded. "Absolutely."

"Then I'm coming along, too."

She sat up. "You? After I've been trying to get you out for weeks now?"

"Well, maybe if the president's along the responsibility will be spread a bit."

"No," she said firmly. "Come on if you want—hell, I'd love to see you. But there's only one person in charge of a boat, and that's the captain. One person in charge absolutely, and one person who's responsible for all aboard and their actions. That's the law and that's the way it has to be. Understand?"

"Okay, Captain," I responded, and kissed her.

It was a foul morning with intermittent rain and mist, so that you were hardly aware it was past dawn. The sea looked choppy and the boats all rode up and down uneasily on the water. That worried me, but Dylan was actually in better spirits because of it.

"We'll all be in rain gear, so if anybody happens to be spying from Akeba House they'll get no clues, not with these slickers and with her hair tucked up under the rain hat."

She had briefed her crew the day before in the privacy of the open sea. Nobody had objected. They knew her almost as well as I did, if not better, and she had their absolute respect.

The boat had a name—*Thunder Dancer*—but it was usually used only officially. Informally, it was always "Dylan's boat" or just "the boat."

We stayed inside the aft cabin where we had schemed and plotted not that long before, and a crewman fitted us with life jackets and briefed us. Dylan, at the wheel, was busy and we respected that.

"You can both swim, can't you?" the crewman asked, half joking.

"Yeah, although I'm not sure how far and how fast," I responded. 'It's a shame we have to go out on such a rotten day."

He laughed. "Oh, this is a *good* day. You ought to be here when we get in really rough weather. Waves over the bow, and even we crewmen puking as we hold it together. Don't worry about this, though. The front's only three or four kilometers out, and we're going a lot farther than that today. We should have warm and sunny weather by midmorning."

And, somewhat to my surprise, we did.

It was an education to watch the fleet move out, the trawlers chugging along slowly with two hunter-killers as escorts while we, as one of the two point boats, cleared the harbor and its buoys and flashing lights. We suddenly rose on two skilike rails, thus tilting the whole boat back as it poured on the speed, suddenly freed of having the bulk of its mass push against the water.

"I have to be at station," the crewman told us. "You can go up to the bridge now if you want, but hold on to the handrails at all time."

I looked aft at the rapidly receding shoreline, half hidden in fog and mist, and at the wide wake we were leaving. The shoreline itself appeared ghostly, the great mass of trees rising from the water in and out of fog, punctured only by some distant lights.

"Oh, God! Isn't this *great!*" Sanda enthused, rushing from one window to another. She was like a little kid again, squealing, oohing, aahing, and just having a grand old time.

And there I was, the grand old veteran space pilot, feeling funny in my stomach. But that old me had been in a different body. Still, Dylan had come out on occasion in this body and seemingly had had no trouble, so that wasn't the whole explanation.

"Let's go up to the bridge," I suggested as we broke through the squall line and were suddenly hit by sunlight.

"Great! Lead on!"

We walked through the interior, past the electronic detection gear and biomonitors that would locate the masses of *skrit* on or near the surface and would also warn of borks, through the small galley and up a small set of steps to the bridge itself. There Dylan was sitting, relaxed, in the broad, comfortable captain's chair with an idle hand on the wheel, looking out. She turned as we entered and smiled. "Well! How do you like it so far?"

"Tremendous!" Sanda enthused. "Oh, Dylan, I can never repay you for this!"

Dylan took her hand from the wheel, got up, and hugged Sanda. The look on our captain's face said that the attitude alone was more than payment enough.

"Hey!" I yelled. "Who's driving?"

Dylan laughed. "The autopilot, of course. I've programmed in the course and set it for automatic after we lifted. No more attention required until we get to our zone for the day."

I felt a bit foolish and even a little ashamed. The same guy who bearded lions in their dens and was confident of taking on Wagant Laroo, who'd piloted starships through trackless voids, was damned scared out here in an alien ocean with no land closer than two kilometers straight down.

"You look a little green," she joked, looking in my direction. "If I were the mean sort I'd find some really rough water and give you a workout—but don't worry, I love you and I won't."

The rest of the morning we sat around talking, occasionally bringing Dylan a cup of coffee or light snack from the mini-galley or doing the same for the crew.

And she'd been right. After a while it got to be damned boring. Not for Sanda, who climbed all over the boat, getting explanations from the gun crews, and lessons from the electronics experts, and asking a million questions. For me, though, and basically for the crew as well, there was nothing exciting about skimming along the ocean at thirty-six knots with nothing anywhere in sight.

Still, they all had within them some extra sense, some deep love for the sea, the boat, and their lives here. They were happy, content, at peace out here in a way I could not understand, perhaps could *never* really figure out.

The ocean itself, though, had a certain academic fascination. It was different colors in different places, and there were obvious currents you could literally feel, as if the temperature rose and fell in a moment depending on what invisible part of the water you were in. In the distance you could actually see the storm front now moving "inland," and out a little farther to the northeast you could fully see a thunderstorm, dense rain, high, bomb-like clouds, and lightning all included, while you yourself were basking in the sunlight of a cloudless sky.

The pattern was generally the same for the boats. We had gone to a sector southeast of Medlam allocated by the Cerberan Coast Guard so that each company had its own area for the day, then had started a wide, circular sweep of the zone, going round and round in ever-smaller circles as the instruments looked for *skrit*.

"Still no skrit in commerical quantity," a speaker told us, "but we've got a bork on scope."

Dylan was suddenly all business. "Does he look interested in us?"

"Nope. Not particularly. Big one, though. Four, maybe five tons. About twelve hundred meters south-southwest and at about twenty meters depth. Not going much of anywhere, maybe going to come up for some sun is all."

"Well, keep an eye on him," she ordered, "and warn me of any changes in behavior." She walked out onto the outer deck around the bridge and I followed. The wind from our speed was pretty fierce, although there was a windshield just forward of the real bridge and actually an auxiliary wheel. She stared out at the open sea, as did I, but I could see nothing.

"Yup. There he is," she said unemotionally as she pointed. I squinted in the indicated direction but could see little. I began to wonder if she was putting me on or if my eyes weren't as good as hers.

"I don't see a thing."

"See—way off there? Look real hard in the sky. Squint a little against the reflection, or put on your dark glasses."

I put on the glasses, which I didn't particularly find comfortable, and tried to see. "Look in the sky?"

She nodded. "See those little black specks?"

I tried very hard, and *thought* I could see what she meant. "Uh-huh."

"They're geeks," she told me.

I tried to remember what a geek was. Some kind of flying horror, I seemed to recall. A carrion-eater. "Do they always follow borks?"

She nodded. "They're too lazy to make kills for themselves, and borks are greedy killers who are not too efficient about disposing of their kill. Oddly enough, the bork feeds mostly on skrit, which is why we have the problems we do, but it attacks and takes bites out of almost everything, including other borks. Some sort of natural balance, really. The borks feed the flying creatures and several other sea creatures by the kills they make and don't or can't consume. That's why we even have limits on the number of borks we can kill."

"He's turning," came the voice on the speaker. "We've got the bed pretty well located now and he's heading right toward it. I've sent a slowdown order to the fleet. Shall we engage?"

She looked thoughtful. "Call Karel. Ask if she's in any position to assist a runaway."

There was a short pause, and I gathered by their manner that it was better just to stand out of the way, and let them do what they knew how to do so well. I had an uneasy feeling about all this, though. I kept hearing that "four, maybe five tons" over and over again.

"Karel says she's about twenty minutes away, and escort's about forty."

She looked at me. "Where's Sanda?"

"In the lounge, last I checked."

She turned back to the speaker. "Make sure the passenger is secure inside, then tell Karel to pour it on. Gun crews to full alert status. Stand by to close." She went to the outside wheel and reached to one side, flipping a switch. The boat slowed noticeably. Then, one hand on the wheel and the other on the throttle, a stick with a big black ball on top, she took full control of the boat from the autopilot.

"You better go inside and get strapped in," she told me. "We're at least going to have to turn the bastard and I don't want to lose you."

I nodded absently, feeling a little tightness in my stomach. Lots of nasty things and nastier situations I could handle, but out here on the open sea facing a creature I'd only seen pictures of, I was totally at the mercy of Dylan and her crew. We were closing on the thing. I could clearly see the nasty-looking geeks, about half a dozen of them, circling a dark patch in the water.

"Qwin! Please!"

"All right, all right. I don't want to distract you. I was just wondering why they called them borks."

At that moment the sea ahead of us exploded wth an elephantine mass at least three times the size of the boat. An enormous slit opened, revealing a tremendous cavity linked with sharp teeth and wriggling, wormlike tendrils. "BOOOOAAAAARK!" it roared, so loud that it echoed like thunder across the open sea and almost burst my eardrums.

"Ask a stupid question," I muttered, turned, and dashed for the lounge. Sanda was already there, strapped into a chair and watching out the window. I joined her, almost getting thrown against the side by the sudden change in the boat's direction.

Sanda's expression was stupefied and vacant, her mouth open, and when I got myself into a seat and stared out the window I probably looked about the same myself. "Oh, man!" she breathed.

The entire side of the ship seemed dominated by the monstrous reddish-brown thing that continued to show more and more of itself. I couldn't translate what I was seeing to the pictures and diagrams I'd seen of the things.

Out of the water on either side rose four huge tentacles with bony spikes all over. The tentacles alone looked as if they could pick up and crush the boat, and those bony protrusions looked as if they could easily penetrate not only the plastiglass but the armor plating itself. Worse, I knew that the entire surface of the bork's skin was tremendously sticky and abrasive at the same time, so that the merest touch could rip flesh from bone.

And we were slowly cruising by now, as if on a sight-seeing tour!

Suddenly I heard the engine rev up, whining as if it were strained to the limit. We had been moving so slowly that we were actually hardly up on our hydrofoil skis at all. Then the guns let loose, shaking the ship from stem to stem and sending cups and such flying. The guns were explosive projectiles; you couldn't use a disrupter system on something mostly underwater because you might not be able to stop the effect. Besides, a weaker laser wouldn't put a dent in something this size, whose vital organs were always well underwater and away from direct attack by boats.

I had to admit that for the first time in my life I felt not only helpless but terrified.

The shells struck the thing and exploded with enormous force, releasing not only a powerful explosive charge but also some kind of electrical one as well. The creature roared and moved faster than I would have believed anything that big could possibly move. But still we remained, just crawling past.

With a splash I thought might sink us by itself, the thing had appeared to retreat and dive at the same time, but I was suspicious of this respite. We waited tensely.

Suddenly we were jerked almost out of our restraining straps as the full power of the engines was released at once and the ship almost jumped out of the water.

In a matter of no more than a couple of seconds, the bork rose with a roar and enfolded an area of ocean astern of us. I realized with a sinking feeling that that area of sea was where we had just been.

The aft gun opened up with a full series of shots, pouring it into the great beast. With its computer laser-guidance system it must have poured twenty or more exploding charges into the thing, and they barely made a dent in it.

Again the bork seemed to shrivel and sink beneath the waves. Outside somewhere over the roar of all the action I kept hearing fierce, loud cries of "Geek! Geek!" like some sort of bizarre cheerleading squad—which in a way it was.

So much for how creatures on Cerberus got their names.

For more than half an hour we played cat and mouse with the beast, luring, feinting, and shooting at it with enough ordnance to totally obliterate a medium-sized city. After a while you could see the areas of the creature that had been shot away, and occasional wounds still bubbling and hissing from the electrochemicals shot into it that water would not extinguish. But no matter how many times it was hit, there seemed to be another section just as nasty and virtually untouched.

I did finally realize what Dylan was doing, though. She

was doing her job—pulling the bork further and further away from the skrit that had to be commercially harvested. All I could do was admire her skill, timing, and guts. I recall thinking, *And they have charter boats for people to do this for fun?*

How far away had she pulled it? I began to wonder. Possibly several kilometers. But while it was clear to me that we were faster in the long run than the bork, we didn't have the ordnance to kill the monstrosity alone. For all that we were doing, we were hitting nonvital parts.

Suddenly, after all this cat-and-mouse stuff, Dylan gunned the engine and we sped up and away from the monster, this time not firing. I wondered if she was going to break off. Then suddenly she made a steep turn, and in that turn I could see another boat like ours—Karel certainly—making a similar turn toward the great beast, which, because it hadn't been shot at the last time had not done its fantastic quick vanishing act.

It had in fact seen the other boat and ours turn and was standing its ground, confident of itself despite all the harm we'd done to it.

We started closing fast—so fast I was afraid we were going to crash right into the thing. Mentally I could see only one of those great bony tentacles crashing down into us, bringing oblivion in the deeps. But as the thing made ready for its swipes I heard four sharp pops from each side of the boat, and we suddenly made a turn so sharp it seemed certain to capsize us. The turn put the aft lounge in full view of the thing, and it seemed that the world was full of nothing but the most disgusting gullet imaginable.

Suddenly the sea behind us erupted in a tremendous series of blasts, tearing into the monster, which roared its terrible defiance. We could see the second boat launch its own torpedoes, the nice kind that went by air or water and did what you told them to do.

I saw two literally jump out of the water and go right down the monster's throat!

Already we had some distance on the thing, which still looked like a floating city. Suddenly, though, it was ripped by two tremendous explosions and seemed almost to fly apart, bits and pieces several meters long of bloody skin, bone, and tentacle flying every which way, some almost far enough to reach our boat. At that moment I saw Karel's boat appear off to our side, though quite a bit astern, and heard above the death throes of the monster a foghornlike signal which we answered.

Confirmed kill.

You could hear the yells and cheers from the men and women on our boat, too—and maybe even a little from Sanda and me.

Sanda seemed to collapse, then shook her head in wonder. "Wow! I read all the books, heard all the stories, saw all the roomvision specials, but nothing was ever like this! Compared to this, what we did for you was a piece of cake!" She paused and looked at me oddly. "You all right?"

"I think I wet my pants," I croaked.

A bit later I managed to get hold of myself, clean up, and go forward to see Dylan. This trip had been an education for me, all right, and one I would remember until my death. I had discovered that I *could* be that scared, and I also finally realized that Dylan not only did this every day but did it routinely, as a matter of course. I had a new, almost awed respect for her courage now. If there was anybody I ever dreamed of wanting at my back, it was definitely Dylan Kohl.

The rest of the day, such as it was, was uneventful. No more borks—although we had one sighting—and no more chases. Just playing shepherd to the fleet of trawlers hauling in the rich, reddish skrit. It was a boring afternoon, and I loved every boring minute of it. The efficient trawlers were quick about their work, reaching capacity in less than two hours. Together, we and the fleet headed for home.

My emotions were more mixed now than they had been earlier. As much admiration as I had for Dylan and the others who did this day in and day out, this sort of tension had to take its toll on all of them. If anything, I had underestimated the danger of the job. I was going to be worried more and more about her as I replayed this experience in my mind again and again.

We reached the harbor uneventfully and settled down into the water, pulling smoothly to the dock. Dylan supervised the securing of the mooring lines to the boat and then came back to see us. "Better wait until dark before getting off," she cautioned Sanda. "That way nobody's going to be sure if you went with us or came on after."

She nodded, and I stood up. "I hope you'll excuse me for not staying as well, but I have to put my foot on dry, solid wood or something or I'll go nuts." My whole body felt as if it were permanently vibrating.

Sanda rose and gave Dylan a big hug and kiss. "Oh, I love you for this! By God, I'm gonna beat the motherhood if it kills me!"

Dylan looked at me. "See?"

I nodded understandingly and took off, heading for the gangplank and dock. I had no sooner walked out than I stopped dead in my tracks. Two unfamiliar people were standing there at the end of the gangplank, and they had the look that seems universal for their kind anywhere in the galaxy. I felt a sinking sensation in my stomach and tensed up as bad as I had during the bork hunt.

The two, a man and a woman, walked on board and stopped, looking at me. One flashed a badge and said softly, "CID. I caution you to remain where you are and not make a sound." He nodded to the woman, who walked aft to the lounge, then in the door.

"After you," said the male cop. I turned, and walked back into the lounge with him.

The two women were both there, having mistaken the woman's approach for my return.

"Which of you is Captain Kohl?" the female cop asked.

"I am!" Sanda spoke up bravely.

"No, I am," responded Dylan, looking then at Sanda with a sadness in her eyes and voice. "It's no good. They'll have to scan us both anyway."

"Look," I said, trying to sound indignant, "I'm the president of this company. What seems to be the trouble, officers?"

"Captain Kohl is charged with willfully violating Section 623½, Universal Penal Code," the man responded. Knowingly subjecting an individual classified as an asset to the state to extreme danger."

"This is ridiculous!" I sputtered. "Both of these women work for me."

"Stow it," the woman snapped at me. "We know who the girl is."

"I'm afraid I'll have to ask you both to come down to the station with us," the male cop added. Then, turning to me, he cautioned, "Please don't interfere. The penalties are quite severe for that."

"Can I go with them, then? I'm married to the captain."

"I don't see why not. But no funny business."

"There won't be," I assured them, feeling that all was suddenly very wrong; that for once luck had run out—not on me, but on the one I cared for most. I would have loved to have pulled some funny business and wouldn't have hesitated in the slightest to do so, but there seemed absolutely nothing I could do, funny or otherwise, except tag along.

CHAPTER ELEVEN

A Judgment

On the way in, I cautioned both of them to say nothing. Dylan squeezed my hand and Sanda's. "It's all right," she said simply. "I knew what I was doing, and I'm not sorry for it even now. Maybe it's a fair exchange, although not one I'd have made willingly. I've had five years of living. Now maybe it's somebody else's turn."

"Don't talk like that!" I scolded her. "It's not the end of the world."

"It's the end of *my* world," she almost whispered.

Once in the stationhouse, in a corner of the Municipal Building, both women were taken into a small room where their card imprints and scans were taken. I was not able to follow, but simply had to pace back and forth in a small waiting area. Even the bork hunt paled before my

feelings now, which were at an all-time low. After
about half an hour, they let me see Dylan for a few minutes while they processed their records and did whatever cops did. Sanda was being held in a separate room,
and I didn't see her.

"Well, it's over," she sighed.

"Huh? What do you mean?"

"They've been laying for me, Qwin. Laying for me
for, I guess, five years. They didn't like the fact that I
wormed my way out of the motherhood, so they've been
waiting for a chance to get me. A clerk in the office—one
I know, one who's worked there almost as long as I have
—was a plant. They had something on her. An old
criminal conviction or something, and she was too low in
skill level to be considered vital. She had to catch me or
when she reached the mandatory age it was the mines for
her."

I shook my head in disbelief. "Five *years?*"

She nodded. "They needed an example. There's been
a lot of rumblings in the motherhood since I sneaked
out. I was their symbol of hope—and I knew it. The
authorities *had* to get me, no matter how long it took.
They said their psychological profiles indicated I'd do exactly what I did sooner or later, and they were sure
right."

"What happens now?" I asked her, both concerned
and mad as hell at a system that would wait this long to
hang somebody.

"Judgment," she told me. "The witness, the cops, and
the scans proved their case automatically."

My mind was racing. "Who sentences you? What kind
of rank?"

"A professional judgment panel. Thirteen of them. I'm
scheduled to meet them in a little less than an hour. They
don't usually hold proceedings this late, but they're making a special case for me."

I thought of all the men in high places I knew. "Is there
someone I can call? Someone who can intercede?"

She shook her head. "I don't think so. Maybe after, but
not now. We don't even know what the sentence is yet
—could be almost anything. All I know is that it was
planned and directed years ago." She looked up at me.

"Don't blame yourself! I did it, all of my own free will. I'm totally responsible."

"I let you do it."

She smiled. a ghost of that old smile. "You couldn't have stopped me and you know it."

"Will they let me in? Will they hear any mitigating statements?"

She shrugged. "I don't know."

We waited together nervously until they called her name.

The judgment chamber was much like any other courtroom except for the thirteen black-robed men and women up there behind a curved table. Since only one had a mike, it was clear that there was a presiding officer. They let me in and I took a seat, noting Sanda in a chair forward of the rest of the seats, which were empty. Sanda looked as if she'd been crying a little, or maybe a lot, but she seemed composed now.

"The State versus Dylan Zhang Kohl," intoned the chief judge, as if there were other cases. "Will the prisoner please rise and approach the bench?"

Dylan stood up and confidently did as she was told, looking the chief judge right in the eye. *Good for you, gal!* I thought.

"Dylan Zhang Kohl, you have been found guilty on the evidence which we have judged to be true and incontrovertible that you did willfully and knowingly violate Section 623½, Cerberan Universal Penal Code. Can you find any reason for sentence to be deferred or mitigated?"

"No, your honor," she said firmly.

I cursed and fidgeted like mad in my seat. Twice in one day I felt real fear, and twice in one day a total sense of helplessness.

"Will Sanda Tyne approach the bench?"

Sanda, looking tiny and nervous, did so, standing next to Dylan. I saw that Dylan took Sanda's hand and squeezed it affectionately, as if to reassure her.

"Sanda Tyne, we find that you did knowingly and willfully violate the Articles of Syndication applicable to Akeba House. This we have judged true and incontrovertible on the evidence. Can you find any reason for sentence to be deferred or mitigated?"

"I talked her into it," she pleaded bravely. "I kept after her and after her. It's all my fault!"

"We have considered all the factors involved, including having both your psychological profiles analyzed completely. One of the principal articles of the code, particularly considering the past history of this planet and many of its founding parents, is that the criminal act is not something to be judged in and of itself, but in the context of society. One can, for example, go into one of the private banks and plead for a thousand units, without credit, collateral, or any obvious means of payback. If the bank then gives you the loan anyway, and you default, it is not your responsibility but the bank's. Now, say you desperately needed the money, for a matter of life and death, and you conveyed this to a bank officer. The officer is sympathetic but should deny your loan because it would injure his employer, and therefore his depositors, and therefore the state. Everyone who had deposits in good faith at that bank would pay for his error.

"But let us suppose that his heart was touched by your plea, and he then arranged for you to get to a console so that you could steal the money. You are desperate, and you do so, thereby committing a criminal act. But who is truly committing the more serious crime? The one who steals, or the one who allows and arranges for the person to steal? This court recognizes this principle, so enshrined in our laws and principles, and in that context applies it to judgment in this case. Examining your psychological profile, we find you, Sanda Tyne, to be a secondary party to this violation, as you did not stow away on the boat or enter it without the permission of its captain.

"This court has studied both your records and has arrived at what we believe is a fair and just verdict. It is the sentence of this court that the two of you exchange bodies by means of judgment, and so be locked into those bodies. We further hold that you, Dylan Kohl, will assume the responsibilities of the Tyne body and are therefore not to assume your former position or take any other employ. In view of your psychological profile we further direct that you be taken after judgment to the Borough of Medlams Public Psychology Section and undergo a series of specific treatments to be set by this court for yours and the public's good."

I jumped up. "You're not going to turn my wife into a vegetable!" I screamed.

The judge paused, and all thirteen gave me the dirtiest looks I ever got from anybody. *Well, you've blown it now,* I told myself, but I didn't care any more.

"You are the spouse of the prisoner Dylan Kohl?"

"Yes, I am, and—"

"Silence! Or I will have you removed and charged!" He paused for a moment to see if I would take the challenge, but I got back a little of my self-control and managed to hold on for a moment.

"Now, then," the judge continued, sounding deliberative but satisfied, "let me state to you, sir, that the days of such things, except in extreme cases, are past. For your benefit, I will outline and explain what we mean."

"Please," I almost begged, shaking a little.

"We believe that the profile of Dylan Kohl indicates a possibility of suicide. We will prevent that, as well as other acts possibly harmful to herself or to others. Everything we do will be in the nature of protections such as that or compulsion to ensure that the sentence is carried out. Her memory, personality, and general freedom of movement will not be impaired, since to do anything else would not be a punishment at all. Does this satisfy you?"

It didn't, but what could I say? Well, there was always one thing, while I had the judge's ear. "Your honor, we are married and we truly love each other. Could she not continue to live with me? Even with her other occupation, she knows my business better than I do and could make a contribution to its management without costing the company or the state anything. It would be a shame to waste this expertise."

I saw the judges whispering among themselves until finally the whisper, like a ripple, reached the chief judge. He looked slightly surprised and a bit uncomfortable, but he considered whatever it was, then turned back to me.

"My colleagues seem to go along with you—to a point. In such a relationship, which is quite rare on this planet, it has been maintained by some of my learned colleagues that an absolute sentence would punish *you*, who have been charged with nothing. Furthermore, it appears that no matter how removed our society seems, there are still some romantics among us. Let me ask you—have you ever had a full physical examination?"

I thought a bit. "Yes, your honor. When I was first on the planet, and again the first week of my employment."

"I see. I note that your form is close to the standard for the civilized worlds, and such are generally sterile. Do you know if you have the capacity to father children?"

"I am told I do, your honor," I answered. "Although the product of some genetic engineering, this body is of the frontier."

Again came conversation, again the whispers and the ripples, the nods and gestures. Finally the chief judge announced, "Well, we find an equitable solution here, we believe, one that is in accord with our past history and is in the interest of fairness. It is quite out of the ordinary, but we feel that if it sets a precedent it will be a rare one, considering the circumstances of the case and the example. We therefore place the prisoner in the Childbearers and Rearers Syndicate, subject to all its codes, rules, articles and provisions, but assign her to you rather than to a specific Guild House, for so long as you choose, with the following provisions.

"One, that you yourself in no way cause the prisoner to violate any of those codes, rules, articles, and provisions. Two, that you perform the duties normally done by insemination at the Guild Houses, or arrange for insemination in case she cannot fulfill her quota. Three, that you assume absolutely all financial burdens, and that the prisoner shall have no credit, no money, and no possessions under law except those which you provide. All joint assets currently in both names or in her name shall be transferred to you alone, and her card shall be invalid for any purchases or other transactions, making

her a total dependent. Four, she shall be totally subject
to your authority, carrying out any such duties large or
small that you permit so long as she follows the guild
code, rules, articles, and provisions. Five, should you ever
no longer wish her company or services, she must immediately report to and enroll in the nearest Guild House,
transferring all authority to the Guild House. Do you
understand the terms?"

"Yes, your honor." I sure did. It was the most de-
grading and demeaning sentence I'd ever heard in my
whole life, one that could only have been pronounced
on this dirty planet. It was in fact the worst punishment
they could mete out to her, considering her independent spirit. Suddenly she was reduced not merely to the
chattel of Akeba House but to outright slavery. Still, I
had to agree, it being as good a deal as I thought could
be made at this time. But someday, Cerberus, I was going to correct it all. Correct it, and pay them back for
this. They might temporarily break her. But that only
spurred me on to break their whole goddamned rotten
system.

"Sentence on Dylan Zhang Kohl is therefore pronounced and ratified," the judge was saying. "Prisoner
will remain in custody and undergo full sentencing as
soon as practicable, preferably within the next few hours.
Release is set at ten hundred tomorrow morning, at
which time she will be released to your custody, Qwin
Zhang."

I nodded and sat back down.

"Sanda Tyne," the judge continued, "you shall be
judged and locked into the body now possessed by Dylan
Kohl. It is further directed that you undergo a process of
psychological conditioning at the Borough of Medlams
Public Psychology Section as prescribed by this court,
and that you be reduced to the status of mendicant. Any
employment you might find is restricted to the most me-
nial of Class II occupations, and permanently fixed in the
lowest position at the minimum wage prescribed by law.
This sentence is to be carried out expeditiously, and not
later than ten hundred tomorrow morning. This court is
now adjourned. Prisoners will report to chambers for initial judgment.

The thirteen filed out, and a cop came up and escorted the two women through a door to one side of the judge's dais. Neither of them looked back in my direction.

I was frankly more concerned with Dylan than with Sanda. As head of Hroyasail. I could hire her even if I was limited in what I could pay her or do for her, so she wouldn't face the fate of others in the mendicant class —a free one-way trip to Momrath. I worried, though, if having her around in that body would bother Dylan.

I waited anxiously in the anteroom of the Municipal Bulding at ten hundred. I didn't have long to wait. I soon saw both of my women, looking very much the same, walk out and head toward me. Both were stopped, asked to sign something, and then given their cards.

Dylan, now in Sanda's slim sandy-haired form, was through first and came up to me. "Hi," she managed weakly.

"Hi, yourself," I responded, and kissed her. "Was it bad?"

"Not really. I don't even remember most of it. No, the bad stuff's to come. I can't believe the sons of bitches actually *gave* me to you!"

"It's not a precedent," I told her, "and not restricted to women, either. It's also done for Syndicate bosses, it seems, and Laroo. Some of 'em have private harems, male or female. It's based on their first principle—you own your mind but the state owns all our bodies."

"Maybe mostly, but they own a little of my mind, too. I don't think they missed a trick to humiliate me. I can't cause myself or anyone else physical harm. The way the psychs adjusted my mind, I'll almost go into heat, like some animal, to get pregnant right on their schedule. I can't even leave your side without permission, and if I'm left in the apartment I must stay there. I can't set foot on a boat, even if it's docked, permission or no. All that sort of shit."

"I'm so very sorry. I'll make it as easy on you as I can," I soothed.

She managed a wan smile. "I know you will. Look, I told you I took the risk freely. We crapped out this time, that's all. Look on the bright side: you won't have to worry any more about my getting killed, and those bastards turned me into an adolescent sex fantasy all for you."

"I didn't ask for that."

"I know." She turned. "Here's Sanda."

Our other woman looked *really* stricken, filled with guilt, a guilt I knew would surface not only every time she looked at Dylan but also every time she looked in a mirror. She had done her idol in, and that was her true punishment.

Dylan grabbed her and hugged her. "Don't feel so bad! Don't feel so guilty! No more babies for you, no more prisoner! And we're still together!" She turned back to me. "You *can* find a job for her, can't you?"

I nodded, feeling relieved that *that* was out of the way. "Sure." I looked around. "Let's get out of this place."

We walked out into the sunshine and sea breeze, and I hailed a cab to take us back to the dock. When we got out, Dylan looked up at Akeba House, out on the promontory. "There *is* one requirement they made that I have to observe, permission or no," she told me. "I have to go up to the House in the next few days and, before an assembly of the women there, tell what happened to me and recant my crimes in front of them. That'll be the hardest thing."

We entered the old, familiar apartment. "You can set that up now and get it over with," I noted, gesturing toward the phone.

She went over, took out her card, put it in the slot, and waited. Nothing happened. She sighed and turned to me. "You'll have to dial for me," she said wearily. "With no credit of any kind I can't even make a simple phone call."

I tried to console her. "I'm going after Laroo and this whole rotten system. You're gonna be free and on the seas once more someday. I swear it."

I was going to try as hard as hell to make her believe that, too.

CHAPTER TWELVE

Project Phoenix

Dylan's luck had gone down the drain, but mine was still holding up. She went up to the House for her obligatory purging, then stayed around a bit, with my blessings, looking up some old friends, getting some consolation and advice, and doing some general talking. Misery loves company, as Sanda pointed out, and deep down, nobody was more miserable than Dylan. Still, when she finally returned, it was with some interesting news. Sanda, after all, had been spending her leave with us and had hardly checked in up there at all.

"There's a couple of women there under Cloister," she told me. "New people I never heard of before. Really gorgeous, too."

"What's Cloister?"

"It means they're restricted to the grounds of the House, and they've had their cards completely lifted. They can't leave the place. It's usually only done by the Syndicate as punishment for offenses, but they don't seem to be like that at all. In fact you'll never guess where they come from."

I shrugged. "What's the mystery?"

"They're from Laroo's Island," she told me. "They were some of his—what? Courtesans? Harem? Whatever."

The news piqued my interest for several reasons. "What did they do? Have a falling out with the old bastard? Or did he just get tired of them?"

"They're not sure. One day—zap! The whole bunch were picked up and shipped to Houses up and down the coast under Cloister. They say they think it's because of some big deal that Laroo's using the island for. According

to them lots of new faces and equipment were coming in
—and have been for the past few months."

She shook her head negatively. "But one of them saw a
name on a stack of boxes—Tooker boxes."

Better and better. "What was the name?"

"Project Phoenix."

I punched up the encyclopedia on the roomvision
monitor and checked the word. A legendary bird from
ancient Earth cultures that was totally reborn by being
completely consumed in flames.

"Can you go back up to the House whenever you
want?"

"As a Syndicate member, sure."

"I want you to do just that. Get to know these women.
Find out as discreetly as possible everything you can
about Laroo and his island and this mysterious project."

"As you wish," she responded. "But I should warn you
if you have any new schemes in your head. One of the
things they psyched into me might foul you up. I cannot
tell a lie. Not only not to you, not to *anybody*."

I considered that. "Can you not tell the truth? I mean,
if somebody asks you a question and you don't want to
give the answer, can you withhold it?"

She thought about it. "Yeah, sure. Otherwise anybody could pump me about you, and that would be illegal."

"Well, use your common sense, but if anybody asks
you a question the answer to which would cause any
problems, tell them you aren't permitted to answer that."

"As you wish," she repeated again in that rote tone.

I looked at her. "What's that 'as you wish' stuff?"

"Conditioning. Any order or direction you give me
that doesn't violate Syndicate rules or my other conditioning I *must* obey. Don't look so upset—you can't change
the rules. You can't even order me to disregard them,
because they thought of that, damn them! I have—a—a
compulsion to serve. They have made me a totally passive
individual and I will, well, suffer mentally if I'm not ordered about, set to tasks—in a word, dominated. Every
time you give me an order and I respond I get—well, a
feeling of pleasure, of well-being, of importance. I'm a

human robot—I exist to serve you, and you must let me. You must—for me."

I looked at her strangely. Was this the same Dylan Kohl who only a day before had coolly faced down one of the most horrible monsters of the sea? Was this the independent, gutsy schemer who got out of the motherhood, worked her way to captain, and helped rig a computer? It didn't seem so. They had certainly done something to her. Something in its own way more horrible than the lobotomies the judge said were no longer civilized. In more than one sense, this was a far crueler thing to do. I didn't know how to handle it.

"What sort of tasks?" I wanted to know.

"Prepare your meals, clean, run errands. Anything and everything. Qwin, I know this is hard on you, and you must know it's hard on me, but it's done. I accept it, and you must, too. Otherwise send me away to the House and forget me."

"Never—unless you want it."

"Qwin, I no longer have wants. Wants have been forbidden me. They stripped the wants away and left only a series of needs. I need to serve. I need to do my work as a mother. I want nothing. If you choose to keep me naked constantly scrubbing the apartment, that is what I will do, and what I *must* do."

"Damn! There must be some crooked psychs I can pressure into getting this lifted!"

"No. These compulsions are so deep-planted that to remove them other than in the precise manner that they were applied would destroy my mind and make me a permanent vegetable—and that precise manner is stored in the master computer alone. They didn't even have just one tech to do it, but many, one at a time, so it couldn't be reconstructed; that is the added hold they have. They alone can restore me. As long as I am a good example to the motherhood of what happens if you try and change your lot, I will remain this way. I would be this way even at the House, only subject to the orders of all the women of the motherhood."

That master computer again! I *had* to crack Wagant Laroo! I just *had* to!

*   *   *

I pulled all my strings at Tooker, starting with Sugal, with whom I had a cordial lunch.

"You want something. You always do when you come up," he told me, sounding not in the least put out.

"What's Project Phoenix?"

He started. "Where did you hear *that* name?"

"I heard it. I want to know what it is."

His voice lowered to a whisper and he grew increasingly nervous. "Man! You're dealing with high explosives here!"

"Still, Turgan, by hook or by crook I *will* know about it."

He sighed. "If you heard of it at all, I suppose you will. But not here. In a public place. I'll get you the information."

He was as good as his word, although even he really didn't know what was going on. Nor in fact did I depend entirely on him. I pulled every string and called in any IOUs I had, as well as using the ever-fascinating Tooker computer network, to which I still had access, to build my own picture. The elements, spread out in front of me in my office, gave a story that would emerge only through deduction and analysis.

Item: As I had already known, every single computer expert pulled from Tooker at the start of the last quarter had been expert in some form of organic computering. Most major organic computers and work on them had been banned long ago by the Confederacy, after some of the early creations, centuries ago, became more than human and almost took over humanity. That bitter, bloody, and costly war had made such work feared to this day. Those who dabbled in it were wiped or—sent to Cerberus? From Sugal and other sources I determined that we weren't the only one tapped for such minds.

Item: A couple of months earlier than this, major construction began on Laroo's Island, partly to create a place for shuttle landings to be made in safety there. But a whole hell of a lot more than that was in progress, to judge from the crews and raw materials ordered.

Item: Interfaces between Tooker's master computer —and other corporations' master computers—were established on a high and unbreakable scramble, relayed

by satellite. The relay system's other end pointed to Laroo's Island, although officially it was interconnected to
the Lord of the Diamond's command space station in
orbit around Cerberus. That raised an interesting question: if the work was so super-secret, why *not* the space
station? It was almost as large as the island, and if one
allowed for the shuttle dock, power plant, and fixed structures on the island, it was a damn sight bigger in usable
space.

Item: Interestingly. Hroyasail's own area for trawling
had been increased by almost 50 percent shortly before
I took over, something I never would have noticed if it
hadn't been reflected in the quota plan for the quarter,
a document I was only now getting to know intimately.
Seaprince of Coborn, about the same distance south of
Laroo's Island as we were north, had an equal increase.
A look at corporation affiliates and a check with the previous quarter's quota plan showed that an entire Tooker
trawling operation, Emyasail, was in the previous quarter's plan but was totally missing now. Its area had been
given to Hroyasail, which was natural, and Seaprince,
which was most unnatural, since Seaprince was a Compworld Corporation subsidiary, not one of Tooker's. You
didn't hand valuable territory to a competitor that close
voluntarily, so Compworld had to have given something
really major in return and nothing like that showed in the
books. In fact records showed that Tooker's *skrit* harvest
since the quarter began was down sharply, indicating a
dip into the reserves by next year. So it wasn't voluntary,
and only the government could force such a move.

These facts alone, put together with what only I really
knew of anyone likely to compile them, painted a stark
picture.

Item: The only folks anybody knew about now using
uncannily human organic computers were our aliens and
their spy robots, robots known to have a connection with
the Warden Diamond. That was why I was here. But
the alien robots were so good that no research project
would be really necessary on them—and even if it was,
it wouldn't be carried out here, not on Cerberus or any
other Warden world, and certainly not by any of our

people, who were definitely behind the aliens in this area.

And yet the conclusion was inescapable: Wagant Laroo had converted his former retreat and resort into an organic computer laboratory, staffed with the best of his own that he could find and supplied by Emyasail's trawlers. Why trawlers and gunboats and not by air? Well, for one thing it would attract less attention and give the appearance to onlookers of business as usual in Emyasail's area. Also, there appeared to be some paranoia about many aircraft in the vicinity of Laroo's Island.

I paced back and forth for several days and also talked the matter over with Dylan, who, having less background in this sort of thing than I did, came up even more of a blank. However, her more parochial outlook gave me the key I was looking for. "Why are you assuming the aliens have anything to do with it?" she asked me. "Why isn't this just a new scheme by Wagant Laroo?"

That stopped me cold. Suddenly all the pieces fell into place, and I had at least part of the picture. "No," I told her, "the aliens have everything to do with this—only they don't know it!"

"Huh?"

I sat down. "Okay, we know that these aliens are able to make facsimiles of people, people with jobs in sensitive places they have to gain access to. We know that these organic robots are so good they fool literally everybody. Not just the machines that check to see who's who, but everybody. Close friends. Lovers. People they've known for years. And they even pass brain scans!" I was getting excited now. "Of course! Of course! How could I be so blind?"

She looked concerned. "What do you mean?"

"Okay, so first your agents pick out the person they want to duplicate. They find their records, take holographic pictures, you name it. And from that, our alien friends create an organic robot—grow is a more apt term, if I remember correctly—that is absolutely physically identical to the target. Absolutely. Except, of course, being artificial it has whatever additional characteristics its designers want—eyes that see into infrared and ultraviolet, enormous strength if need be. Since it's made up of incredibly tough material instead of cells, with a skin more or less grafted on top, and powered perhaps by drawing energy from the fields that surround us—microwaves, magnetic fields, I don't know what—it can survive even a vacuum. The one that penetrated Military Systems Command seemed to have the power to change its components into other designs—it actually launched itself into space. And yet it fooled everybody! Bled the right blood when it had to, knew all the right answers, duplicated the personality, right down to the littlest habit, of the person it was pretending to be. And there's only one way it could have done that."

"All right, how?"

"It *was* the person it was pretending to be."

She shook her head in wonder. "You're not making any sense. Was it a robot or a person?"

"A robot. An absolutely perfect robot whose components could provide it with whatever it needed, either as a mimic or as a device for fulfilling its mission or getting away. An incredible machine made from tiny unicellular computers that can control independently what they are and do—trillions of them, perhaps. But the aliens solved the problem we never did, and never allowed ourselves the research time to do—they discovered how to preprogram the things indelibly, so they'd be free and complete individuals yet never deviate from their programming, which was to spy on us. So now they build them in our images, and—what? They bring them to Cerberus. No, not Cerberus, probably to the space station."

Dylan frowned, puzzled. "You mean they're around here?"

I shook my head. "No, what happens next has to be something like this. The target is snatched—kidnapped. Probably on vacation. At least at a time when he or she won't be missed for up to a couple of weeks. The victim is brought to the station and infected with the Cerberan version of the Warden organism and allowed to season there. Then—Dylan, you remember that drug you stole to get out of the motherhood?"

She nodded. "I—I got it off a shuttle pilot."

"Great! It's coming together nicely. So, after seasoning, their target is given some of this drug and introduced to the similarly infected robot facsimile. The target's mind and personality goes into the robot's, but the robot is already preprogrammed as an agent."

"As they programmed me," Dylan said emotionlessly.

I nodded. "Only a far more sophisticated method. A psych machine wouldn't do the job, since they need the complete person—and only that person's attitude is changed. No, it's in the original programming of the robot when it's made by the aliens, of that I'm sure."

"But how can this robot return and replace the original?" she asked. "Wouldn't the Warden organism destroy it when it left?"

"No, not necessarily. Remember, there are several items, several products that even now can be sterilized. Apparently these robots can too. Basically, all they do is get out of the system. The Wardens die, but so adaptable are the quasi-cellular components of the robot that they can make immediate repairs. The target returns to work from 'vacation,' the absolutely perfect agent-spy. It's beautiful."

"It sounds too much like what happened to me," she noted.

"I'm sorry," I said gently. "I was admiring a finely crafted gem. I don't want to make light of the human tragedy involved. Still, considering the size and complexity of the Confederacy, it'd be almost impossible to block them all out, and the major damage has probably already been done."

"And Laroo's Project Phoenix?"

I considered it a moment. "There's only one possibility I can come up with, and it's a terrifying one in some respects. The aliens have no reason to use the island, and less reason to use people who know less about their robots than they do. To put any of their operation directly on a Warden world would eventually tip off the Confederacy anyway, and they know the Wardens are 'hot' for them right now. No, for the answer you have to think as Wagant Laroo thinks, from the perspective of the Warden Diamond, and the answer becomes obvious."

"Not to me it doesn't," she said.

"All right—all along we've wondered just what the

aliens could offer the Four Lords other than revenge. Well, here's the payoff. When they win, the Four Lords, and those others whom they choose—maybe even the whole population of all four worlds—will be given new bodies. Perfect bodies, those of organic robots. You see what the Four Lords were offered? A way out. Escape. The freedom to leave. If these agent robots can do it, anybody can. But there's a hitch, one that necessarily paranoid Lords like Laroo would immediately think of."

"I can follow this part. What's to stop these aliens from preprogramming the payoff robots as well, so they have a population of superhuman slaves?"

"Very good. High marks. So here you're given a way of escape and you dare not use it. What would *you* do?"

She thought a moment. "Study theirs and build my own."

"All right. But it's unlikely that you could do it without such a massive plant that the Confederacy watchers wouldn't take notice. Besides, it might well involve construction materials or support materials not found anywhere in the Warden Diamond, maybe unknown to anybody on our side at this point. What if you couldn't build one?"

"Well, I guess you'd order a few you didn't need as agents from the aliens, who have to trust your judgment in these matters, and use them."

"Right again! But these will come preprogrammed by a method unknown to our science. To make them work you have to find out how they are programmed and eliminate the programming. No mean trick, since it's probably integrated with instructions on how the robots function and those you have to keep. The best you can do is hope. Gather everything you can, and everybody who might know something about it, lock 'em up on the island with the robots, lab, computer links, and whatever, and try and find an answer. And that's what Project Phoenix is all about."

"Laroo's not only getting back at the Confederacy," Dylan said in an almost awed tone, "but double-crossing the aliens, too!"

I nodded. "I have to admire the old boy for that, anyway. And it's probably not just Laroo but all the Four

Lords. And I think I know, at least, how the robots are getting in and out, too. It has to be in the shuttle system. But aside from the Diamond they go only one other place —the moons of Momrath. Out there someplace, possibly inside those moons' orbits, alien and Warden human meet."

I sat back, feeling satisfied. In one moment I'd solved at least half the Warden puzzle. I didn't know anything about the aliens, true, and I had no idea as to the nature and scope of their plot, but I now understood, I felt certain, much of the Warden connection.

"And what good does it do you to know these things?" Dylan asked. "You can't do anything about them."

Good old practical Dylan! Her comment was on the mark. What *could* I do?

Or more accurately, what did I *want* to do?

Kill Laroo and topple the system, yes—but even if I figured out how, did I really want Project Phoenix to fail?

At the moment I knew only one thing. The biggest deal in Warden history was happening out there on Laroo's Island—and I wanted in on it.

CHAPTER THIRTEEN

The Easy Way Into an Impregnable Fort

A few days later I had Karel take me out in her boat and go through all the routine motions, but this time we went almost as far south as we dared go. I remembered Dylan's comment about chasing a bork to within sight of Laroo's Island, and I had questioned her on the incident. I felt certain we could get as far chasing an imaginary one as she had chasing a real one.

The "island" was really pretty far out in the ocean, far from any sight of land and exactly the kind of place a dictator would love as a refuge. It was a small stand of major trees, giving an area of perhaps a hundred or so square kilometers. Not a really big place. At some point this grove had obviously been connected to the main body, but something had happened, probably ages ago, leaving only isolated islands of trees out here now. There were several dozen in the area, none really close enough to be within sight of the others; still, they pointed like a wavering arrow toward our familiar "mainland" bunch.

We skirted the island just outside the main computer defense perimeter, an area clearly visible on electronic scans of the place. It was a mass of orange, purple, and gold foliage atop the thick, blackish trunks, and even from our vantage point of almost fifteen kilometers out, my spotting scopes revealed an extraordinary building in the center of the mass. Gleaming silvery in the sun, sort of like a fantasy castle or some kind of modernistic sculpture, it was both anachronistic and futuristic. The exiled concubines and even Dylan herself had given rough descriptions of it, but these paled before the actual sight.

Still, thanks to Dylan and contacts throughout the Motherhood, at other Houses where Laroo's women had been sent, I knew it pretty well. Knew, at least, the basic room layouts and the locations of the elevators, the key power plant, the basic defense systems, and things like that. From it all, I concluded that it was as close to an impregnable fortress as was possible to build on Cerberus.

The electronic screens were not only domelike over the place but also went down to a depth of more than two kilometers—right down to the ocean floor itself. With a few million units of the right equipment and a force that would be more than obvious, it might be possible to tunnel under the screens, but even then it would be risky once you were through the initial barrier. There were not only inner defense screens but physical ones as well. Both robotic and manned gunboats constantly were patrolling.

Karel, a big, muscular woman with a deep, rich voice, was all too happy to help, and she at least suspected what I might be up to. She and Dylan were very different to look at, but they shared a lot deep down and had been close to partners for more than three years.

"Suppose we drove borks in there? Lots of them?" I suggested, thinking of various plans.

She laughed at the idea. "Sure would be fun, but it wouldn't get you in. There *are* ways to attract borks, for sure, but those screens are pretty powerful. You'd need a regular stampede even to make a dent, and if two of *our* boats in skilled hands can usually finish one, you wouldn't believe what the defenses there can do, even to a dozen."

I nodded. "Yeah, I know. But—say! Did you say there were ways of *attracting* borks?"

She nodded. "Certain high-pitched sounds, and certain odors in the water that simulate a *skrit* colony. You might draw three or four, if you were lucky, but no more. They aren't as common as all *that* around here. If they were, there'd be no way for the *skrit* to survive and reproduce."

I nodded idly, but I was already thinking. When we got back to shore I'd do a bit more, and see what could be done. I was sure that given enough time—and I had no idea how much time I had—I could have gotten through those screens, but that would have gotten me only to the island—where just about every step required a brain scan.

No, there *had* to be some easier way.

"Dylan?"

"Yes, Qwin?"

"How do those torpedoes on the boats work? I mean, how do they explode?"

A detonation device screwed in the side, with a minicomputer aboard. You tell it when to arm and when to explode by remote control."

"Uh-huh. And how do you know one from the other? I mean, how can you use a single remote to trigger the whole bunch?"

"Why, you don't. Each uses the same frequency and all the torpedoes are universal. Each also comes with a code stamped on it. You just read the code for each into your transmitter, then fire them by the code numbers, which is all they'll answer to. Once you have the numbers in your weapons control computer you don't really need to know anything else."

I nodded. "And who feeds the new numbers in? Do you take 'em off the invoices or bills of lading when new ones arrive, or what?"

"Are you kidding? Would *you* trust your life to a bill of lading? No, each captain loads each torpedo into his or her own boat, then physically reads the numbers off and puts them personally into the weapons control computer."

"Uh-huh. And where's this number stamped?"

"On the detonator hatch. A small door that's welded shut after the minicomputer for each is placed inside. Go down and see for yourself in the warehouse here."

I did—and liked what I found. They didn't bother to stamp each number on the door, just stenciled it on. Talking with others, I found that, indeed, sometimes the numbers were wrong, but there was a test code to check it that would send back an acknowledging signal to the weapons control computer verifying the number. It was a rather simple test: you just took a number like, say, FG7654-321AA and changed the last A to a T.

I found the information most interesting, and asked Dylan a few more key questions. "The minicomputers come preprogrammed and the doors welded shut. I assume, then, that they're shipped live, so to speak?"

She nodded. "There's no danger. A test must be run to arm them, no code is ever duplicated or used again, the frequency used is used only for that purpose, and the transmitters are controlled devices built into the gunboats. Why this interest in torpedoes all of a sudden? Are you planning something?"

"What you don't know can't violate your psych commands," I told her. "Of *course* I'm planning something."

"Just changing the codes won't work," she noted. "They wouldn't pass the test."

I grinned. "What's the transmitting range on these things?"

"As an additional safety measure, only three kilometers. That's more than enough for a good captain."

"And more than enough for me, my darling," I responded, and kissed her.

*   *   *

The next day I dropped by Tooker and checked the shipping section and bills of lading. Even if Emyasail was now working only for Laroo, it was still *our* company and supplied via our transit routes. And of course they needed torpedoes in case they ran into a bork or two on their way to Laroo's Island anyway.

Nobody kept a large stock of the things on hand—no matter how safe they were claimed to be; they terrified the fire department, and even local governments didn't like to think of all those explosives in one place. A little warehouse fire and you could wipe a whole section off the map.

I *did* have to wait, though, a bit impatiently, for over ten days until Emyasail put in another order, and then it was for only twenty. Still, that was enough, considering that they would at best be replacing used ones in the tubes, not completely refitting the boats.

A bit of creative routing on the forms made sure that these torpedoes would come first to Hroyasail and little ol' me.

Dylan could have nothing more to do with this one. She would be prohibited from assisting in anything that would almost certainly cause someone to come to harm. Sanda, however, was only too glad to help out.

I had been worried about Dylan's reaction to having Sanda around, but the true problem had turned out to be the reverse. Sanda felt tremendous guilt and remorse and blamed herself completely for what had happened, and she really didn't want to face me or, particularly, Dylan any more than necessary. I had put her to work as a maintenance worker around the docks, refinishing the wharf, painting the boats, stuff like that, and she seemed content with her lot. Now, however, I had a different sort of painting to do, and it had to be done quickly and quietly.

The flaw in their torpedo system was that, since there was little to be perverted concerning them, they'd stand-dardized it. Thus Sanda and I, working through the night with Emyasail's new torpedoes, were able to remove the numbers and, with some expert stenciling, replace them. I had some admiration for the manufacturing process:

those numbers were *baked* on and hard as hell to get off, but my trusty computers at Tooker had come up with a solvent, and I had no trouble with a replacement stencil and paint, although the numbers would not be on as solidly as before. Oh, they'd *look* right, but they weren't as permanent. I hoped nothing rubbed off during the transshipment.

Sanda was puzzled, but there was a slight glow of excitement in her as she realized another operation was underway. "I don't see what good switching the numbers will do," she commented, sounding more curious than anything else. "I mean, they just won't test out and they'll be rejected, like those three over there of ours."

I grinned. "But they *will* test out," I told her. "We aren't just changing numbers. We are exchanging the numbers. All the numbers are still good, just for the wrong torpedoes. When they load these and test them, they'll get a response from their computers—from the torpedoes in the warehouse—but the computer won't know that, or at least won't tell. So they'll sail off with a batch of torpedoes that will test out perfectly, but when they have to use them, they won't work."

"Sounds like you're gonna blow up the dock instead," she noted.

"No. It's highly unlikely that any borks will come within three kilometers of land. The danger zone's out past five kilometers. And that's too far. Still, if there's a really thorough investigation, *I* can always blow the docks—from one of our boats."

She stared at me, looking slightly shocked. "Oh," she said.

Rigging the torpedoes was only part of the problem. The other was making certain that there would be an occasion to use them. For that, I began a thorough search for everything that turned borks on.

It turned out that the most reliable and effective means were pretty simple—some soluble sulfides would draw them if they were anywhere close and would drive them into something of a frenzy (as if that weren't their normal state anyway). But for long-range attraction, I needed something more. Again the solution was rather simple. Like marine creatures on many worlds, the borks were supersensitive to ultra-high-frequency sounds and apparently used them for territorial claims, fights, lovemaking (hard to imagine with something like that, but, then again, there were a lot of borks), and such. The vocabulary was not extensive, but it was clearly known, so much so that various boat engines and the like were made to specific noise standards to avoid any such sounds within their operating ranges.

On such a simple idea I didn't go the circuitous route, but simply got some modified UHF broadcasters from Otah myself, then worked with them, a circuit diagram, and some easy modifications of tiny programmable chips to create a remote transceiver that I could tune to any selective frequency from anywhere within an area of fifty to a hundred kilometers. Various shops specializing in special underwater gear provided easy cases that could be adapted to the transmitters without much problem. A couple of chemical supply houses sold various standard compounds that together would in my makeshift kitchen lab create one hell of a glue to reinforce the magnets on the inside of the case. I didn't want the things falling off under battle stress, as magnets might risk—and a magnet powerful enough to stay regardless would be a magnet powerful enough to be detected by ship's instruments. More electronic modification and I had a small charge I could also set off by remote control—enough to melt the little transmitters into a nondescript goo, but not enough to cause harm to the hull.

Although they were curious, I dared not tell Dylan or the boat captains and crews what I was doing, since in Dylan's case she might try and stop me because of her prohibition against any violence, while the boat people would hardly be enthusiastic about my possibly doing in several of their own. I didn't like that prospect much myself, but more was at stake here than a few lives. This was Laroo I was going against, not some minor executive or fire department employee. At least my way they had a chance and so did I. Simply to have sabotaged the boats might not accomplish what I wanted, but would certainly alert Laroo and his security forces that somebody nasty was up to something.

But I would need somebody to help me plant the things and that meant Sanda—and I wasn't 100 percent certain of her. Up to now she had gone along, it was true, but before I actually put anything into practice I had to be certain she wouldn't cross me up at the wrong time—not by choice, I knew, but I had no real idea what *her* psych inhibitors and commands were. So I had to see somebody who could tell me.

Most doctors were pretty bored on Cerberus; the Warden organism was extremely efficient at keeping the natives ultra-healthy. Still, some were around for emergency services and for research, and one group, considering the culture, was absolutely necessary and always busy— the group I was most concerned with, the psychiatrists.

Almost all were exiles, of course, sent here for a variety of infractions. Most were not adverse to a little under-the-table money for private work of a less-than-official nature. A large number of people, some otherwise quite ordinary, recommended Dr. Svarc Dumonia as the ultimate psych expert who would do anything for an extra unit, so it was he I went to see, taking Dylan along—not because I felt he could help her, but because it would make seeing him more natural, and the big fee look legitimate. Dylan, however, would undergo an extensive series of mostly useless tests while Dumonia and I had our real little chat.

He was a thin, wiry, nervous little man who wore horn-rimmed glasses, something I took particular note of, since everyone on Cerberus had eyesight in the same condition as the rest of their bodies—near perfect. He caught my glance and shrugged.

"The glasses. Oh, call them an affectation. I'd like to think I wear 'em—the panes are perfectly clear, of course —to be more of an individual, to stand out in the crowd. Truth was, I'd been getting a tad nearsighted back home and never seemed to have the time to have the matter attended to. I just got some glasses, liked the look, and kept wearing them. After I got here I felt unnatural without 'em."

I smiled slightly and took a seat in his office. My record of never meeting a psych who didn't need a psych was holding firm.

"Doctor," I began carefully, "I'm here so I can understand more about the process of psychological conditioning. As you're aware, I live with its results almost constantly."

He nodded and flipped through a folder. "Hmmm . . . interesting treatment, I must say. Highly creative. The design team that worked out your wife's pattern had to be one of the best. It's a highly skilled profession, you know, and getting the results you want from what's ordered is often nearly impossible. Every time you implant *anything* beyond, say, a simple command, as in say, posthypnotic suggestion but making it permanent, you're taking risks with the entire mind, the entire personality. Information is filed scattershot throughout the brain in tiny electrochemical bytes, you know. It's put together up front by the cerebral cortex, which reaches at the speed of light for whatever it needs to create holographic memory, personality, whatever. To do something this complex takes —well, not technicians but *artisans*."

"Some artisans," I muttered. "They destroyed her."

"Oh, sorry. Didn't mean to offend, but when you're in the business and you see it as a mathematical abstract rather than in human terms it's, well, like admiring a skillful heart restoration back home. If you don't know the person, you admire the work in isolation, even if afterward you find that the person died."

I accepted that notion, or at least understood it. "Still, she was changed into someone, well, very different. The result seems somehow more awful than death or imprisonment."

"Oh, no! Actually, it's not that way at all. Back home, where both of us come from, the procedure is so common you probably met hundreds, even thousands of people with some psych work and never knew it. In psychiatry, for example, we can actually go in and get at the deep psychoses, do things our forefathers never dreamed of. There are no more hopeless cases in my profession. And in the case of your wife, think of the alternatives. *You* might not agree that she did anything wrong or that the law or judges were just, but who does in any society? Isn't that why we're both here?"

I had to smile and nod at that.

"Well, in your wife's case, from the point of view of society, they took someone who violated the law and made her into a productive member of that society who won't violate any laws. Not the important ones, anyway."

"Important to whom?"

"To the state, of course. To understand my job, you have to remember that our task is to restore abnormal people to normal. Normality isn't an objective standard, but rather a subjective term imposed by each society on its people by laws and culture. Ancient cultures used to sacrifice people to appease the gods. In those societies, anybody who objected to that sacrifice or doubted the existence of the gods wasn't normal. The social fabric of the civilized worlds would be horribly abnormal to many of our own ancestors, but it's ours. We were born into it and accept most of its values, even if we question or violate one or two. Cerberan culture is nothing but a modification of the civilized worlds' own culture adapted to local conditions and limitations. Deep down you can understand that."

This line of conversation was making me slightly uncomfortable, and I couldn't really figure out why.

"Now, in your wife's case," he continued, "we have somebody with a couple of problems from the state's point of view that made her abnormal. First, she escaped from the motherhood, something which is culturally forbidden and which held the threat of undermining a basic underpinning of Cerberan society. But since everybody here in any position got there by getting away with breaking the rules—and she had only bent them slightly —they couldn't do much to her at that point without questioning their basic values and themselves. Besides, she overcompensated for her previous cloistered life by taking on a profession most Cerberans consider suicidal."

"Overcompensated?"

He nodded. "Sure. The unhappy ones in the motherhood are basically of two kinds—those really unfit for the role, who are usually given psych treatments, and the romantics. Extremely bright and very limited by her assigned role, Dylan had only one view of outside, in this case outside her House—that dock and those adventurous seamen. She fantasized about what she knew and could see, and that really was Hroyasail. But when she *did* get out and *did* attain her dreams, they weren't all they were cracked up to be. The fantasy was far more romantic than the reality. It was either as dull as the motherhood or horribly life-threatening, and when you take risks like that day after day, knowing the odds, even *that* becomes unsatisfying. Like most people who work on the boats, she was really past caring. The motherhood was dull and repressive, and her fantasy was dull and in its own way equally repressive. So she continued going through the motions without much hope for the future, knowing that sooner or later her luck would run out and she'd be killed. Being killed in her work became her new romantic fantasy."

I was a bit shocked at this. "You mean she was suicidal?"

He looked back down at his charts. "In a sense, yes. Oh, she wouldn't try to kill herself, but she herself must have told you that you get to be captain mostly by attrition. Everybody likes thrills, but with the kind of odds in *her* business you have to have a death wish. It shows up clearly in her profile."

I shook my head in wonder. "I can't believe that of her."

"Oh, it's true. What in fact her profile suggests she really wanted was to be what she is—a mother. But a *complete* mother, one who not only bears but raises her children, frontier-style. In fact, for all her rationalization, the addition of a new factor in her life, when her odds were surely running low, was the final trigger for her to take the action she did."

"New factor?"

He nodded. "You. She fell in love with you. And suddenly she found it more and more difficult to go out on her daily hunts. For the first time she started getting scared because she no longer was content to die at the helm, so to speak. When you restored her will to live, you shortened her odds of surviving to a tiny fraction. She couldn't *consciously* face this, but her subconscious knew, and that's why she decided to give in—to violate the law —and take the girl Sanda along that day. She was at her peak, of course, because she had both you and Sanda to protect, but you have no idea the risk you took that day. Half of her, I'm sure, considered the idea of going down with those she loved, a tidy and romantic ending. She didn't, because she loved you too much."

"You're saying she knew she'd get caught?"

"I'm saying she wanted to get caught. If she hadn't been caught this time she'd have done something else. She wanted out so she would no longer be faced with inevitable death and separation from you."

I felt at once touched, uncomfortable, and incredulous. "But she could have quit. We'd have created a place for her with the company."

"No, no. She couldn't consciously face that either. I suspect that the idea never entered her head, since she also feared losing you. You admired her courage, even as you feared for her life. She was afraid that any such move would be interpreted as cowardice on your part and might leave her without you—and that was the only thing that mattered to her. You."

"But that's ridiculous! I wouldn't have—"

"You probably wouldn't," he agreed, "but the human mind is more than a computer, which is why we have psychiatrists at all. We're individualists, with emotions and a streak of irrational thinking that both makes us humans great and is our biggest weakness."

"I still can't really accept this," I told him.

"Ah! Love!" he sighed. "Our craziest failing. It has almost been eliminated on the civilized worlds, and it's pretty damned rare here on Cerberus, too. But give it half a chance, give it a little crack to slip into and it raises its head nonetheless. Look, Zhang, I can tell you really don't like Cerberan culture very much, but next to the frontier the Warden worlds—all of them—allow one thing that makes them, I think, better places. Here we still dream, we still fantasize and romanticize. On the civilized worlds they've eradicated that, and they know it. That's why the frontier's a continuing operation. It's the only place where people can still dream. All of humankind's advances—since the precursor of Man came down from the trees on ancient primordial Earth—have resulted from dreams, fantasies, imagination. Dylan broke free of the motherhood for a dream—she found a way. But as with the civilized worlds, which were begun with the most glorious of dreams in mind, the reality proved less than that. Hollow. If you search inside yourself *you* know it, too."

I gave a dry, humorless chuckle. "I can see how you wound up here."

He gave a genuine chuckle in return. "They made a mistake on me. Sent me off to the frontier because they had a shortage of medical officers for a short tour. When I returned to the civilized worlds I couldn't believe how hollow and empty they were—the same places I loved and yearned for only a year before. I became convinced that civilization as I knew it would continue of its own momentum much as other ancient empires had continued, but being hollow, it was also fragile. I knew that we'd crack against any good assault from outside, and I started a campaign to restore some vigor, some mental health." He spread his arms. "And here I am. And know what? I really haven't been that sorry about it."

"Suit yourself," I told him. "I certainly see your point, even if I don't accept your conclusions on the civilized worlds or on Dylan."

"An interesting metaphor, one that appeals to me. Your wife and our old civilization. History will eventually prove me right on the civilized worlds, but I can prove my point on Dylan easily."

"How could you do that? From reading psych profiles taken in only one night?"

He grinned like a man about to lower the noose. "No, because I know from your cover application on her what she told you was done to her. I knew in a minute it couldn't have been like that—that sort of complete turn-around takes weeks, maybe months, if it can be done at all. So I just got the test results on her, and they confirmed my suspicions."

"Which are?"

"Considering the time, it was a masterful job, as I said, but it was hardly *that* extensive. Dylan believes they did all of it—she is convinced of that. But what the psychs did was far slighter and more subtle. They simply gave her a nudge here, a tap there, a *very* subtle working of her subconscious desires, ones she herself was not fully willing to admit to herself. She did the rest to convince herself and you that those things she wanted to do and be were involuntarily imposed from above. Look, Zhang, if we could do such a complete job on somebody like her overnight, the syndicates would put us all through the ringer and you know it."

"Are you telling me that there's no psych command that says she has to obey my every wish? No psych plant against going out on the boats?"

"I'm saying there is not. The first, the obedience thing, comes partly from her early training and psyche, partly from inner needs, and partly out of her very real total dependence on you financially. She is convinced there *is* such a command, but it comes from her own subconscious—and is no less real because it does. Furthermore, there is absolutely nothing preventing her from going near the boats except the laws governing the motherhood, but it's a damn good way of not having to face up to the fact that she doesn't *want* to go any more. You see, she's taken the things she doesn't want to face and transferred them to a third party—the psych. That way *she* can accept it, and that way *you* have to accept her."

I had half risen from the chair, but now I sat back down again. "What you're saying is that she's living in a fantasy world completely now. One of her own making."

"Somewhat," he agreed. "Now, we can schedule a series of sessions that will allow her to accept the truth, but it may take time. With your help we can bring her face to face with herself again, so she'll be a whole person. Nonetheless, she'll be more the *present* Dylan than the past one—you understand that?"

I nodded, feeling slightly dazed. "All right. We'll schedule it. But I'm—stunned. What psych commands *did* they put in?"

"Well, the prohibition against taking any human life is real and pretty standard for sentencing," he told me. "It protects her and you. She's also got a command that prohibits her from ever leaving the motherhood of her own accord again, although that's mostly reinforcing—under judgment she can't switch bodies anyway. The rest, as I said, is all subtle. The brain triggers hormones and the like. Reinforcing her natural drives, so to speak, as defined by that body. This has the nice by-product of reinforcing her feelings for you, which is damned clever, since that in turn feeds her psychoses and gives them the force of commands, too."

"From what you're saying, maybe we shouldn't snap her out of it," I noted. "You claim she's happy."

"No. She'll never be happy until she *realizes* that this is what she wants and until she is convinced that what she wants is also all right with you. Not doing something about these convictions, particularly the second, could in the long run turn her into the very robot she thinks she is. Which is fine for the state and the state's psychs, but not for her or for you."

"Okay, you convinced me. But what about my original purpose for coming?"

"Sanda Tyne. An interesting case, quite unlike Dylan, you know. She's one of those never really cut out for the motherhood, but she hasn't nearly the intelligence potential nor the vision to really be somebody in the outside world, although she has great dreams. She enjoys thrills and adventure, but only as a child might, with no real understanding of the dangers to herself or to others. As with Dylan and with all the best psych work, they simply took what was there and used it, although in her case they more or less froze it. Hard as it is to believe, Sanda is more psyched than Dylan."

"What!"

He nodded. "She feels no real guilt about what happened to Dylan. Not really. In fact she's somewhat disappointed that she didn't replace Dylan in your life; she still hopes to one day. That's the limit of her ambition and vision—and now you understand why she doesn't call on you both more often."

"Jealousy?"

"Envy, mostly. Her whole life has been nothing but envy. The grass is *always* greener to her. Physically and intellectually she might have lived for twenty years, but emotionally she's somewhere around eight or nine. The psychs merely damped down whatever ambition was left and much of that active imagination. They reinforced the envy, but also lay down prohibitions about doing anyhing about it. The way they have her damped and oriented, she'll be perfectly happy chipping paint and collecting garbage, secure in the knowledge that someday her prince —you—will come to her."

"What about that business concerning harm to self or others? You said it was standard?"

"True, but there's only so much you can do in a few hours, and they did a lot. Much the same thing was accomplished by the other conditioning, as I mentioned. She isn't going to hurt Dylan because that might alienate you. Besides, she's sure you'll dump Dylan sooner or later and come down and see the errors of your ways. She isn't going to hurt you because she's patient, as long as she's near you. And secure in the knowledge that she'll win in the end, she's hardly going to do anything to herself. That being the case, no prohibition was necessary. In fact I can foresee only one way in which she could harm *anybody* for the rest of her judgment, and only one, so you're safe."

"Oh? What's that?"

"If you asked her to. She'll do anything to demonstrate to you the mistake she thinks you made."

I grinned, feeling a bit more comfortable. "No chance of that, of course."

"Of course," Dumonia agreed.

The torpedoes had been rerouted to Emyasail, where they were supposed to be all along, and my devices were ready. Confident now of Sanda's complete cooperation, we went down one evening to scout out the place and found it similar in layout to Hroyasail. It would be, I told myself, considering it was built by the same parent corporation at the same time for the same purposes.

Of course there were guards all over the place, and all sorts of electronic security as well, but it was oriented toward the warehouses.

Sanda, like all Cerberans, knew how to swim. When you lived in giant trees with an eternal ocean always underneath, that was one thing you absolutely learned from the start.

We were using just basic wet suits and snorkels. I

wanted no giveaways should there be underwater devices
for picking up sounds like mechanical rebreathers or an
underwater cycle. As a check, we donned the suits and,
starting from more than two hundred meters beyond the
docks, actually swam up to and under the boats, checking out the lay of the land. We found some small sensors
along the docks themselves, but not only was there nothing to keep us from the bottom of the boats but the area
was floodlit so they were nicely silhouetted.

But then why should Laroo suspect sabotage? What
would be gained? It was sure to be discovered. But even
if it wasn't, it would just slow him down slightly—he
could get boats from other places, if need be. The only
irreplaceable stuff, the organic robots, would come in
from space to his new landing pad. Anybody else
would be more interested in the warehouses, which *were*
heavily guarded, than in the boats—since, any good security officer would reason, why would anybody attack
them? Not only expendable, but you'd lose the cargo to
the depths. Nothing to gain.

They were wrong.

The next night Sanda and I returned, this time with
the bag of little goodies I had made up from Otah's materials and other sources. We easily and silently affixed
the devices not only to the gunboats but to several of
the biggest trawlers as well.

The work went so easily, in fact, that Sanda was more
than a little disappointed. It was exhausting, yes, but not
thrilling. It was in fact as easy as writing a letter.

The devices triggered at different points, and I arranged for them to be triggered from our boats when we
came within range during routine operations. Nobody on
our boats knew, of course, that they were doing anything
like that, but that didn't matter. The one thing I couldn't
control was when those defective torpedoes would be
loaded and used. I could only give them an intermit-
tently bad bork problem that would cause torpedoes to
be used up at a fearful rate. Otherwise, all I could do was
go about my normal routine and wait it out. I wouldn't
even hear the horror stories. I just hoped that the after-
math of their troubles would, otherwise unbidden, wash

right over me. It was the easiest, if least certain, way.

The best way of doing what you want to do, of course, is to create a situation wherein your enemy invites you, even commands you, to do precisely what you wanted to do in the first place—which was the plot here. If *that* worked out, then the solution of how to get into Laroo's fortress would work out, too. The easiest way into an impregnable fortress is to be invited in by the owner.

CHAPTER FOURTEEN

Facts About Myself, Some Psych Work, and Fruition

During the waiting period, Dylan began her sessions with Dumonia—and so did I, since convincing her that I loved her no matter what incarnation was at the heart of the whole thing. It was true. I *did* love her, and if frontier wife was her new goal, then that was fine with me. I wanted her to be happy, and as Dr. Dumonia had noted, under the present circumstances she was not. What was intended was to give her a sense of *security*—which in its own way was somewhat ironic. I was arranging to kill Wagant Laroo and at the same time trying to make Dylan *secure*.

What was really interesting about the process was that during a few sessions some of her visions of me and my earlier caper slipped out, as inevitably they would. Although I was paying Dumonia enough to ensure he kept his medical ethics about him, I was more than slightly amused when I discovered that he totally misread this one as another of Dylan's romantic fantasies in which I had somehow become involved. That computer fraud scheme had been so nutty and unbelievable that even her psych refused to believe it. That, of course, had been precisely why I had done it the way I had.

Naturally, during the process, I had to undergo a bit myself, but I wasn't really worried. My early training and conditioning automatically switched in under such probes, giving the psychs whatever information I wanted them to have. My probing also wasn't deep, but was only directed toward my feelings about Dylan and so I was on relatively safe ground. At the end of the second session with the psych and his machines, however, I got one shock.

"Did you know you have two surface-planted command impulses?" He asked me. "Been to a psych before?"

"No," I answered, slightly worried. "I know of *one* that should be there. Basic data about Cerberus. It was a new process they were trying with me to help people get acclimated."

He nodded. "We got that. Some of it, anyway. Quite thorough. But there's another."

I frowned and leaned forward. "Another?"

He nodded. "Actually, as I said, two. Two commands, in addition to the briefing."

I was beginning to get worried, not only because I didn't know what these were—all my agent conditioning would be beyond these machines—but also because they might betray me and who I really was. "Do you know what they are?"

"One is treasonous," he replied, sounding as objective as he did when discussing mundane matters. "It appears to be a command to kill Wagant Laroo if you can. Actually more of a reinforcement—designed to make you detest him enough to kill him. Very nice job, really. I wonder if *every* new exile is being sent in with this sort of conditioning? Still, I wouldn't worry about it. The read-outs state that you're really not violent or self-destructive. Though this impulse is enough to ensure that you're never going to love the state and its glorious leader, it's no stronger than your common impulses, which would be to damp down the actuality. We'd *all* like to kill *somebody* at one time or another, but few of us do. The impulse is no stronger than that. Unless you have a specific pre-Cerberan reason for wanting to do him in? Revenge?"

"No," I responded smoothly. "Nothing like that. I

never met the man, never even *heard* of him until I was told I was being sent here."

"All right. But that makes the second one all the more puzzling."

"Huh?"

"Basically it boils down to an instruction to call your office every so often when the opportunity's offered you, then forget all about doing so. Do *you* understand that?"

Instantly I *did* understand, but the trouble was finding a way to explain it away, all the while mentally kicking myself for not thinking of this before. The sons of bitches! Of course! How could they track me, know what I was doing on Cerberus? The organic transmitter would cease functioning the moment I switched bodies. The answer was simple and staring me in the face, but I'd been too cocky to think of it before.

There were other agents here somewhere. Probably local people, perhaps with something they wanted from outside, or perhaps exiles with close friends, family, something to lose back home. Blackmailable, to a degree. How many times had one of these come to me, perhaps when I was walking alone or on the road, and told me to call the office? Lead me, then, to a transceiver of some sort so I cold send my doings up to my other self, sitting there off the Warden system.

Done it, then promptly forgot it.

"I think I understand," I told him. "My—ah, previous activities, well, they involved some complex dealings and some people in high places. These people need certain—codes, basically, to continue to enjoy what I no longer can. This, I think, is a form of blackmail."

He smiled blandly at me. "You're a plant, aren't you? A Confederacy agent. Oh, don't look startled. You're not the first, nor the last. Don't worry, I won't rat on you. In fact it wouldn't matter much if I did, all things considered. Your profile indicates you are highly independent, and that Cerberus, and particularly Dylan, has changed you, as something always does. They keep trying though."

I sat back and sighed. "How did you know?"

"From the start—Qwin Zhang. Woman's name. Woman's body, when you came down. But you're no woman. You've never been one, except for that brief and quite brilliant cover entrance. There are differences in the brain scans between males and females. Not ones you'd really notice, but not only am I an expert, I'm also on a world where such swapping goes on all the time, so I see all sorts of switches. Remember the physiological differences between the sexes. The brain governs them, and while new patterns might emerge, there are always traces of the old. Not in your case, though. So from your appearance here, I infer that the Confederacy's finally figured out how to do what we can do naturally."

"Not exactly," I told him. "The attrition rate's high. But they're working on it."

"Fascinating. They'll have to suppress the knowledge, you know, except perhaps for the leadership and essential people. They'll have to—such switching would disrupt their society enormously, perhaps beyond repair." He smiled at the thought. "Well, it's no big thing, since the Confederacy still has the unsolvable problem. Anybody capable enough to really cause damage as an agent that they send to a Warden world changes into one of the Warden Diamond's best and most dangerous citizens. Tell me, do you really intend to kill Laroo?"

"I *should* kill you," I noted icily. "You're the most dangerous man on this planet to me. More than Laroo."

"But you won't," he responded confidently. "For one thing, that would add lots of complications to whatever you're doing now. For another, it would draw attention to you, even if you got away with it, since you'd be linked to me by your scheduled visits. I doubt if a man like you could stand being under a microscope right now. And finally, I think you realize that I couldn't care *less* if you bump off Laroo, or settle down and enjoy life, or take over the whole damned place. If you did, it'd be a change, anyway. You must believe me, Zhang, when I tell you that you're the seventh agent I've met and I haven't turned one in yet. You surely must realize by now that my own fatal psychological flaw is that I'm a romantic revolutionary anarchist with no guts, but with a taste for the good life. If you weren't sure I would stay bought, you wouldn't have come to me in the first place."

I relaxed, in spite of my old instincts. He was right, of

course—and it was unlikely that I could do anything *but* trust him. This was a smart man who'd protect himself.

"Can you remove that 'call the office' command? At least the part about forgetting I did it?"

"Sadly, no. Not with what I have. However, both commands are simple enough that they could be canceled out."

"Huh? What do you mean?"

"Well, using the level and intensity of the patterns I have here, I could lay on a new set of commands of absolutely equal strength. For example, I could lay on one that said you *liked* Wagant Laroo and had good feelings whenever his name was mentioned. This would negate the other. If I phrased the command exactly right, you'd wind up in a love-hate relationship that would cancel. As for the other—well, I could give an equal command that you will *not* use a transceiver for off-planet communication. Same effect. You'd still go when called, but you wouldn't tell 'em anything."

"I'm not too concerned about those," I told him. "At least not now. Later I might want to have that call command negated; right now it might be useful, although I'm not sure how. But I want to remember doing it, and what I did. Any tricks there?"

"After the fact, perhaps. After all, it's all there, in your memory. You're just barred from consciously recollecting it. I suspect that with a very strong neutral field under a psych converter, together with a hypnotic series, for example, we might be able to get the information out of you and recorded. When you awoke you still wouldn't be able to remember it, but you could then examine the recording and get the data no matter what."

"All right," I told him. "Let's do it."

The trick worked, after a fashion. I really don't know what is being transmitted even now, you bastards, but I now know how it's done and by whom. And how damnably obvious the whole thing was once the truth was out.

Who better to have such a spatial link with you than old fat, friendly Otah? An electronics shop with black-market connections. No wonder Otah could get whatever he needed in the way of bootleg gear! That's how you pay him, right? Very clever. I should have thought of it as soon as I figured out that you had something to do with my being sent to Medlam, so close to Laroo's Island, in the first place. Medlam, and associated with Tooker, a corporation well suited to my talents. And waiting there, where you knew I'd eventually go, was Otah.

Well, it didn't matter now. In fact it helped. Now at least I knew who—and when.

Three weeks had passed since my dirty deeds at Emyasail, and I was beginning to feel nervous. Something, I felt sure, should have happened by now. I began to turn my mind to more direct, less devious, but more risky alternatives.

The one bright spot was Dylan, whose treatment was really helping. I'll say this for Dumonia: although he is crazy as a loon and more amoral and cynical than I am, he really knows his stuff. I began to believe that in his own field he was one of the most brilliant men I had ever known. This is not to say that Dylan was anything like back to normal, but she was more comfortable with herself and with me, more like a real human being, and she seemed happier. Dumonia explained that he could do a lot, but the key breakthrough eluded him, the point of her own insecurity regarding me. It was a wall he couldn't get past, a wall erected of her deep-rooted conviction that without the pity angle I would not like her as she wanted to be and would tire of her and leave. She was very wrong, of course, but her fear was deeply rooted in her understanding of the culture from which I came and the culture of Cerberus in which she had been raised— cultures minimizing close personal attachments and emotional factors. In the Cerberan culture you held your power and position by the favors owed you or by blackmail or by some other hook. So the idea of such things not being necessary was a cultural gap that seemed impossible to bridge. In reversed circumstances, I could see myself having the same hang-ups.

"If she weren't under judgment, there *are* things that might be used," Dumonia told me. "Unorthodox, maybe dangerous things, but quite effective. But as long as she's trapped in that body we're stuck."

That thought depressed me a bit, since I most wanted the old Dylan back, a partner I could deal with as an equal, almost the part of me I'd gotten used to having. It was peculiar that I, the consummate loner, born and bred to be above such things and never before touched by them, should suddenly have this need, almost a craving, for someone else. I instinctively knew that it was my Achilles' heel. Still, the fact that I had these weaknesses, didn't matter to me as much as it had, and there was also the corner of my mind that said that everyone, even me at my old top form, had flaws and weaknesses anyway. Nobody was immune. The important thing was to recognize your own and get to know them so that perhaps they could also work *for* you.

A few days later, when I'd just about given up, my scam paid off. I was visited in midmorning at my Hroyasail office by a big, burly man whose dark eyes indicated an intelligence his general appearance belied.

"I'm Hurl Bogen," he introduced himself, offering his hand, which I shook, then gestured for him to have a seat.

"What can I do for you, Mr. Bogen?"

"I'm the security coordinator for Chairman Laroo," he told me, and my heart almost stopped. This was either very good or bad news. "You know he has an island resort south of here?"

I nodded. "I'm afraid I've even taken a vicarious look at it from one of our boats," I told him honestly. If he didn't already know that he should have. "Just out of curiosity."

He grinned. "Yeah, lots of folks do. I don't blame 'em and I don't worry about it. Basically, though, we've run into a big problem with a project we're working on over there and we need your help. We've contracted with Emyasail to keep steady supplies coming and going to and from the island, and it's worked out fine until a couple of weeks ago. We got just creamed by borks—never saw so many of 'em in my life. We got most of 'em, but they did a pretty good job on Emyasail's fleet. We're down to a dozen trawlers, all smaller types, and just one gunboat."

I feigned shock. "But hell, how many borks could you

have? Those were good crews, and we haven't had any problems of that sort. Matter of fact, we've been pretty damned peaceful around here the last few weeks, with only one or two reported and only one actual engagement."

He nodded ruefully. "No wonder. They were all down our way. The bio boys say that something attracted them down there, possibly a run of some chemical in subsurface currents. Rotten luck."

I held my breath. "How many people were lost?"

"We were pretty lucky there, although we did lose a dozen or so. Luck of the job, really. You should know that. But the main thing is, we no longer have enough boats to meet our supply needs. We've limped along with what we had for a while, using some air supply for the emergency stuff, but we really need some boats. Not trawlers—we're commandeering some big freighters now —but gunboats. We need a full four to make it out to the island okay."

"I can understand that," I replied, "but I've only got the four here myself."

"We need one of 'em," he told me matter-of-factly. "We're also pulling one each from two other companies along the coast here. You'll have to make do with three." It wasn't a request but a command.

I sighed. "All right. But I'm responsible for those boats and crews and I don't like the idea of a high-risk bork area being worked by four crews unused to each other." I pretended to think for a moment. "Look, for your safety as well as ours, why not do this instead? Pull all four of my boats and crews off—that is, let Hroyasail take over entirely from Emyasail. We'll use your surviving Emyasail boat and the other two to fill in here. The Emyasail skipper knows the territory around here, and putting three crews from three spots into a routine trawling and protection operation is a lot safer than cargo."

He considered my suggestion. "Makes sense," he admitted. "In fact I'll recommend it if you and your crews check out okay."

My eyebrows went up. "Check out? Come on, Mr. Bogen. You're a security man. You've already checked us out."

He smiled and gave a slight shrug. "Well, yes. Your boats and crews check out nicely, I admit. You, however, are a question mark to me, Mr. Zhang. You don't fit. You don't quite add up to me. Your psychological profile feels funny. I have the funny feeling I should take the rest of Hroyasail and not you."

"What! I don't understand."

"Don't ask me why. It's just a gut feeling. Still, my gut feelings are often correct. Besides, we don't really *need* you, you know."

This guy was good. I hadn't quite counted on this and I had to make some split-second decisions on him based on risky and incomplete data.

"Look," I said. "What do you think I am? A Confederacy spy or something? You have my old records."

"Yes, we do. And more completely than you can believe. We find your whole personality and profile too much at variance from Qwin Zhang's to dismiss." Then he thought for a moment, as if wrestling with himself, while I suppressed my rising tension. *Damn* Security for that sex switch! First Dumonia, now the infinitely more dangerous Bogen, smelled a rat because of it.

"Tell you what," he said at last. "I don't know your game, Zhang, nor whether you're who or what you say you are. But I'll admit I'm curious—and more than curious, I'm interested. So I'm going to take a mild risk and let you come along. What throws me is that your current profiles indicate a strong, almost overriding attachment to your wife, and she to you. That's enough of a lever for now."

I relaxed, pleased that I hadn't had to play any trump cards at this point and take some real risks. "When do you want us to move down?"

"Day after tomorrow," he told me. "Brief your crews, then switch over your computer nets." He stood up and again shook my hand. "I don't know why, but I have the feeling this is going to be very, very interesting."

I nodded. "Somehow I think so, too, Mr. Bogen. Now, if you'll excuse me, I have a lot of work to do. I want to brief my crews this afternoon and make the adjustments with Tooker."

"The day after tomorrow, then, at Emyasail." And he was gone.

I sighed, and didn't like the vibrations I got from Bogen at all. I think I knew the final step he'd taken in deciding to invite me along, and it was another one of those gut feelings. We had stared into each other's eyes—and seen each other there. One good pro always deserves another. That would mean that he'd be out to get me, perhaps out to give me enough rope.

One against one, Bogen, I thought, feeling better than I should. With the best man winning.

Moving down was no real problem since we were taking only the gunboats and the administrative staff. The layout was similar to the one we had, except the upstairs offices weren't in very good shape and hadn't been used for more than storage for some time. Dylan threw herself into getting the place into at least reasonable shape, although for the first week we felt more as if we were camping out than being in familiar surroundings, cooking over a small portable stove and sleeping on a mattress on the floor. I offered to get her some help, but she was determined to do everything herself and seemed to really enjoy it.

One major change was the large number of scanning machines you had to pass through to go just about anywhere. We all had to have new imprints taken for the benefit of the security system. I had no intention of trying that security system. I was in the big leagues here, and the schemes that had brought me to this point were no longer valid. Bogen would have me under a microscope, and I had no intention of giving him an opening unless it was on my terms. A dozen lives had already been spent getting me here; I felt a strong sense of responsibility to those innocents to do what I had been sent here to do. I owed them at least that.

Dylan suspected I had somehow engineered my way here. Hell, she more than suspected—she had worked with me before and had given me the initial information about it. Only her feeling that I would not deliberately cause the deaths of any innocents kept the peace. I had no intention of ever telling her differently.

One of the first things I had to do, though, was check the torpedoes still in the weapons warehouse against my little list of serial numbers. None of my old numbers were still there, but since we'd come down with a full load of our own in our boats I felt safe.

The stuff we ferried out to the island varied from the usual stuff—food, general electronic and maintenance supplies, that sort of thing—to major communications and computer links and lots of biolab stuff. The fact that so much was still going out, along with an occasional new face from one of the corporations, told me that Laroo wasn't having a lot of success with Project Phoenix. Still, though I was allowed to ride the boats out to the island and back, I had not been permitted off the island dock and was closely watched at all times when I went over. The strange, futurisitc structure in the center appeared even more imposing close up, but that was as near as I could get.

I kept going through everything I knew or had surmised or deduced and what I was seeing, though, and I understood the dead end I was at. Merely having access to the island dock wasn't enough, but even if I managed to sneak in I'd be caught in short order, as would anybody else I might send.

"I'm frustrated," I admitted to Dylan one day. "I'm at a dead end, and I can't figure out any way to proceed. I've been here a year now and I've accomplished a great deal—but now I'm stuck. The most frustrating thing is to be this close to all of it and not be able to move."

"You're still bent on killing Laroo, aren't you?" she responded. "I wish I could help you, but I couldn't and wouldn't. You know I can't be a party to taking a human life."

I nodded and squeezed her hand. "I know. Still, killing isn't my major objective. I want to find out about those robots. I don't like the idea of a legion of those things, all under Laroo and Bogen and perhaps the others of the Four Lords, unleashed on the Confederacy. Those things are so perfect they scare the hell out of me. If they could negate the obedience programming, that would in and of itself create a new form of life, human-looking but not at all human. Imagine such people able to think with the speed of a super-computer, literally able to control every 'cell' of their bodies, to give them whatever they want—the ability to fly, to survive in a vacuum, and all the rest. People like that mentally reduced to great super-computers in human form with only one drive, their own ultimate drive—power. They'd be nearly immortal, too—and if they ever *did* have problems or wanted a new shape or mass, they would just return here and take on a new one."

"Surely the Confederacy could track them down and destroy them!"

"Maybe. I keep remembering that one of them got into the most absolutely secure area of the Confederacy, survived all the traps and both human and robot security personnel, and was caught and destroyed in the end only because its programming demanded that it report back to the Warden Diamond. It was basically a senior clerk! Put the best, the crookedest, the nastiest minds of the Warden Diamond in those forms and—well, Dr. Dumonia suggested that the Confederacy was fragile, continuing to be a success mostly because it had never met a real challenge to it. These people alone would be a challenge. Put them together with a sophisticated alien culture and it could very well be the end of all we know. I've got to stop him, Dylan."

"You're sure he can do it, then? Did you ever think that maybe these aliens are advanced enough so that the tools simply aren't available here to get around their creations?"

I thought it over. "The Four Lords' reach goes far beyond the Warden Diamond. Although trapped here themselves, they have powerful people all over the Confederacy in their pockets."

"But would they dare it? I mean, they know the Confederacy knows about their robots, right? And Laroo can't risk tipping the aliens off, either, to what he's doing. Doesn't the fact that he's doing the research here rather than having it carried on outside show that he doesn't want to risk getting anybody outside involved?"

"I think you may be right," I told her. "Okay, let's make a few assumptions based on what we know. First, the work's being done here. Second, despite unlimited

Cerberan—and maybe Diamond—resources, and the best scientific minds around, he hasn't been able to crack it yet. The Four Lords are also in a bind: they risk the intervention of the Confederacy, and they also are risking relations with their allies." I leaned over and kissed her. "Maybe you're right. Maybe they *can't* solve their problem without outside help, and they can't get that help."

We sat there silent for a while as I considered all my options and all my possibilities. What *did* I know, and what didn't I know?

I wanted to get on the island and into the project. If in fact it was a project of the Four Lords rather than just Laroo's, as seemed likely, knocking off Laroo wouldn't matter a bit in the long run. Bogen or somebody else in this highly organized society would simply slip in and keep things going.

So what, then, did I really want to accomplish? I wanted the project abandoned, at least for now. I wanted to be in a position to change this rotten world a little, make it more human, while at the same time protecting what was important to me. Most important, I wanted to wind up a good guy to the Cerberans, to the Four Lords, and to the Confederacy all at the same time.

The idea floated in and I grabbed it, turned it first this way, then that, then decided it was so crazy it couldn't possibly work—just like the first one. I would have to be *right* on a lot of close, perhaps uncallable calls, 100 percent of the way. If I was wrong just once in this whole thing I was a dead duck.

"Dylan?"

"Yes, Qwin?"

"Suppose—now just suppose—that there was a way to put a stop to this, at least for now. Put a stop to it, cause a minor revolution that would change Cerberus to a more open and humane society, and put us on top of it?"

"You're getting crazy again. I can see it."

I nodded. "But suppose all that was possible—and if everything worked, we would kill no one, not even Wagant Laroo?"

She laughed. "Are the odds as bad as the Tooker operation?"

"Worse. I would estimate that right up to the end, to

the very last second, the odds would be five to one for discovery, double-cross, or even death. The odds of the whole thing coming off might be a hundred to one, or a thousand to one, or even worse. Depending on where and when things go wrong, it could mean anything from packing up and forgetting all about it through a really nasty judgment to death or Momrath, which is much the same thing. The risks start the moment I put the plan into operation, and after that it might not be stoppable."

She looked at me with that puzzled fascination she'd shown in the past, a flash of the old Dylan indeed. "I know you want to do it anyway. What's stopping you?"

I drew her to me. "You don't know?"

She sighed. "The alternatives, I guess, should be considered. If you don't do it, you'll wonder about it for all time, and if anything really terrible like what you were saying comes to pass, you'll never forgive yourself. I'm not sure I could, either. I don't know much about your Confederacy or what it's like outside or even on other Warden worlds, but sometimes I think we're the last two really true human beings around."

"But what about you?" I responded gently. "It might be the end of all this."

"Then it's the end. If we continue the way we are, our relationship will be hollow anyway. I'll have kids and they'll be taken away, as always. And they aren't very likely to lift my judgment, so in twenty years or so I'll be ready for Momrath or whatever it is they do to the expendables. What kind of life is that?" She stared seriously into my eyes. "You go ahead—and if my psych blocks won't interfere, include me in. You understand? If anything goes wrong, and it probably will, I don't want to keep going. One big gamble for the two of us. Everything we want—or we go out together."

I grabbed her and pulled her to me and kissed her long and hard, and we made love as if it might be the last time we would ever have the chance.

The final, the ultimate scam was about to begin.

CHAPTER FIFTEEN

Laroo's Island

I walked into the dockside security office with a sense of
doom, yet also with a feeling of intense excitement, as if
my whole life had prepared me for this moment. Enough
of the idea was necessarily left to improvisation, and
knowing I was going up against the best the planet had
to offer added to the challenge of it all.

The security officer was surprised to see me, since we
had no shipments today, but he just nodded and looked
curiously at me.

"I want you to get in touch with Security Coordinator
Bogen," I told him. "I want to see him as soon as possible."

"Bogen's on the island," the man responded. "Besides,
anything about security concerning you is more my problem than his."

"No offense, but you're too small. Besides, it's not a
breach. You're a good cop, Hanak, but this is out of your
league."

That nettled him. "What the hell are you spouting off
about, Zhang?"

"Radio Bogen and tell him I want to talk to him right
away. Just *do* it, Hanak, will you? It won't cost you anything."

"He won't see you," he sneered back at me. "He has
more important things to do."

"If you send this message just the way I dictate it, I
guarantee you I'll not only see him, but he'll break the
galactic record to get to me."

"So what's this big, important message?"

"Tell him . . ." Here goes. "Tell him that he'll never
solve the deprogramming problem no matter how much

time, money, and effort he puts in Project Phoenix. Tell him I can do it."

Hanak stared at me. "You ain't supposed to know about that."

"Just send it. And let me know when he wants the meeting. I have work to do back in my office." And with that I turned and walked out the door and back to the administrative complex. I had no doubt that Bogen would take the bait. None at all. I figured I'd hear the explosion from the office, and I wasn't far wrong.

Just a few minutes after I'd settled back down to try and get some work done, Hanak rushed in to see me.

"Well, big shot," he said, "I sent it out to the island and they threw a half-dozen shit fits. Bogen's up on the satellite but he's coming back down, personal, just like you wanted. You're to meet him in ninety minutes."

I nodded and grinned at him. "Where?"

"In his office in the Castle."

"On the island?"

"What other castle is there?" He paused a moment, looking at me strangely. "You know, Zhang, you're either the dumbest guy I ever met or the nerviest. Which are you?"

I gave him a wide, toothy grin. "Guess!"

It was harder to get up a crew on this day off than I'd figured, but with backup and emergency services I was able to muster a gunboat crew in about half an hour, leave a note for Dylan reading simply, "It's started," and head for the island.

Bogen, although coming from the space station, would probably arrive before or at least at the same time as I did, assuming he left right after sending his reply. In point of fact, his "ninety minutes" was unrealistic for me to make, short of flying over, which security really wasn't prepared for. Even at top speed of something around seventy kilometers an hour, the boat would take almost ninety minutes just to reach the island, and we'd had a half-hour delay in starting. That was just fine with me. I liked to keep people waiting and fuming a bit—knocks them off balance and makes them somewhat emotional in a situation where I'm perfectly rational and as calm as I can be given my training.

Still, it seemed like an eternity crossing that stretch of ocean. I kept having nightmares about being attacked by a bork on the way over and having the whole thing end right there.

The crossing, though, was uneventful, and soon the shining tower of the Castle hove into view, rising eerily up out of the trees. The sky was darkening, and I could feel a slight chill that told me that rain was due. It hardly bothered me. The executioner might care what sort of day it was, but not his victim.

We pulled up to the island dock and secured quickly. I walked off and up to the security building in back.

"Zhang," I told the duty officer. "Here to see Bogen."

She checked a screen and nodded. "You're cleared to his office and no other areas. Pick up your escort at the security gate."

"Escort, huh? Well, well!" I turned and walked out, then over to the gate I'd never gone through before. I had to put on a scanner to enter. Finally it confirmed that I was me and slid open, allowing me to step into a second chamber, where the procedure was repeated. Finally a far gate opened, and I walked through, meeting two khaki-clad and very serious members of the National Police, both very large men and both heavily armed.

"Walk between us and don't deviate from our path," one of them ordered. I gestured for him to lead the way. As we walked along the tree-lined paths I couldn't help but notice the special security systems all over the place and the fact that just about every step we took was being closely watched by somebody. Still, we were almost to the Castle when we had to get through yet another double gate with scan, and from there we walked on into the inner courtyard.

I was impressed. Although artificially surfaced like the docks and landing areas, and made from careful cutting of the trees, the area around the Castle was something I hadn't seen since leaving the Confederacy. They had imported sod from somewhere—probably Lilith, since that was supposedly the garden planet—and there was a huge, brilliant green lawn complete with exotic

plants and flowers. I was impressed a little more with Laroo; this was the sort of thing *I* would have done in his
position, but few others would have.

After another scan at the Castle entrance as we approached, we were inside double sliding doors. I had to
admit, despite the tales from the concubines, I wasn't prepared for what I saw. We walked through huge open
areas with incredibly opulent furnishings. Beautiful rugs
and carpeting blended into furlike couches, chairs.
and recliners. On the walls were beautiful works of original—I supposed—artwork that matched the mood of
the rooms. The only jarring note was the policemen
standing guard just about everywhere, that plus the
knowledge that cameras were following us everywhere
and seeing everything.

I never saw any stairways, although they might well
be somewhere if only for safety reasons. We went up in a
large elevator that was basically a glass tube wrapped
completely around its supporting pole. Very neat, I
thought. *They* control access to and egress from the elevators, can see you at all times, and make sure you go
only where you're supposed to.

We got off on what I thought was either the fourth or
fifth floor, walked across to the main building on a small
ramp—which had emerged when we stopped there and
pulled back into the wall once we were clear, another
nice touch—and down another corridor. This floor was
filled with rooms resembling national museums, complete with display cases and lighting. Weapons, coins, and
gems from many worlds were all there in their respective
places. I was more than impressed. I knew, too, that this
stuff wasn't Wagant Laroo's—it was just put in his
charge. Everything here was a type of object that could
survive Warden sterilization from the Cerberan organism,
and all of it belonged to somebody else, put here for
safekeeping until its owner needed it or was in a position
to enjoy it. I began to appreciate just what Bogen secured
most of the time.

Finally we reached the end of the hall and a door slid
back to reveal a modern office waiting room, complete
with receptionist but lacking, I noticed, anything to read
or look at.

My two guards flanked me while I presented myself. The receptionist nodded at my name. "Go right in. Director Bogen is waiting for you."

"I'll bet," I muttered and walked to the inner office door, then turned and looked back at my guards. "Not coming?"

They said nothing, so I opened the door and stepped inside.

It was a small, cramped office, one that looked really lived in—all sorts of books, magazines, print-outs, you name it were scattered over the place, practically obscuring an L-style office desk with computer access terminals on one side and a pile of papers and other stuff, even a dictawriter, on the other. Bogen, dressed in casual work clothes, needed a shower and shave. Clearly he wasn't prepared for this, and his eyes had an angry look.

"Clear that junk away and sit down," he snapped, gesturing to a chair. I did so and just looked at him.

"Well?" he shot. "Just what kind of shit are you trying to pull on me, Zhang, or whatever your name really is?"

"I wanted to prove a point about your operation, and I think I proved it to your satisfaction," I told him, controlling heart rate, blood pressure, and everything else, to keep as calm and relaxed as was humanly possible.

"That my security stinks? Is that it? Look, it's easy for you to have picked up that Project Phoenix name just from some of the stuff around the docks, and maybe to guess a little that we're doing some kind of biological experiments out here. But you put your finger on the heart of the research, and that just isn't possible. Aside from the Chairman, me, and six or seven other people on Cerberus—and the other three Lords—there's nobody, and I mean nobody, who knows what we're doing who ever gets off this island. I want to know how you know, and I want to know why you told me you knew, before I have you killed."

"Charming," I responded dryly. "I'll bet that line is a big hit with all the girls."

"Cut the clown act, Zhang! I'm in no mood for it."

"Would you believe I deduced it?"

"Ha! From what? You'd have to know more than almost anybody on this planet to do that."

"I do," I replied coolly. "I'm not *from* this planet. And to judge from your accent, neither are you originally. I know about the aliens, Bogen. The aliens and their fancy robots."

"How *could* you know? Or are you admitting you're a Confederacy agent, like I thought?"

"I'm an agent," I admitted. "My old employer was the Assassination Bureau of Security. They took me and using a process that seems to have been developed based on what happens here on Cerberus, they put me in Qwin Zhang's body and sent me here."

"For what specific purpose?"

"Basically because they already suspected how the robots were so perfectly programmed," I told him, lying profusely and knowing that I was being monitored by lie-detection gear of the first water. That was all right. I had been trained to fool the best of them.

"That's bullshit and you know it!" he shot back. "If they knew that they'd be on us like a ton of bricks, connections or no connections."

"They know," I assured him. "And I'm almost certainly not the only one here, although I don't personally know of any others. Sure, they could knock down your fancy space station, maybe fry this island with a deep beam—but what would that get 'em? They want the aliens, Bogen, and Cerberus is the only place so far where they have a direct link to them. They'll fry us, maybe the whole damned planet, one of these days, that's for sure —but not as long as they can gain as much or more than they lose."

Bogen chuckled. "Well, they'll have a long wait for that. I don't think even Laroo's ever met one. If any of the Four Lords have, it's probably Kreegan of Lilith. This whole thing was his idea, anyway."

"It's to our advantage not to let anybody know that— to *our* advantage, really. I don't want to be fried, Bogen."

"It won't make any difference to you, anyway," he noted. "You're a dead man right now."

"I doubt it," I responded, sounding less than upset by his threats. "Now, I'm going to make a point, and I think you're intelligent enough to realize that it's the truth. I *could* have just reported my findings on Project Phoenix to the Confederacy and let them take drastic action. I didn't. Instead I reported them to you."

"Go on."

"You know the old problem with agents sent to the Wardens. We're trapped here, same as you."

"They must have been pretty sure of you, since they could hardly keep any kind of trace on you from body to body," he noted.

"They were—and with good reason. I was born and bred for a job like this. It is the sole reason for my existence, what I live, eat, sleep, and breathe for. Once the objective's accomplished, there's no further reason for living. You've heard of the assassins before."

He nodded. "Met a couple, and I agree. Fanatics. I think old man Kreegan used to be one, in fact. So I know what you are and what you're like. I know out of your own mouth you're the most dangerous man on Cerberus to me and my boss."

"But they screwed up," I told him. "Believe me, it surprised me as much or more than it's gonna surprise them, but they slipped up. This place—well, it changed me, too. I have something to live for beyond the mission—or rather, some*one*."

Bogen seemed to relax a bit. I saw, though, that one eye kept glancing down at something beyond my field of vision. The lie-detector screen, probably. "So now you want in and you're trying to bargain with us, right? But you've got no cards."

"I think I do," I responded carefully. "The fact is, they were so sneaky they put in a deep psych command for me to report and forget I reported. I didn't even know that until I put my wife and myself under Dumonia up in Medlam."

Bogen tensed. "Then you might already have reported."

I shook my head from side to side. "No, not this much, anyway. My last report was more than two months ago, and I haven't been near the agent who can trigger the command. But I know who he is now, so they don't own me any more."

"Who?"

"Does it matter? If you nab him, they'll just establish a dozen more, ones we don't know. No, from the point at which I learned of all this stuff, I started getting ideas of my own. First, I definitely wanted in. I don't like being a prisoner any more than you or any of the rest of us, and I don't like living under the Confederacy's gun. Whether I succeeded or failed, I was a dead man—and I don't want to be dead, Bogen, and I don't want the kind of stasis my life's now in, which was the other alternative. So that got me to thinking about you and Laroo and Project Phoenix. It occurred to me that you're dealing with a product of alien technology using people who have no experience even in our end of things. Organic computing's on the proscribed list, as you know, so there are few experts in it, and those who are, are basically industrially oriented, toward the parts the Confederacy *does* use. You don't have the people or the years of research and development to solve the problem, and I think you know it."

"All right. I'm not about to grant that, but I'll admit progress has been almost nil. We know *what,* but there's just no way to take the programming out selectively— and if you take it all out, you destroy it, since life support and all the other normal functions are part of the programming molecules within each tiny cell. Basically you need a full-blown organic computer to do the job, and we haven't been allowed to get near those things in hundreds of years, not since the war."

I nodded. "There's only one place other than the aliens where the kind of expertise you need exists at all. You know it and I know it. I'm sure you've sicced some of your robots on it, but the data are too diffuse to get at. It might take years to put it all together, even assuming you can break the codes. I don't think you feel like you have years to spare."

"Go on."

"Security. Confederacy Security. They could easily tap the data, put it together, and send it to as complex a computing network as necessary to solve the problem. *They* use organic computers, you know. Not like these— not at all like these. Bt they *do* use them in their ships and modules. *They* could solve your problem for you."

He laughed. "And just like that—you ask 'em and they comply, right? Don't be ridiculous!"

I relaxed a little. "Not at all. I told you I knew who the communications agent was. If I walk in there and force him to put me through, there'll be no force, no coercion, and no forgetting. Now, just suppose I call upstairs and tell them I've got a crack at stealing one of the alien robots?"

"What!"

"Uh-huh. And I tell them how I'm going to do it. I'm going to clear it of all prior programming, then take control myself. Let my mind go into it and bring it—and me—out of Cerberus."

"They won't swallow it."

"I think they will. Remember, they don't have any way to check on the truth of what I'm saying, and the mere fact that I'll be coming to them with this will prove an unbroken line. I'm a pretty good hypnotic subject when I want to be. Let's say I tell 'em some of the robot programming is being done on this island—they already know almost as much anyway—and that I've wormed my way into the project through my Tooker associations. Some of the experts working on the project don't like the idea of working for unknown aliens, and I've got some underground help—if I can get a robot out. And the only way to ensure that is to walk out as one. They'll buy it. It sounds just like me."

He thought it over. "Too risky."

"There's no risk, if you think about it. They already know that the Cerberans are involved in the programming, and it doesn't take a master detective to figure that it has to be the space station and the island. I'm giving them a convincing scenario that meshes with my previous reports and also with what they already know. They themselves then have the choice. Either they okay the plan and give the solution to me—if *they* can solve it—or they turn me down as too much of a risk for that kind of information. I think I know them. As long as they know they have the power to destroy this whole planet, they'll okay it. The temptation, the bait, will be too great."

"Supposing they do? What happens to Cerberus when you don't deliver?"

"We have the key, and that solves the problem. Beyond that—well, I would assume protection for my wife and myself, perhaps eventually cleared robot bodies of our own. And if the Confederacy makes a move to atomize Cerberus, we'll have a lot of advance warning. You just can't make that kind of decision easily, so we'll have th opportunity to call on those aliens for help."

"And if they won't?"

"Then at least *we* get away."

He thought it over some more. "Well, what you say is true—up to a point. My only concern is that, unbeknownst even to you, this is a subtle Confederacy plot."

"Huh? What could *I* do to *you?*"

"Oh, not you. But suppose they use all this to get a authorization for planetary destruction? Suppose that's what they really want—direct cause they can get through the Councils? Their primary, maybe only, objective is to bring these aliens out of the woodwork. Maybe the authorized destruction of Cerberus is the way they're planning to do that—and we have no guarantees the aliens will protect us, or be able to. It seems to me that if they could defeat the Confederacy militarily they wouldn't have needed us in the first place."

It was a glum thought, one I hadn't really considered. As sneaky as my bosses had been, *was* this, then, their goal? Certainly it would be the ultimate goal, to smoke them out. I didn't like to think of the idea that they expected it all along, though, from me.

"It's a possibility. A risk. A big risk, I admit. But which is the bigger risk? *Not* to try it, not to crack this programming code, and still be sitting here when they eventually *do* get around to excising us? It's going to happen. You know it and I know it. If they go along, at least we have a chance—all of us."

Bogen sighed and shook his head, but all his belligerence was gone. "This is too big a decision for me to make, you know. I'm going to have to buck this to Laroo. You, too, probably."

"Suits me fine."

I sent back word with the boat crew that I would be remaining at least overnight, and gave Dylan some encouraging news, in the simplest form of code. I didn't really care if Bogen's people figured it out or not; if he didn't have some foreknowledge of me and my nature he didn't deserve to be in the business.

Then I waited for Bogen to call his boss, and finally he returned. "Okay," he said, "he's coming in tomorrow afternoon. Earliest he can get away. You're to stay here as his guest until he hears you out and makes a final decision."

"What about my wife?" I asked, somewhat concerned. "She has no credit, remember."

"She'll be all right through tomorrow. My people will be there if she needs anything. After that, well, we'll see. Remember, your future and hers are hanging by a thread right now."

Didn't I know it! Still, I was committed now. "Well, since I'm either in or dead, mind letting me see one of these wonders of the universe?"

He thought it over. "Sure. Why not. Come on."

We rode down in one of the transparent elevators, far beyond the ground floor and into the vast trunk of the main support tree itself.

The lab facilities down there were quite modern and impressive. Along the way I ran into several old Tooker employees who saw and greeted me, but Bogen wasn't in the mood to let me renew old friendships.

The center of all this activity was an eerie lab in two parts, with a monitoring and control panel of unfamiliar design on one side and a series of small booths along an entire wall. A young and very attractive woman with long black hair trailing down over her traditional lab coat was checking a series of readings on one of the machines as we entered. She glanced up, saw Bogen, and rose to meet us.

"Here's the best mind on Cerberus, and one of the best in the whole galaxy," Bogen beamed.

She smiled and put out a hand. "Zyra Merton," she introduced herself.

I was startled even as I shook the thin, delicate hand. "Qwin Zhang. Did you say Merton?"

She laughed pleasantly. "Yes. You've heard the name?"

"I sure have. Somehow, though, my vision was always of some little old man with wild hair and a beard."

"Well, I *am* pretty old," she replied good-humoredly. "In fact, I'm close to a hundred and eighty. The reason why I came here, almost ninety years ago, was not only to study the Warden processes on Cerberus but also because it was at the time the only way to save my life. However, I assure you that I am and have always been a woman, and I've never once had a beard."

I laughed back. She was charming, and a surprising answer to the question of just who Merton really was.

"But tell me, where did you hear my name?" she asked.

"I'm a product of what the Confederacy calls the Merton Process," I told her.

She seemed very interested. "You mean they solved the problems? It cost too many lives and too many people's sanity ever to be very practical, I thought. I abandoned that research when I turned entirely to researching Cerberan processes. That was—let me see—fifty years or so ago."

"Well, they solved some of it," I told her. "Not the attrition rate, though."

She looked disappointed and a bit angry. "Damn them! Damn me! My biggest regret has always been that I developed the thing to begin with and sent out the data in so incomplete a form. Still, in those days there were few people here, and not much technology or governmental structure, and I was dependent on outside support to get anywhere. Still, I'd like to give you a complete psych scan sometime, just to find out how far they *did* go with it. It's a dead end beyond what you say, I fear."

I decided not to tell her how much of a success the Confederacy thought it was. Out of respect for my counterparts on Lilith, Medusa, and Charon, I didn't want to blow too much right now.

"I'll be glad to—sometime," I told her sincerely. If I could trust anybody on this crazy ball it was probably her, if only for her scientific detachment.

"Zhang's interested in our friends," Bogen told her. "Can you give us a bit of a demonstration?"

She nodded. "Glad to. Got one that's just about ripe."

"Ripe?"

"Finished. Complete. Ready to go." She went back to her instruments and punched in a series of instructions. A slight buzzer sounded over one of the booths, and a red light came on. After a moment the red light went out and was replaced by an amber standby, then a green.

She left her panel, went over, and opened the door to one of the booths. The sight revealed startled me. It was the body of a tall, muscular man to civilized worlds' norm. He looked recently dead.

"Two one two six seven—awake and step out," she instructed.

The cadaver stirred, opened its eyes, and looked around, and into its whole body came an eerie sense of life, of full animation. It walked out of the box, suddenly appearing very natural.

I went over and looked at him. Doing so made me a little uncomfortable, because suddenly it was a person and not a thing I was eyeing as I would a piece of sculpture.

"The most amazing marriage of organic chemistry, computer, and molecular biology I have ever seen or known," Merton told me.

"This is a *robot?"*

She nodded. "They don't come packaged exactly like this, I should tell you. They arrive in a roughly humanoid shape and with the same mass, but that's about all. From cell samples supplied us, we're able to graft an entire skin onto it so perfectly that it is an exact duplicate of whoever's cell we use. The material we use for it is similar to the stuff used on the entire device, but it's capable of following and using the genetic code of the original. When we have the original subject handy, it can add in moments any scars, blemishes, or oddities to make itself a complete duplicate."

"How the hell can you *make* something like this?" I gasped.

"We don't, and can't. The Confederacy could if it wanted to. Even then, the design would be different. It takes very little time in close examination to see these devices are the product of a society and culture that is extremely alien to our own. Not that scientific laws are violated—they aren't. But the whole evolution of science up to this point came from a far different series of steps."

"Where *do* they come from, then?"

She shrugged. "We have only a few here, partly for seasoning and partly for experimental purposes. They don't let us have too many, and only when we have a specific individual in mind. They're pretty careful."

"But the whole thing is done here? All the mind-changing?"

"Oh, no. It can be done anywhere in the Warden system out to a point roughly one hundred and sixty million kilometers beyond the orbit of Momrath. Just as long as it's done in an atmosphere containing only Cerberan Wardens. I don't know the details."

"And this doesn't disturb you? That we're using these to spy on the Confederacy?"

"Not really. Why should it? Everything that government does turns to dust or ashes, including the people. We have an entirely new, fresh technology here from an entirely nonhuman evolution, and that's far more interesting. I can hardly blame them for not announcing themselves to the Confederacy. Every alien race we've ever touched we've murdered, literally or culturally."

"You sound like you would have gotten sentenced here if you hadn't come voluntarily," I noted.

"Probably," she laughed. "We'll never know. But it worked out, anyway."

I stared at her, thinking hard. "And *you* haven't been able to solve the programming riddle? If *you* can't, can anybody?"

She looked questioningly at Bogen, who nodded, and then she turned back to me. "It's not all that simple. Here, let's go over to the scope."

We walked over to the instrument cluster. "I don't recognize any of this," I told her. "Whose is it? Your own design?"

"No. It's supplied by the makers, too. That's part of the problem. Here. Look in the screen."

I looked, and saw a close-up of a cell. No, not a cell. Some sort of unicellular animal, it seemed, like the amoeba.

"That's a cellular unit from one of the robots," she told me. "It really isn't a cell, although it acts like one. It's a complete self-contained microcomputer using organic molecules and an organic structure." She fiddled with a dial and the tiny thing was gone, replaced by a horde of tiny thngs swimming in a clear river.

"The molecular chemistry itself's a nightmare," she told me. "It's not that we're seeing anything unusual. No special elements we've never seen before, nothing like that. But they're put together in a way I couldn't even imagine. There is in fact no way I know to build or grow something like that, composed of all those elements and compounds, and make it work. For example, I can take carbon chains and sulfur and zinc, potassium, magnesium, and a hundred other compounds and elements and put them together—but never would I get something like *that*." She shifted the focus to the cellular wall and blew it up almost impossibly large. "See those tiny little hairlike things? They're the electrical connectors to the surrounding cells. Like nerves, yet not like them. Connected up, they form a *conscious communications system* from cell to cell. The brain can tell any cell, or any cell group, what it wants the little bugger to do, look like—you name it, and it can do it. Mimic almost anything. Even functional things. Impossible. Inconceivable. Even in our best bad old days of the robot war we had nothing that could do that. We might have had, though, had they not banned further research and development."

"I get the point. What you're telling me is that even the Confederacy couldn't reprogram or deprogram the things."

"Nothing of the sort! Given one of these, they probably could. But we—we're at a dead end. We are able to see how it's done, but we can't do it—or undo it—ourselves. And most important, we can't tell the necessary programming from the unnecessary stuff. See?"

I *did* see. "But you think the Confederacy could?"

"Only because they have bigger, faster, quasi-organic devices themselves. I doubt if they could *duplicate* this, but they could probably tell it what to do. That's why each cell has a self-destruct switch. If it's incapacitated or in danger of capture, it simply melts down. All of it."

"Seen enough?" Bogen asked impatiently.

I nodded. "For now, anyway. I'm impressed, I have to
say that." I was more than impressed. The damned
things scared me to death.

CHAPTER SIXTEEN

Wagant Laroo

I spent an extremely comfortable night in one of the guest
rooms, surrounded by old masters and sleeping in the
kind of computer-controlled luxury I'd almost forgotten
existed. I slept late, knowing I might need all my wits
about me, and had a sumptuous brunch; then, with the
permission of the National Police, and under their extremely watchful eyes, I toured the collections upstairs.
All in all it was a fascinating day as well as providing
solutions to enough unsolved spectacular thefts to earn
any cop a seat in the hall of fame, if they have one.

In the late afternoon a flier approached and landed on
the front lawn I still found so nice. Out stepped five men,
each carrying a briefcase. There was nothing particularly
unusual about any of them, so I could only stare out the
window and wonder which was Laroo.

That, it seemed, was the real trick.

"You never know which one of the party is him,"
Bogen warned me. "He has about two dozen people that
are so good at acting that they actually represent him at
various functions, and he usually travels with a group. He
can be any one of them—and you're never sure if you're
talking to the real one or not."

That made me a little nervous. "So the real one might
not be here at all."

"Oh, one of 'em's him, I guarantee. This is that kind
of decision. The best way is just to treat *any* of 'em as if
he were Laroo. The real one'll get everything."

I nodded uneasily, and we went down to the Lord of

the Diamond's elaborate office. The idea that Laroo played such tricks made me a bit uneasy. Another thing that could go wrong, I thought nervously.

I was ushered in and introduced to a tall, handsome man with prematurely white hair that gave him the look of a distinguished politician. I looked over at the others. One of them was short and fat and looked a little like Otah, but hardly anything like I imagined the Lord of Cerberus should look. *I'd* pick that one, I noted to myself. Nobody could ever take somebody who looked like that seriously as a dictator. I looked around at the others sitting there, relaxed, eyes on me. I wondered if *they* knew who was who right now.

I went up to the Laroo indicated, stopped, and bowed slightly.

He put out his hand and flashed a politician's smile. "You don't have to go through that shit," he told me pleasantly. "We're all businessmen here. Here, have a seat and make yourself comfortable."

I did as instructed. He just sat there a moment, looking me over. "So you're a First-Class Assassin," he finally said.

"Was," I responded, relaxing a bit. "I'm no longer interested in that part of the work."

"I've viewed the tape of your conversation with Bogen yesterday and checked the instrument readings. It seems we have a truly valuable and interesting man in you, Zhang. I'm curious, though. If you volunteered for all this, why did you turn yourself around?"

"I didn't volunteer," I told him truthfully. "I was nominated, elected, put to sleep, briefed, and woke up on the prison ship."

He laughed at that. "Sounds like 'em, all right. And now you're in business for yourself. Well, I have a few more questions of a more practical nature."

"Fire away."

"First, assuming we let you go ahead with this, what guarantees do we have that you won't double-cross us?"

It was my turn to laugh. "Double-cross *you?* All by myself? Look, turn it around. Once I've done it, what guarantee do *I* have that you won't then decide just to terminate me?"

"Fair enough. So we're starting on the basis of mutual trust. A good foundation. You know what *we* expect to gain. What about you? What do *you* want out of this?"

"Well, before we go anywhere with this, I'd like my wife's judgment set aside. She's got some mental problems and the judgment stands in the way of solving them. That comes before anything—as a gesture of trust. Also, I'm going to need her, since she's the only check I have that the Confederacy's agents won't pull a fast one on me."

Wagant Laroo seemed more than a little amused, as did the others. I noted with some discomfort that their reactions to my statements were virtually simultaneous—and identical.

"You know, I like you, Zhant, or whatever your name really is. Here you are, a prisoner on my island, and with a flick of a finger I could sweep you away as if you'd never been. Considering this, you start demanding terms and advance payment! I really do like that."

"If you accept my idea, then it's perfectly reasonable," I told him. "If you don't, then I'm gone anyway."

He nodded, liking the answer. "That's true. You already know I'm interested, or I wouldn't have interrupted my very busy schedule to get here. More, there's an extra feeling of urgency on my part to accomplish something, purely for my own protection. Marek Kreegan, Lord of Lilith, was assassinated yesterday."

"What!" I felt a rise of excitement within me that I could not suppress.

He nodded gravely. "Actually, it was something of a fluke, I'm told, but it was a direct result of the Confederacy putting somebody there to do it. I, and the other planetary leaders, must assume that there are Confederacy assassins out to get all of us, a clever and backhanded way to strike at us. Tell me, wasn't that really *your* assignment?"

Honesty was the best policy. Besides, they probably had already burglarized Dumonia's office and records anyway. "Yes, it was. Deep down there's still a psych command to that effect in my brain, but if you'll check with Dr. Dumonia he'll tell you it isn't an imperative in any way—and I have already changed my game plan. I would have anyway after discovering that. I don't like people, even those people, messing with my mind."

"I think I believe you," he told me. "But that doesn't alter the fact that you're probably not the only one."

"Almost certainly not," I agreed, feeding his paranoia with the truth. "They told me at the time that there might be others."

"Exactly. That means Project Phoenix is even more urgent in my case. You know, I was giving your proposal much thought, and I got to wondering why I shouldn't just have a robot made of you. That would most certainly assure your loyalty, honesty, and cooperation."

I felt a tinge of panic. That was a line I'd thought of as one of the major risks—and one I had no real counter for.

"It won't work," I lied as smoothly and convincingly as I could. "The kind of mental training I had for my entire life would be placed into direct conflict with the robotic programming. An internal war would ensue, and at best, insanity."

He thought it over. "Maybe. Maybe not. I don't know. We've never had someone of your unique training and upbringing before. Still, I can see the logic in it, and I'll check it out with a psych. Go get some dinner now—Bogen will show you where—while we discuss this and while I check out that particular point."

The interview was over, but I didn't feel too good about it nor did I feel much like eating. Bogen, who stuck with me, seemed quite satisfied with himself, so I knew immediately where the idea had come from. After killing some after-dinner time, we were summoned back into the five presences, this time with even less ceremony.

"All right," Laroo began, "you win this round. We contacted five of the top psychs in the area, including your own, and two out of five agreed with you while the other three weren't sure. All things considered, I can't take the chance on you right now. I also toyed with the idea of replacing your wife—a very simple procedure, really."

I tensed, but said nothing.

"However," he continued, "Dumonia said that doing so would eventually turn you into a suicidal assassin of the first rank, which would mean killing you immediately. It's still an attractive idea—and you might consider that you won't know if and when I decide to do it —but I won't for now. The fact is, your kind of mind comes along all too seldom around here, and your type is one I find fascinating and useful."

"Aside from the fact that if you replaced Dylan I'd know the first time we swapped minds, assuming I survived the swap."

He sighed. "Yes, that *is* the compelling reason. See what I mean? You think right. And because you think right, I'm inclined to give you a chance. I'm inclined to let you try."

I relaxed. Second big hurdle crossed. "When?"

"As soon as possible," he told me. "Ordinarily I'd take this up at the semiannual meeting of the Lords of the Diamond, which is the day after tomorrow, but with Kreegan gone I can no longer afford the luxury of committee decisions. *He* usually made them, anyway. I will, however, bring the matter up at the time." He rose, as if to dismiss me.

"My wife," I reminded him. "The down payment."

He hesitated, then sighed. "Very well. Call Dumonia when you get back to shore. I'll arrange things through him. Get it done quickly. But the psych commands and network remain. You understand that? And the credit dependency. If she tries to get out of the motherhood again, I'll fix it so she'll beg for mercy—and you, too. Also, her life as well as yours is in your hands as of now. *One* cross, *one* little slip by either of you, *one* thing going even slightly off—even if it's something beyond your doing or control—and both of you won't be dead, but you'll wish you were. You understand?"

I nodded seriously, noting the vicious undertone in his voice. It was an edge, a *very* slight chilling undertone, that had been absent before. I realized suddenly that I was facing the real Wagant Laroo, although I hadn't the first time, and I felt the odds tilt very slightly back to me. I could recognize him if I was careful. Could pick him out in his room full of doubles. Those others, that first one, were damned good actors, but the kind of emotional undertone here had to be, I felt, unique to the real one.

Bogen suddenly paled as a worthy opponent in my eyes. I could see him shrink into insignificance in my mind, a minor-league security chief. Wagant Laroo was the most chillingly dangerous human being I had ever met. I never doubted for a second his threat, or his ability to make good on it.

CHAPTER SEVENTEEN

Creative Psych and Proposition Time

"I still can't believe you managed it," Dylan told me on the way over to Dumonia's. "My God, Qwin! In one year you've come here, framed a big shot, become a company president, wormed your way into a high-level security project, and now you've even managed to get a judgment reversed—a judgment not too many months old!"

I nodded and smiled, but that dark edge that came in when things were underway and out of control was irrepressible. "Still, we're only halfway home. The trickiest parts are yet to come, and this guy Laroo really bothers me. Dylan, I looked at him and I knew real fear, real danger. These Four Lords are the best of their kind, an ultimate evolutionary type. The whole Warden Diamond concept was the dumbest thing the Confederacy ever accomplished. I see that now. They put the absolute best, most brilliant criminal psychopaths together on one spot. The survivor of such struggles has to be the perfection of their kind—thoroughly brilliant, totally amoral, totally ruthless. He thought of every way to screw me up just while I was sitting there, and I think he knows, or at least suspects, what I'm up to."

"But you talked yourself out of his traps," she pointed out, "and he went along with you. If he's *that* good, why did he?"

"I think I know. Consider his position. His biggest weakness is his fear that at any moment his enormous and growing power may be snuffed out. It was already a fear before, but now that one of the Four Lords is gone, it has become an obsession. He has the best minds on Cerberus working on his ultimate solution—including Merton, who may be one of the best minds in that area, period. And they can't crack it. He *needs* Project Phoenix. So even figuring on a double-cross of some kind, he's willing to let me go ahead anyway. He has no choice. The only thing he can do is let me go all the way, using Merton and the others to uncover my tricks, in the hopes that I'll still solve the problem for him. It's the ultimate challenge, Dylan. He's betting his ego against mine that he can outfox me before I can outfox him."

"You're sure he knows you're planning something?"

I nodded. "He knows. Like Bogen said, you get a gut feeling, pro to pro. Like the gut feelings you relied on most heavily in the bork hunts. He knows simply because of the bottom line. Once I deliver, he has everything to fear from me and nothing to gain by keeping me around. We both understand that. He knows I'll have to pull something, and he is betting he can figure it out. That's why the free leash right now, the giving in to my conditions. It doesn't matter—as long as I deliver the goods."

She looked at me. *"Can* you deliver?"

I shrugged. "I haven't the slightest idea. That'll be up to Otah and my brother and Krega and those above *him*. In the end, I have to bet on their being able to come up with the solution to the problem."

She just nodded and turned and looked back out the window of the helicab.

Soon we arrived at Dumonia's offices and were quickly ushered in. Laroo had wasted no time in setting all this up, since he saw assassins in every corner. He was probably right.

Dumonia, too, seemed impressed. While Dylan was off with the thirteen judges assembled on Laroo's orders just for this purpose, we sat, relaxed, and talked. I liked Dumonia, although I didn't trust him.

"Well, so you blew the lid off your cover," he noted casually.

I nodded. "Why not? It was always shaky anyway.

And frankly, if *you* knew, it'd eventually get out in any event."

He winced. "Am I *that* disreputable?"

"For all I know, you're exactly what you seem to be. Or you *could* be Wagant Laroo himself. On this world, who can tell?"

He found the idea amusing. "That's the most common problem we face, you know, here on Cerberus. Paranoia. Fear of who's who. It's the thing that keeps the people in line. We have a really nasty element in our population, courtesy of the Confederacy, but it takes something like that to keep us as peaceful and relatively crime-free as we are. That and the threat of a judgment, or death, if caught. I suspect that that's why I love this place so much. Think of the *business!*"

I had thought a lot about Svarc Dumonia over the past several weeks, and had been extra careful even in choosing him. The man was a total contradiction—a totally amoral, cynical person with criminal tendencies in the mass and abstract sense, yet totally devoted to helping and curing his individual patients.

"Just your idea that I might be Laroo is a good example," he said. "Total paranoia reigns. But I'm *not* Laroo. I couldn't ever *be* Laroo, for the very simple reason that I hate governments. I hate *all* institutions, from the Confederacy to the Cerberan government to the local medical society. Organized anthills, all of 'em. Designed to stifle and straitjacket the individual human spirit, and doing a damned good job as well. Religions are just as bad, maybe worse. Dogma. You have to believe this; you have to behave like that. Run around wasting time in silly rituals instead of being productive. You know we have a hundred and seventy different faiths in Medlam alone? Everything from the Catholic Church and Orthodox Judaism—consider the problems with sex changing, circumcision, and the rest *they* face in our changeable world—to local nut cults that believe the gods are sleeping inside Cerberus and will awaken to take us to the Millennium someday."

"You're an anarchist, then."

"Oh, I suppose. A comfortable, upper-class anarchist of a sort, wearing tailored suits and having a seaside resort home I can get to in my private flier. That's where the old philosophers went wrong, you know. Anarchism isn't the way for the masses. Hell, they *want* to be led, or they wouldn't keep tolerating and creating all these new bureaucratic institutions to tell them what to think. It's an individual philosophy. You compromise, becoming as much of an anarchist as you can without worrying about man in the collective. The only thing you can do in the collective sense is to shake them up periodically, give 'em a revolutionary kick in the pants. It never lasts—it creates its own dogmas and bureaucracies. But the shake-up is healthy. When the Confederacy got so institutionalized that even a little revolt here and there was impossible, that's when dry rot set in."

I began to see where he was heading. "And you think I'm a local revolutionary?"

"Oh, you'll probably get your fool head blown off, but maybe you'll give 'em a kick. Eventually you'll become what you destroy even if you succeed, but then some new smart ass will come along and do the same to you. It'll keep the juices flowing for the long run."

I accepted that. I *liked* Dumonia, although not necessarily all that he said or believed. I certainly couldn't see myself as another Laroo and said so.

"But you *are*," he responded. "You told me you felt real apprehension and fear when you met him. Know why? Because you looked at Laroo and knew, deep down, that you were looking at yourself. Knew that you were looking straight into the eyes of somebody whose mind worked just like yours."

"I don't worship power."

"Because you've never had that degree of power, so you can't really imagine what it might do to you. But you *do* love it. Every time you took on an opponent, a system, something, and won, you exercised power and demonstrated your mastery over those people, that system."

"I hope not. I sincerely hope you're wrong. But tell you what. In the incredibly unlikely event that I ever get to be Lord of Cerberus, I'll continue to see you often just to have you kick me in the rear. How's that?"

He didn't laugh. "No, you won't. You won't like, or will choose not to believe, what I tell you, and you'll eventually grow sick of it. I *know*. You see, twenty years ago I had almost this identical conversation with Wagant Laroo."

"What!"

He nodded. "I've seen 'em come and go. I helped put him in, and I'll help put *you* in if I can, but nothing will change."

"How do you stay alive, Doc?"

He grinned. "My little secret. But remember, everybody now running this place has at one time or another been a patient of mine."

"Including me," I muttered, more to myself than him. I suddenly realized that here in this office was truly the smartest, most devious man on Cerberus—and oddly, not one to be feared, at least yet. Dumonia could have been Lord any time he wanted, but he didn't want it. Running a place was against his religion.

"Well, let's get on to more direct matters," I suggested, feeling more and more uncomfortable. "You said that if Dylan were out of judgment you might effect a complete cure. Well, that's going to be the case. Now, what needs to be done?"

He assumed a more professional tone. "Frankly, the easiest thing to do is to stop here and let it ride. The safest, too. She's quite a bit better now. She knows who she is and what she is and understands herself pretty well. Most of her old personality is back, and some of the confidence, too. The remaining block is that she's scared deep down of losing you. If not now, then years down the pike. Not by violence, which seems likely—she could accept that, I think. She lived with friends and co-workers dying for five years. But, well, losing your *heart*, so to speak. There's really only one way to show her it's a groundless fear, and it involves tremendous risk to both of you."

"I'm rolling for all the marbles now, Doc," I told him. "What's a little more risk at this stage?"

He sat back, thinking. "All right. You've heard of Cerberan-induced schizophrenia? A misnomer, by the way, since it not only has nothing to do with schizophrenia, it doesn't even have any related symptoms."

"I'm not really sure," I told him honestly.

"Well, in very rare, freak instances during the personality transfer process, we wind up with one of two very strange conditions. If we can control the transference between two minds and interrupt it at a precise spot, the data from both minds will be present equally in both brains, so to speak. We have more than enough room in there, you know. The two primary results are either eventual merging of the two into one new personality after a period of acute identity crisis, or winding up with two complete, distinct personalities in each body, alternating. Timing, mental and physical setup, and the like, is crucial and not guaranteed."

"I think I remember hearing something about it. Early on, in the briefings after I came."

He nodded. "Very rare—but we can do it in the lab. The problem is that every individual is physically different, and the time tolerances are incredibly fine to get any result, let alone the desired one. And there's very little margin for error. We've occasionally been able to get the splits to merge, but that's about it. The process is irreversible and permanent."

"And just what does this have to do with Dylan?"

"Well, barring the discovery of mental telepathy in practical form, the only way to reassure her totally—if you really are sincere and her fears are groundless—is to try something akin to this process. Control it, and stop the transference *just short* of the induced split. This will put a strong imprint from the other person in each mind. It'll be as if you could read each other's innermost thoughts and secrets—which is why almost nobody has the guts to try it. No more secrets, period. None. But if timed correctly, it'll fade over a period of weeks, leaving only the original personality and the intimate memory of knowing the other. If we could do this with the two of you, she would *know*, would have been inside your head so to speak, and there would be no more doubting you—if you really don't, deep down give cause for the doubt. For a brief time, a few days at least, she would have total access to your mind, memories, and personalities inside her own head—and you, hers."

I whistled. "That's a pretty nasty load. Do I even know *myself* what I really want or feel?"

"Yes. You see the risk. And there's the additional one. To be really effective, the timing is crucial, and as I said, individual factors not all quantifiable come into play, making it an educated guess. Split or merger is a very real possibility."

"I see. And what are the odds of something going wrong like that?"

"Fifty-fifty, frankly."

I sighed. "I see. And, just on the off-chance I still wanted this, and Dylan was willing too, how much prep time would you need? How much notice?"

"At least a day. Several weeks would be better, since I'd have to cancel a lot of my appointments, but it'll be worth it. I haven't done anything like this in a long, long time."

"How many times *have* you done it in your twenty or thirty years of practice?"

He thought a moment. "Four, I think."

"And how many times did it succeed?"

"Well, that's relative. Two worked, and two caused the induced state I mentioned. Of the two that worked, one couple became the closest duo I'd ever known, and seemed to almost reach nirvana."

"And the other?"

"Wound up hating each other's guts. That was partly my fault. I really didn't dig deep enough into one of 'em."

"We'll have to think about this," I told him. "It's a big step. And right now I can't afford to have anything less than a clear head. It's a pretty drastic step."

He nodded. "That's understandable. But I might mention something that might come in handy, maybe not. The brain-scan devices have a preset pattern they look for, allowing for variances if bodies have been switched in the electrical and chemical requirements of the new body. It's a points-of-similarity thing, like partial fingerprints. If it gets twenty points of similarity with what's recorded, it says it's you. Under *any* of the induced states, at least for a period of days, the scan machines would recognize those points in either mind. I've been playing with that idea for years, but never had a use for it. Maybe you will."

I looked at him strangely, then had to laugh. "You old anarchist bastard!"

"Things are so bright and clear again," Dylan told me as we sped away from the office. "You don't realize how much you see and hear the Warden organisms between people and things until you're deprived of that contact for the first time in your life. It's like being blind and then suddenly being able to see again."

I could only partly understand that. True, I was aware of the things, and you *could* feel 'em and hear 'em if you concentrated, but they'd become just something that was, something you damped out and never gave a thought to. And that of course may have been what she really meant. You don't notice the noises of the sea, but if they stopped, you sure would.

"You've got to watch yourself now, though," she warned. "You can wake up automatically inducted into the motherhood some morning."

I laughed and kissed her. "Don't worry about it. I can always get my body back if I want to."

We went on to talk about a lot of things, including Dumonia's radical ideas.

"You'd be willing to do that?" she asked. "For me?"

"If that was what you wanted and needed," I assured her. "That is, if we survive the next few days."

She hugged me. "Then we don't have to. Just knowing that you would is more than enough for me. Partner."

"Lover," I retorted, and hugged her back.

Otah's shop hadn't changed at all, nor had Otah himself. He hadn't seen me in some time, though, and looked surprised and pleased to see me, although less so at the sight of Dylan. Still, he pulled himself up as straight as he could and came over to us.

"Qwin! How delightful! I'd given you up for dead!"

"I'll bet," I responded dryly, then gestured with my head to Dylan. "This is my wife, Dylan Kohl."

"Your wi— Well, I'll be damned! And to think you two first met here!"

"We didn't," Dylan told him. "That was somebody else, same body."

That news befuddled him a bit, which I took as a good sign. That meant that Otah had no idea what I had transmitted, or he'd have known of Dylan, Sanda, and the rest. He didn't listen—or couldn't.

"Well, what can I do for you two this lovely day?" he asked pleasantly, and I could see that behind that fat face his mind was trying to figure out how to separate the two of us so he could force a report.

"You can can the act, Otah," I responded, a slight edge in my voice. "I know about the transmissions. I know you get your black-market electronics from the Confederacy somehow in exchange for triggering folks like me."

He laughed nervously. "Why, Qwin! That's insane!"

"No, it's true—and you know it, I know it, even Dylan knows it. Otah, this has grown bigger than you, bigger than the bootleg stuff. I need to call in. I need to call in *now,* consciously, and with full knowledge and memory of the call. You understand?"

"I don't have the slightest idea what you're talking about!"

"No more games!" I snapped. "If you want to keep this sham up, fine. There are other sources. But you'll be long gone to Momrath for inconveniencing me, I promise you. Otah, I'm in the middle of Wagant Laroo's own circle, including the man himself. One word about your off-planet bootlegging activities and you know what will happen."

He sputtered and swallowed hard. "You wouldn't."

"In a minute. Now, let's stop this old school uniform stuff, huh?" We got to be friends because that was how you got your payoffs. You used me, and that means I can now use you—or discard you. Which will it be?"

He swallowed hard, shook his head, and sighed. "Come on, it was nothing personal, Qwin. You gotta believe that. I always liked you. It was just—well, *business.*"

"The transceiver, Otah. Let's get this over with. I can only promise you that if you go along, with no funny business, no one will ever know. But we're stuck for time. We're being followed, and I had to get a doctor to remove a couple of small tracking devices placed under our skins without our knowledge. We're going on a real shopping spree and celebration today, hitting all our old haunts, and you're one. But if we take too long here, they'll know."

He looked around nervously. "Come on in the back," he turned and we followed.

The workshop was the usual mess, out of which he dug a helmetlike device and plugged it into what looked like a test bench console, then turned on the juice.

"Looks something like the brain-scan things—the big stuff," Dylan noted, and I nodded.

"It probably is something like that. Otah, without saying the magic words, how's it work?"

He shrugged. "I dunno. The transmission just goes out through the antenna on the roof I use for routine communications. I guess it's scrambled and picked up somewhere else on Cerberus, then beamed to satellite, and then to who knows where. All I know is you come in, we talk, I wait until we're alone and say—well, the key words—and you and I walk back, turn the thing on, plug it in. Then you put it on and go into a trance for a couple of minutes. Afterwards you take it off and come back out, and I spot you and make some inane comment and you pick up the conversation from there, just as if you never left."

I nodded. "Okay, good. Go on back out to the shop until I need you. Dylan can stand watch."

"Suits me," he responded nervously, and left.

I looked over the helmet. "It's a simplified version of a readout used by the Security Clinic," I told her. "It *is* something like a scan device, only it transmits the information."

"I thought that was impossible," she responded. "Nobody but you would be able to receive it."

"That's pretty much correct. Now, don't get alarmed if I go into that trance. Just let it go. Make a brief appearance out front if you want to—I want no interruptions. When I'm through, we'll see what's what."

"Qwin, who's on the other end of that thing?"

I sighed. "A computer, probably. Quasi-organic type. And eventually me."

*   *   *

And so that's where we stand to date. I hope you will evaluate this information and pass it on to the Operator at this point, rather than waiting for a final report which I *will* make—if I'm able.

There is a mild pause, like a break in the static. Suddenly a voice—no, not a voice, really, just an impression of one, forms in my mind.

"*I will inform him that the report should be read,*" the computer says, "*but not of its incomplete nature. He will make his own decision.*"

"*Fair enough,*" I tell the computer. "*How long?*"

"*Unknown. He is distraught over the Lilith report and has refused immediate reading of this one. Perhaps a day.*"

"*How, then, will I get back into contact? I can't draw attention to here.*"

"*We will contact you. Do not worry.*"

That's easy for you to say. You're only a machine, and you aren't down here with your neck in a noose.

END TRANSMISSION. READ OUT, HOLD FOR FURTHER INSTRUCTIONS.

The observer removed the helmet and sank back in the chair, looking and feeling exhausted. He just sat there for several minutes staring at nothing, as if unable to focus his thoughts or get hold of himself.

"You are upset again," the computer said.

He pointed at nothing. "Is that *me* down there? Is that really me? Is that me so romantically linked, so crazy and so ambitious?"

"It is you. The verifications and patterns show it so."

He chuckled dryly. "Yeah. Quantitative analysis. Boil everything down to nice, neat little numbers and symbols. It must be nice to be a computer, not to give a damn that everything you ever thought, ever believed, about yourself and your society is being ripped apart bit by bit, piece by piece."

"Both of us are the sum of our respective programming," the computer noted. "Nothing more—or less."

"Programming! Aw, what's the use? You're incapable of understanding this. I wonder if anybody is. Nobody's ever been put through this before—and shouldn't be, again."

"Nonetheless, we have learned much. If the Cerberan unit were to be terminated right now, we would be far ahead. We know now how the robots are programmed. We know that the point of contact between alien and Diamond is inside the orbit of the moons of Momrath. We also are in a position to strike a blow against those robots, even if we have not yet solved the puzzle."

"I'm not going to recommend frying Cerberus!" he snapped. "Not now, anyway."

"The station and Laroo's Island would be sufficient, don't you think, to put more of a crimp in the operation than even killing one of the Lords, or even all four?"

"Yeah, you may be right. But if I report this, they're going to recommend taking the whole planet out anyway. As Laroo, I think, pointed out, that might provoke a confrontation—and it would eliminate the robot threat. Without Cerberus, they couldn't program the things with real minds."

"Why do you hesitate? Ordinarily you would think nothing of such a step."

"Why—" He paused, sitting back down. "Yeah, why do I?" he asked himself aloud. "What's it to me?" That was his training and experience talking, but that was only his intellectual side. There was another side of him, one he had never suspected, that had now revealed itself not once but twice. With Lilith he'd finally convinced himself that it had been an aberration. He was a technological agent, and in a nontechnological society he'd had to change and compromise. But Cerberus? The excuse was gone in that situation. And yet, and yet—had only his twins down there changed?

Still, there was only one thing to do, and he knew it.

"If it makes your decision any easier," the computer put in, "the elimination of Cerberus would not stop the robot operation, only set it back. As long as any of the Cerberan variant of the Warden organism remained in alien hands, it could be used anywhere in-system. We had the indication that it already was being so used. Nor is it yet the time to provoke a confrontation. We have insufficient data yet to get such a resolution through Council for the sector's elimination. All we might accomplish at this point is a refusal to defend by the enemy, the elimination of the Warden system or its neutralization, and we would then lose all links with the enemy."

He considered that, and it made sense. "All right. Transmit the proposal and problems to Security Central and get an evaluation and recommendations."

"Being done," the computer responded.

CHAPTER EIGHTEEN

R&D—And a Split Decision

I notified Bogen that I had initiated the contact and could only wait for results. It would be a nervous time, I knew. The only bright spot was that Dylan was so much fresher, so much more alive, her old self again in spades. If it hadn't been for the noose, those next three days would have been among the happiest and most satisfying of all my time on Cerberus.

At the end of the third day, though, I received a call from someone I didn't know and from a place I couldn't guess. I knew Bogen had the phone bugged and traces all over the place, but somehow I doubted his ability to do much about this.

There was no visual, only audio. "Qwin Zhang?"

"Yes?"

"Your proposal has merit, but nothing can be done without a physical sample."

I held my breath. "How much of a sample?"

"About fifty cubic centimeters of brain tissue and another fifty of other random tissue should suffice. Is this possible?"

"I'll see," I told whoever or whatever it was. "How do I let you know?"

"We'll be in touch." The line was dead.

Dylan came in. "Who was that?"

"You know who," I responded. "Time to call Bogen from the security shack."

Bogen insisted on talking to me directly, so I got on the line.

"They contacted me. They need two tissue samples."

He nodded. "Figures. We anticipated that. Just out of curiosity, though—how did they do it? You haven't been out all day and you haven't received any phone calls or messages."

"They called. On my phone. Surely you tapped it."

He looked more than a little nervous. "We sure did. And your quarters, too. I'll check it out, but nobody called me from the monitors like they were supposed to. I don't like this at all. They shouldn't have power like that—not here."

He switched off, but I understood his concern and waited at the shack for a reply, which wasn't long in coming.

"Did you check the phone?" I asked him.

He nodded worriedly. "Sure did. No calls of any kind. And we ran the recording of our bugs in your place, too. You wouldn't be kidding us, would you, Zhang? There's nothing on that tape but normal noises. No conversation on the phone at all, although we do hear your wife come in and ask 'Who was that?' and you reply."

I whistled. I *was* impressed, and so was Bogen—although not in the same way. "So what's the answer?"

"You'll get your tissue."

"Shall I pick up or do you deliver?"

"Very funny. No, it should be picked up, if only because I want to see how they collect the sample."

"I'll get a boat started up," I told him.

"No. As a precautionary measure, Chairman Laroo has ordered that you never set foot on the island again, and security will fry you if you try."

"That wasn't part of the deal!" I protested, feeling a sinking sensation in my stomach. If Security went along, I *had* to be there.

"We changed it. You're an admitted assassin, Zhang, and we don't minimize your skills. We can't afford to take the chance."

"But I'll *have* to come in if they give me anything."

"Nope. If anything physical is required that we can't handle, you will send your wife. Between the psych implant against killing and the fact that she's native here, we feel more secure."

"I don't want to involve her! The deal's off!"

He laughed evilly. "Well, that's okay, but if it ends here, so do the both of you. You knew that when you started this. Our terms, or forget it. Now, send her over in two hours exactly."

"All right," I sighed. "We'll play it your way—for now. But wait a minute. She's of the motherhood. She's prohibited from ocean travel."

"By whom? By authority of Chairman Laroo she's been waived of that requirement. Anybody gives you trouble on it, tell 'em to call me."

"But I thought she had a psych implant against it."

"We had Dumonia remove it. It wasn't much anyway. Go ahead. We're wasting time."

I switched off, feeling less than confident now. This change in the ground rules was hairy indeed.

Dylan, however, didn't mind at all. "We're in this together, remember."

I nodded, and could do nothing but see her down to the docks and off. She was excited to be on a boat again, for she really *did* love the sea. She was gone about five hours, a time in which I became increasingly worried and nervous. When she finally returned I was still apprehensive.

"They didn't do anything to you, did they?" I asked her.

She laughed. "No. Mostly I took the wheel and had a little fun. That's a gorgeous place inside there, though. They only let me on the main floor, handed me the sealed, refrigerated case here, and marched me back."

I looked at her nervously. Would I know if they'd replaced her with a robot? Would I *know* if they'd pulled a fast one with the psych machines?

Well, I'd know the robot situation if we swapped during the night, and I felt reasonably confident that at this stage they wouldn't risk it. For the other, I'd need Dumonia—if I could trust him.

Suddenly I stopped short. "That son of a bitch!" I muttered. "That crafty old anarchist!"

She looked at me, puzzled. "What? Who?"

"Dumonia. He's ahead of both Laroo *and* me. He knew this all along, set me up for it."

Points of similarity indeed. He knew damned well what he was saying when he told me that.

We just brought the case into the apartment and then waited for more instructions, which didn't come. Finally, we got tired of waiting, caught up on some routine paperwork, and went to bed.

In the morning the case was gone. I reported the theft to Bogen, who sounded none too thrilled about it all. He'd had lenses, agents, and a full security system trained on the place, and nobody had seen a thing. Worse, at least five separate tracing devices had been placed inside the case, all of which had functioned perfectly, apparently. At least they still were—they said the case was still in the apartment. The trouble was, no amount of detection and searching could reveal it, although they finally came up with a tiny recording module, something like a tiny battery, wedged inside the floorboards.

Sure enough, it nicely broadcast exactly all five tracing signals.

Bogen was both furious and unnerved by it all. I knew damned well that a far different account would reach Laroo, one in which Bogen didn't look so bad.

I had to admire the Confederacy's other agent in this area, who seemed head and shoulders above even me, at least in audacity. In fact I was so impressed that when he called and made an appointment for us to go and see him, I could hardly wait.

The samples had been gone nine days, and during that time little of interest happened in any direction, except Bogen was becoming more impatient and threatening toward us. Both Dylan and I started becoming a little fidgety.

Finally, though, the call I'd been expecting came, and off we went, almost certainly unsuspected by Bogen and his other people.

"I always wondered how and why you thought you could talk so freely in here," I told the agent.

Dr. Dumonia smiled and nodded to the two of us. "Oh, it's a couple of modern wonders, really. The fact is, the place *is* bugged and Bogen's people are right now hearing us talk. They're just hearing something quite different. It's so pleasant to work in a technological environment that's a few decades behind what's current."

"You and your anti-Confederacy anarchism. I *knew* there was something funny about you, almost from the first, but I missed which side you were on."

"I'm on my side, of course. So are you two—on your side, that is. I'm not a fraud, and everything I told you is true. I *detest* the Confederacy. If I could be sure these aliens of ours wouldn't eliminate our whole race I'd cheer 'em on as they attacked. There would be no better shot in the arm for humanity than a good old war, as long as the race survived to build and grow. I'm a psychiatrist and I like my creature comforts and my profession, too."

"Then why—why work for them?" Dylan asked, puzzled.

"Oh, I don't *work* for them, exactly. On Cerberus, I just about *am* the Confederacy, which I consider a delicious joke on all of them. It has to do with the way I look at history and society. Qwin here might tell you more about that. I don't really feel like philosophical chats right now, there's too much to be done. Let's just say that I use them, and they use me, and we both profit. I also use Laroo and his people and system. All to the end of living exactly the life I want, doing what I most love to do."

"I don't understand why they sent me at all," I told him honestly, and with the respect one professional offers another. "You could have done everything easier and with less risk yourself."

"Well, that's not true. If I got anywhere near Laroo, or particularly his island and his projects, I'd put myself in severe and immediate danger, and I'm just not willing to do that. As I said, my activities are designed to keep me in my own personal nirvana as long as possible. Indefinitely, I hope. So I'm not the active sort. Laroo wouldn't trust me near him or his babies simply because I know too much about him, know him too well." He grinned. "He thinks I had a partial mindwipe about that, which is the only reason I'm still here. But on a secondary level, I'm too close to the problem. I've been here too many years, know too many people. My objectivity is askew. A fresh analytical mind was needed to filter the information. Besides, this way it's *your* neck, not mine."

"But you said you didn't care if the aliens attacked," Dylan noted, still trying to figure him out. "Then why help against this thing at all?"

He became very serious. "The ultimate threat is those creatures out there. Perfect organisms, superior in every way. *Homo excelsus*. And all totally programmable. Totally. Everybody's programmed, of course, by what we call heredity and environment. But we have the ability to transcend much of that, to become what the programming never intended. That's why no totalitarian society, no matter how absolute, in the whole history of mankind has been able to eradicate the individual human spirit. These—robots—are the first true threat to that. *They can't outgrow their programming.* Speaking euphemistically, I have to say they scare the shit out of me."

We both nodded. "So where do we go from here?" I asked him.

"All right. We've analyzed and dissected and played with all those samples. I'll tell you the truth: Dr. Merton is correct. We have no idea how to duplicate that stuff, how to make it ourselves. It's beyond us. Which is all to the good, I think. I wouldn't want us in that business, either, although Lord knows they'll try. That's the bad news, sort of. The good news is that though we can't make it or quite understand how it works, we know how to work it, if that makes sense."

"Not a bit," I told him.

"Well, I don't know how to make a pencil, but I know how to use one. Even if I'd never seen one before, I could still figure it out. The operation, that is. We have an infinitely complex variation of that same idea here. Now, if the basic obedience programming were in the very chemical makeup of the thing, we'd be up the creek. No way to deprogram without dissolving it. Fortunately, it's not. There *is* a programming device inside each quasi-cell, and it's quite complex and we don't understand it at all. However, knowing that, we can *add* programming information and be sure that the information is transmitted and stored via the Wardens the same way as we swap here. There's an interesting implication that the thing is designed with Wardens in mind and might not work without them, which may mean that these things were developed by our aliens specifically for us here and now on Cerberus, rather than just being a variation of something common in their culture."

"So? What does this all mean?" Dylan asked impatiently.

"Well, half the samples went elsewhere and the other half stayed here, where my lab handled the practical stuff. Wardens were essential, which we have in abundance here. It became a fascinating exercise, really. Using an organism we can't understand at all to influence another we can't build or duplicate. But with the aid of computers Outside and my lab here, we finally managed to get a readout. The chemical coding language is quite complex and not at all human, and that's what took the time, but we finally got it. Fortunately, the basic obedience stuff is duplicated in every cell. In fact all the cells, whether brain or tissue, are pretty much the same and can simply become what they need to be. The programming is rather basic, as it would have to be, since it's serving as a single base for all the different robot agents being sent back to all sorts of different worlds, jobs, and conditions."

"Then you can get rid of it?" I pressed.

"Nope. But we can do the same thing I suggested as regards psych implants. The aliens have made it impossible to separate the basics without lousing up the cell and triggering this meltdown process. But the cells are programmable, remember. They have to be. So we can *add* programming to override these initial steps. Cancel it out completely, leaving an unencumbered mind in a super body."

"Surely Merton would have thought of that," I pointed out.

"Undoubtedly she has," he agreed, "but she hasn't the computer capacity and resources to get a complete readout of the codes, let alone actually break the language used. That's what stuck them. You wouldn't believe how much time had to be devoted to *this*. Laroo was right: not every string he could pull could commandeer that much computer time for that long without drawing Security like a magnet."

"So we can give him what he wants," Dylan sighed. "How does that gain *us* anything?"

"Well, for starters, we'll need to give you some absolute protection. That can be accomplished simply by making it a complex psych implant using the Security system. Laroo can't break it. Nobody here could break it —or if they can, we've already lost the war. In other words, you can't give the information to 'em unless you want to, which is the only time you'll know it—and you'll just know what to do, not what you're doing. And it'll have to be done one at a time, one robot at a crack."

"But he's only allowing *me* on the island," Dylan pointed out. "Doesn't that mean he'll just make a robot out of me and have it any time he wants it, block or no block?"

"No, and there's an easy way to handle that. Very easy. We add another block, similar to the dozens Security's placed in Qwin's brain over the years, as insurance. There is no human who cannot be tortured, or chemically or mechanically made to spill his or her guts. None. So we use the same methods to make sure that such operations will be fruitless. It's what stopped Laroo from going the robot route with Qwin here right from the start. I'm sure he has some implants like this himself. It's really simple, and one they'll understand and accept right off because they all know the type. Basically, it's a psych command that erases other information if any sort of coercion is used, and can even be triggered voluntarily if need be. He won't *dare* try anything with you. He'll need you totally—and he can use his own psych staff to verify the existence of the erase commands. It protects you— and it protects us."

Dylan looked puzzled by that, but I understood him exactly. "He's telling us that not only can it be triggered voluntarily or involuntarily to erase, but it can be triggered externally, as by a Confederacy agent. Similar to what the good doctor here must have used on Laroo to ensure his own well-being."

Dumonia smiled and nodded.

"But you're *still* going to give him the answer he wants!" Dylan protested.

Dumonia kept smiling.

"Think about it, Dylan," I urged her. "You've seen the way we think long enough. Remember the cells are *programmable*."

She considered what he said, and I was beginning to think we were going to have to spell it out. Then suddenly I saw her mouth shape into an oval. "Oooh . . . Oh, my!"

"My only regret is that Dylan's going to have to do this all alone," I grumbled. "I hate missing out on the climax of the big scam. After all, it *was* my idea."

"There's a way, you know," Dumonia reminded us softly, but I could see that eager gleam in his eyes. "I set things up in case you wanted to do so."

Dylan looked at him, then me. "I—I'm not sure I want to," she told us. "I'm a little scared of it."

"I told you there was a big risk," the psych admitted. "And I understand the cautions. First, you could split. No big deal there, as long as you wanted to stay together forever, and that's a long time. You could merge into one new personality. Or you could find out that deep down neither of you really like the other. That's particularly the case in Qwin's mind, since he was a *very* unpleasant person until he came here and found his humanity."

She nodded. "I know. That scares me the most, I guess. I love him the way he is now, but I don't think I would like the old Qwin very much at all. He sounds too much like Wagant Laroo."

I looked at her strangely. Her, too?

"There's another possibility," he suggested, sounding slightly disappointed at her reluctance. I think he really *wanted* to pull off that merger or whatever, strictly for professional curiosity or maybe just for fun. "I could manipulate the psych plants so that it would require *both* of you to complete the programming operation."

I looked up at him accusingly. "That's what they recommended right along, wasn't it? To make sure that neither of us could be held hostage to the other's cooperation."

He coughed apologetically, then shrugged and gave a wan smile. "So would I be a good doctor if I didn't point out all the interesting alternatives?"

"Then we go together, whether they like it or not," Dylan said firmly. "That's good." She hesitated. "But won't this operation point an arrow straight back to you? Won't they *know* who had to be the one to give us the information?"

"If it works, it's academic," he told us. "If it doesn't, or if anything goes wrong, well, I have contingency plans. Don't worry about me. I cover myself pretty well."

"I'll bet you do," I said dryly. "Well, let's get on with it."

As I predicted, Bogen *didn't* like the revised plan, not one bit.

"What could I do?" I asked him innocently. "Here we were going down the elevator from Dumonia's office and suddenly, bang, out go the lights for both of us. We wake up half an hour later halfway across town, with the briefing identically planted in our minds and the blocks in place. You know your men lost us."

He didn't much like *that,* either, but could only glower. "Well, you got it, though?"

"We got it." I had already explained the terms and conditions, spelling out the protections in pretty absolute terms.

"The boss isn't gonna like this," he growled. "Too much to go wrong. Tell you what, though. Both of you come out to the island this afternoon. Bring your things—it might be a long stay."

I nodded and switched off.

"You really think Laroo will buy it?" Dylan asked worriedly. "After all, he's putting himself in the Confederacy's hands."

"He'll buy it," I assured her, "although cautiously. He doesn't have any choice, as you know who assured us."

"Imagine. The most powerful man on Cerberus, one of the four most powerful in the Diamond, and maybe one

of the most powerful men around today, period—and
he's scared to death."

"Or *of* it," I responded. "Let's go pack."

CHAPTER NINETEEN

The Final Scam

Dumonia and his psych computers had built a tremendously impressive psychological profile of Wagant Laroo
over the years, back from when he first appeared on
Cerberus. Like all the world's most powerful men
throughout history, his one fear was assassination or even
accidental death. This fear had actually been com-
pounded, on Cerberus, where one had the potential of
eternal life—and that was the kicker. By now Laroo felt
almost omnipotent, but to feel like a god and know you
were potentially mortal was unthinkable. The robot was
the closest thing to total security he could ever hope to
achieve. Even more, it would allow him to leave the
Warden Diamond—and return—at will, thus making
him certainly the most powerful man our spacefaring race
had ever known. Surrounded by a small army of the
more obedient sort of organic robots, he would be virtually invulnerable. Freed from all wants and needs of the
flesh, and armed with a mind that could operate with the
swiftness and sureness of a top computer, he would be a
monster such as mankind had never known.

He knew this, and knowing this, his psych charts said,
he *had* to take the risk. Add to that the knowledge that
one Lord had already been done in, a Lord he obviously
respected and feared—and you had the clincher.

I couldn't help but think that Dumonia had had a lot
to do with my decisions. I'd been seeing him—and he'd
made sure it would be him—about Sanda and Dylan
before I ever made the Project Phoenix move, and then
I'd done nothing until just the right psychological time—

for Laroo. Then and only then had I been willing to take the ultimate risk and had done so practically without hesitation, and with Dylan's full support. I couldn't help wondering how many little pushes and suggestions I'd gotten from him even before I ever heard of him.

It really didn't matter now, though. Now everything would come together—or it would all come apart. Either way, I had no doubt he was protected. And I suspected that if we *did* fail there was a cruiser even now prepared to come in close to Cerberus and fry Laroo's Island to a crisp and us with it.

Dylan and I spent almost a full week in the Castle, mostly enjoying ourselves, although always under the watchful eyes of guards and scanners. She was fascinated by the broad, green lawn, something she frankly had never even conceived of before, and by the museums of stolen goods, many of which I could take pleasure in explaining both the history and something about the culture they came from.

When we first arrived we were taken to Dr. Merton, who ran some tests to verify our psych commands and blocks, as expected, and had done so. Unlike the first time I'd come to the Castle, I wasn't bluffing now, and they confirmed it.

We also revealed, without really knowing or understanding what it was we were describing, the type of equipment necessary for the deprogramming process. Merton checked the information over with interest, obviously understanding it, and assured us that it could be assembled quickly.

Finally, though, and without any real warning, a big transport landed on the front lawn. Out stepped five people as before, only these were far different. Dylan surveyed them curiously from the window. A teenage boy and girl. A tough-looking woman pushing forty, with short gray-brown hair. A short, wiry man of very dark complexion. And finally, a young executive type in full dress suit and black goatee.

"He has quite a collection," I said approvingly. "Nobody there I recognize, from last time or any other time."

"They walk alike," Dylan noted. "Even the women walk just like the men."

"I see what you mean. They're good actors. Damned good."

"How will we know which one is the real Laroo? Or if *any* of them are?"

"That's simple," I replied. "The real one will be the one left alive and kicking at the end."

We were summoned by National Police to the downstairs lab complex, and left immediately. All five of the newcomers, plus Merton and Bogen, awaited us in the lab, where seats had been provided—five seats.

"They even cross their legs the same," Dylan whispered, and I had to suppress a laugh.

We stopped. The goateed businessman proved the spokesman this time.

"Well, well. Qwin Zhang. I hadn't intended that we meet a second time, but you made it unavoidable."

"I'll make it worth your while," I promised him.

"You better," he growled. "I don't like people who make themselves indispensable. You should understand that."

I nodded. "You have a choice. We can call this off and all go home."

He ignored the comment and looked over at Dylan. "A pleasure. I trust all is satisfactory with you now?"

"Extremely," she responded with that old confidence. I could almost read her mind, and I loved her for it. Wagant Laroo would be a pantywaist in a bork hunt.

"You understand there'll be some, ah, tests first?"

We both nodded. "We're ready when you are," Dylan told him. "The truth is, we no more understand this than you do." She looked them all over. "Who goes first?"

"None of us. Yet." He nodded at Bogen, and the security man went out. Two technicians wheeled in a device that was pretty much what we'd described several days before to Merton. It was a hybrid, and obviously had been knocked together, but if Merton thought the thing would work, well, I was willing to trust the expert.

The machine looked essentially like three hair driers on long, thick gooseneck poles leading into a rear electronic console. They brought it in, and with Merton's help fitted it against the instrument cluster that was a permanent part of the lab. Cables—lots of them—were taken from the top rear of the console part and plugged into the instrumentation, and switches were thrown. Merton checked the whole thing out, then nodded. "It's ready."

I looked at the gadget and couldn't shake the feeling that I was about to be electrocuted. According to Merton, it was a variation of the basic psych machine itself, although without a lot of the electronics and analytical circuits. In effect, it would allow Dylan and me, if we concentrated, to send impulses from our own minds to a third. What we were going to do could have been done by computer, of course, but then they wouldn't have needed us. Chairs were brought in and placed under the gadget, and the helmets or whatever were adjusted to hover just over each one.

"Now what?" Laroo demanded.

"We need a robot," I told him. "First we feed the signal into the robot, then you slide a mind in there any good old Cerberan way."

"Merton?" he said expectantly.

The doctor walked over to one of those booths and opened it, obviously prepared for this. The robot inside didn't look like a cadaver this time, but was fully prepped and animated. Still, it had a totally vacant look that would be impossible for a human being to duplicate.

Dylan and I both gasped at the same time. "Sanda!" she breathed.

No, it wasn't Sanda, but it *was* a perfect facsimile of Sanda's current, and Dylan's old, body.

"I see I haven't underestimated the old boy," I muttered. "What a rotten trick."

Laroo—all the Laroos—looked at us with smug satisfaction. "I thought that if you were going to try any funny business, you'd be less likely with somebody you both know and like," he told us.

"You're going to kill her after this works!" Dylan accused. "You know I can't be a party to that. I *won't* be."

One of the Laroos stopped, thought a moment, and I thought I could see his eyes divert to his side. For a moment none of the others moved. Then, interestingly, I saw the teenage girl very naturally reach up and scratch her nose. Goatee paused a moment, then pretended to consider things while glancing idly at the ceiling. Finally he said, "All right. But for reasons you obviously understand, you're making a test *very* difficult—and I will not proceed without one."

I shrugged. "Don't look at me. *I'm* not the one who insisted that the psych inhibitors remain on."

"It wouldn't matter. I wouldn't do that kind of thing anyway," Dylan snapped.

Laroo sighed, and thought again. Finally he said, "Leave us for a minute, both of you. Just wait outside."

"Stuck you, didn't I?" Dylan stated smugly. I nudged her to keep her from baiting him further. Paranoia, psych profile, or not, Laroo was psychotic enough to call the whole thing off if we pushed him far enough. We left and stood outside.

"Don't bait him," I warned her. "There are some things more important to him even than this."

She just nodded and squeezed my hand. We didn't have long to wait, and were soon called back in by Dr. Merton.

"All right," Laroo said, "let's start one step at a time. First we'll just try and clear a neutral body, so to speak. Then I want Merton to check it over, see what can be done, what we can learn. Will you go that far with me?"

We looked around and found that the robot Sanda had been replaced in its booth. I looked over at Dylan and shrugged. She sighed. "What choice do we have? All right."

The robot body produced was impressive. A huge bronze giant of a man with great, bulging muscles. If any one of them looked the part of a superior human being, this male body did.

It too was as blank as you could conceive, and had to be helped to the chair by Merton and two assistants.

"I gather they don't have much basic programming when they arrive," I commented.

"Activate, deactivate, walk forward, walk back, stand, and sit—that's about it," Dr. Merton told us. "They don't need much else, although in a pinch I can feed in some basic additional commands. When you're putting a complex human mind in there, you don't need much."

I could see her point. I took the seat next to the thing and Dylan sat next to me as Merton pointed out which helmet was which.

This point was the most nerve-racking to me personally, since I knew Laroo was as close to totally evil as anyone I had ever met and I hardly trusted him a moment.

The helmets came down and I felt clamps and probes fit into place.

"All right," Dr. Merton said. "You're all set, just like you told me. Do whatever it is you do."

I relaxed, took a couple of deep breaths, heard Dylan doing much the same, then concentrated—no, *willed*— the transfer.

I felt a momentary dizziness, or disorientation, and then it was over. So quick I could hardly believe it.

"That's it," I told them. "Dylan?"

"I guess so. If that funny feeling was it."

The assistants flicked switches retracting the probe helmets and gently lifted them off our heads—all three of us. I got up, as did Dylan, and we stared again at our giant. He looked as blank as ever.

Laroo looked over at Merton. "Anything?"

"Well, we recorded *something*," she told him. "Who knows what?"

Realization came suddenly. *Countermove*, I thought. Laroo's move, really. Merton had created the Merton Process, by which I was here—and in four other places, too. A process that didn't transfer but *recorded* and *duplicated* information in the brain! If she had the key from both our minds, then Laroo no longer needed us at all. It had been a major mistake on my part. I fervently hoped that this hadn't been overlooked by Dumonia or Security.

Two assistants came up with a crazy-looking vertical hand truck, and as we watched, the giant was told to stand, then tilted forward, the platform slipped expertly under, then tilted back so it could carry the thing, which remained rigid. They wheeled him out a side door as we watched, Merton following.

"Where are they going?" I asked curiously.

"First we'll hook him up to some analytical equipment to see if the change took—or if it did, whether or not we can see it at all." Laroo told us. After—well, one step at a time."

Several nervous minutes passed, after which Merton reappeared. "Nothing I can measure has changed in the slightest," she told us. "As far as I can see, everything's the same."

Laroo sighed. "All right, then. We have to try a live test. Is Samash prepared?"

She nodded, went to a wall intercom, and called somewhere. I could recognize Bogen's voice, and the surprise when she said Samash. But in less than a minute an unconscious figure was wheeled into the lab, one that looked nothing like the giant. In fact he was the oldest man I'd ever seen on Cerberus, although he was probably no more than in his middle fifties.

"Samash is a technician here on the island," Laroo told us. "He's very loyal and not very bright, but he's handy. And you can see, he's more than overdue for a new body."

"Some new body," Dylan noted.

"Well, now he'll look the part."

"Is he—drugged?"

"Kabash leaves, a substance about which, if I remember, you also know something."

"Oh."

I got the picture. This was the stuff that forced a transfer if anybody else in the area had it or was receptive. Samash was wheeled into the other room, and soon Merton and the techs all emerged. "Give him, say, an hour," she said confidently. "I'll call you."

And with that, we were dismissed. As before, we were fed, and very nicely, too.

"I'm still worried about all this," Dylan commented.

"Want more?" I told her about my fears of Merton.

She sighed. "Well, we did our best, right?"

"We'll see. It isn't over yet."

An hour or so later we *were* called back and found the lab the same except that now the great giant seemed to be sleeping on the table in the center. Of the old body I saw nothing, and guessed it had died from lack of interest.

Even though the giant robot was sleeping, there was

no doubt that there was a *person* inside it now. It looked natural and normal; somehow even its sleeping face was filled with an indefinable *something* that had not been there before.

"Wake him up," Laroo ordered.

Dr. Merton and the two assistants stood back, and there was a sudden, almost deafening cymbal-like sound all around. It subsided quickly, and Merton called, "Samash! Wake up!"

The body stirred, and we stepped back to the wall and held our breath. Even the Laroos seemed extremely tense.

Samash's eyes opened, and the face took on a puzzled look. He groaned, a deep bass, shook his head, and sat up on the cart and looked around. "Wha—what happened?" he managed.

"Look at yourself, Samash," Laroo told him. "See what you've become! See what I have given you!"

Samash looked and gasped, but seemed to realize instantly what had happened. He jumped off the cart, stretched, smiled, and looked around, a slight smile on his face. I didn't like the looks of that smile.

"Samash, I am Wagant Laroo. Activation Code AJ360."

The giant hesitated a moment as if puzzled, then started to laugh.

"Samash, Activation Code AJ360!" Laroo repeated uneasily.

Samash stopped laughing and started looking mean and irritated. He turned and pointed to goatee. "I don't take orders from you," he sneered. "Not any more. I don't take orders from nobody! You don't know what you did, Laroo! Sure, I know what Activation Code AJ360 means. But it don't mean nothin' to me. Not me. You fouled up this time, Laroo." He turned, ignoring us all, and said to himself, aloud, "You don't know the feeling! The power! Like a *god!*" He turned back to goatee. "Greater than you'll ever know, Laroo, whichever one of you you really are. You're *through* now!" With that he lunged for the five Laroos.

"Protect me!" screamed the teenage girl we'd rightly fingered, real panic in her voice—and to our shock the other four, plus Merton and the two assistants, all leaped upon the giant with almost blinding speed. In seconds they had pinned him to the floor.

"Oh, my God!" Dylan breathed. "They're *all* robots!"

The girl—Laroo, the real one—stepped nervously to the far wall and tripped the intercom. "This is Laroo. Security on the double!"

On the double was right: we were suddenly flooded with National Police as well as Bogen, arms drawn.

"Stand away from him!" Bogen shouted. "Let him up!"

As quickly as they were on him, they were off. Then it took only a split second for Samash himself, in one motion, to get to his feet and charge Bogen and the NPs.

He never had a chance. As lightning-fast as he was, they were even faster. Beams shot out, covering the giant's body. It was an incredible display, since any one of those beams would slice steel in two and burn, melt, or disintegrate almost anything we knew—and all they did was stop Samash. No, not even stop him, exactly— just slowed him to a crawl. He was almost at them, but they kept firing and stood their ground—and suddenly you could see the beams finally taking effect.

There was a sudden, acrid smell. Samash stopped, looked surprised and more confused than anything, and then, with a bright flash that almost blinded us, ignited and melted down into a horrid little puddle of goo. At the moment of ignition, all weapons stopped firing at the same moment, so no beam went astray—an incredible display.

"*All* of them," Dylan was saying. "Even Merton and Bogen and the cops. *All* of them."

"Except her," I noted, pointing to the still frightened face of the teenaged girl. "That's Wagant Laroo for today."

Laroo regained some of his—her—composure.

"Yes, that's right. All the important people on the island are robots," she admitted. "Normally only two of my party are, but I didn't want to take any chances this time. You can see why."

I nodded. "But you took one anyway. He almost got you, even after taking enough blast to melt the Castle."

She nodded nervously. "We'll have better precautions next time. I really didn't quite expect that."

"Well? What did you expect?" Dylan asked caustically. "You're not exactly the most popular person on Cerberus, you know, and you suddenly gave the old guy tremendous power and a real shot at you."

"Enough for now!" Laroo snapped. "Get out of here, you two! Go back upstairs until I call for you again."

If you need us again, you mean, I thought grumpily.

"Well, at least we proved the system works, I think," I noted, and both of us exited at that line, carefully stepping around the NPs, Bogen, and the still smoldering pile of goo.

"How *did* they stop him?" Dylan wondered later that evening.

"I suspect they trained a bunch of different weapons at different settings on him," I told her. "His cells kept compensating for one kind of charge and he was finally faced with too many contradictory conditions to fight at one time. One got through, damaged something vital, and triggered the self-destruct in the cell units."

She shivered. "It was horrible."

"I don't think we'd have liked Samash, either," I pointed out.

"No, not that. The fact that they're all robots. Even that nice Dr. Merton."

"I know. Even *I* didn't think of that, which shows how paranoid he really is. And damn it, they're so stinking *real!* Bogen, Merton—they were real people. Natural. Understandable. They looked, talked, acted just like normal people." I shivered a bit. "My God! No wonder they haven't found a defense against these things!"

"So now what do we do?" she asked.

I sighed. "We relax, get some sleep, and find out if we still wake up in the morning."

We *did* wake up and were served an excellent breakfast to boot. It was a good sign. After we ate, dressed, and cleaned up a bit we were summoned back down to the lab. Laroo had not changed bodies and was alone now, except for Merton, Bogen, and a figure we both recognized.

"Sanda?" Dylan called.

She saw us and smiled. "Dylan! Qwin! They told me you were here! What's this all about? I don't remember anything since I went to sleep last night back in Medlam."

Dylan and I both suddenly froze, the same idea in our heads, and Sanda, sensing something wrong, stopped too, her face falling and looking a little puzzled. "What's the matter?"

I turned to Laroo. "You did it anyway."

She shrugged. "She was here, prepped and available. We decided to see if Dr. Merton's process would work from what we took off of you."

"I gather it didn't, or we wouldn't still be here," I noted.

Sanda looked genuinely bewildered. "Qwin? Dylan? What's all this about? What are you talking about?"

"That's quite enough, Sanda," Laroo told her wearily. "Go report to housekeeping on the third level."

Suddenly Sanda's manner changed. She forgot about us and her bewilderment, turned to Laroo and bowed. "As you wish, my lord," she said, then walked out. Our eyes followed her in stunned amazement.

"How does it work, Laroo?" I asked. "I mean, what does the programming we're canceling *say?*"

"You don't know? Basically it states that you love, admire, worship, or whatever whoever gives you the activation code, and that you wish to serve only the wishes of that person or that person's designated agents. It's sort of an emotional hook, but it's unbreakable. They genuinely love me."

"Surely you don't activate all of them yourself!"

"Oh, no. But if one of my own robots is the activator, it works out to the same thing, you see. Complicated, though. Takes a computer to remember who loves whom."

"Well, I gather your process doesn't work in recording, anyway," I said, relieved, then turned to Dylan. "Don't worry about Sanda. She's still all there. She's just finally in love with somebody else."

Laroo sighed. "Well, we've done what we could. Merton assures me that the language is still gibberish. There's no reason why it shouldn't record and work—but it doesn't. We tried it out not only on Sanda but on three others, varying various factors. It didn't work with any of them. I sadly have to admit that I need you."

Back to my move, I thought, and *thank you, Dr. Dumonia or whoever.*

"Ready now to take the plunge yourself?" Dylan asked Laroo.

She nodded. "But I'll need a half-hour or so in prep. However, I want to warn you—both of you. *Any* funny business, anything wrong with my programming, even accidentally—*anything*—and you won't live a moment. My robots will tear you to pieces, slowly."

"There won't be any double-cross," I assured her. "We have some stake in this ourselves, remember. We're the only two people who *can't* become those robots—and as such, we need you for new bodies at the proper time. It's an even trade."

"It better be." It was that little girl's voice, but that same threatening tone was there.

We waited anxiously for the prep.

To our surprise, the body Laroo had chosen was rather nondescript. Average in almost all respects—civilized world standard male, nothing exceptional, wouldn't stand out in a crowd.

"Still, it makes sense," I told Dylan. "The last thing he wants is to attract attention to himself."

"It's not too bad," Dylan said critically. "Looks a little like you, really."

"Thanks a lot."

In a short time the girl's body was wheeled in by Bogen and the two attendants, and off into the back room. We wasted no time at all giving the jolt to the selected body on the helmet machine, and watched that body get the same hand-truck treatment to the back.

I spent the time looking around the lab, asking Merton a few inane and useless questions and taking in what I could. Something bothered me. Laroo had given in too easily, even considering the stress. Particularly after last night. Something just felt *wrong*. It was a while, though, before I figured out what it was and whispered to Dylan. "Another trick. Don't fall for it."

She frowned and whispered back so low I could barely hear, "How do you know?"

"Those were cameras up there yesterday, I'm sure. Now they're laser cannons."

"You sure they weren't there before?"

"Sure. Otherwise they'd have used them on golden boy. They can track anything in the lab on those camera mounts."

"So he switched during the night."

"Uh-huh. Clever bastard, but hold tight. We got him." His move. No countermove.

A little over an hour later they wheeled the body back out and went through the wakeup routine again. At least this time we held our ears when the cymbals clanged. The man on the table went through much the same experience as Samash had the day before, and when he jumped to the floor, he looked around wonderingly. "Well, I'll be damned!"

Merton went up to him. "Activation Code AJ360," she said to him.

The man paused, smiled, and shook his head. "Nope. There's a little tingle when you say it, like something inside wants to be let out, but it's suppressed, all right." He sighed. "I can see now what Samash must have felt. Like a god!" He turned back to Merton. "You have no *idea* what it's like—oh, of course you do. I forget. It's—unbelievable!" He turned to us.

"Well," he said, "it works. It really works! You have no idea of the *power* I feel. It's almost a strain to slow myself down to your speed just to converse with you. Every cell in my body's *alive!* Alive and sentient! Sentient—and obedient! The power in each is phenomenal! Even I had no idea until now just how powerful and versatile these bodies were. And *no pain!* Every single body has some pain at all points after they're born. We live in it. The rush of freedom—to be totally immune to it—is almost awesome!"

"I wonder, though—if these aliens are so smart, why did they allow this loophole to slip by?" I commented. It was a genuine question that really bothered me.

He shrugged. "I don't know. That bothered me, too—but not now. Nothing," he added darkly, "will ever bother me again. Nothing and no one." He looked back at us. "Now, tell me. Give me one reason why I should allow either of you to live one moment longer."

Dylan looked up at me questioningly, as if to ask, are you *sure* this isn't Laroo?

"Trust me," I whispered beneath my breath, then turned to Laroo once more—the fake Laroo, I was convinced. "Insurance," I told him aloud, hoping his superior hearing would mistake her glance and my comment for reassurance and nothing more sinister. "Remember Samash. And that robot they caught in Military Systems Command. Hard to kill—yes. Superior? Yes. But immortal? No. Not only that, but I think I know, or can at least guess, the alien's insurance policy."

Both Merton and "Laroo" looked startled. "Go on," he urged.

"They—these robot bodies. They'll wear out. They have to, no matter how good they are. What's to prevent a little bit of that programming we dared not touch, the autonomic system's, say, from suddenly stopping at some predetermined point in time?"

He looked nervously at Merton. "Is this possible?"

She nodded. "But not insurmountable. Remember, I have recorded your and other key people's imprints. As long as you update them periodically, as they do in Confederation Intelligence, you can die over and over again —and still live again."

That explanation satisfied him, and also me. "Might I point out, though, that if somebody's not there to clear the next robotic programming, you'll have to go back into a human body again."

"Never!" he snapped. "Once you've been in one of these you can never go back. Not for an instant! Never!" He realized the implications of what he was saying. "Yes, all right. You're right. But you will remain here on the island as my permanent guests. For all time, and from body to body. You say you want to keep your children, raise them yourselves. Very well, do so here, in the midst of luxury."

"Luxury prison, you mean," Dylan responded.

He shrugged. "As you wish. But it's velvet-lined and gold-plated. You'll want for nothing here. It's the best I can do. You and I both know the Confederacy will quickly know that you played false with them. They'll want you at all costs, to erase that information which is probably easily done with a simple verbal trigger—so I can afford you no contact except with my own."

"And if they fry the island?" Dylan asked pointedly.

"They won't," he responded confidently. "Not until they're *sure*. And we'll give them corpses to look at and a really convincing story, not to mention obviously dismantling Project Phoenix. Everything back to normal. They'll believe something went wrong, all right—but it'll be convincing. Believe me."

I sighed and shrugged. "What choice have we got?"

"None," he responded smugly. At that point I noticed he was alone in the center of the room. The laser cannon opened up, and after an incredible time he too was melted. I looked over at the brownish patch left from Samash, still there despite a strong cleanup effort. My move—success. And check.

Dylan gasped and whispered, "You were right!" Then she hesitated. "How will we know the real one?"

"We won't," I told her. "Just trust me."

We went through three more acts, each one as or more convincing than the first. Each time the robot was suddenly melted. I kept wondering if they'd all be so confident if Laroo told them what had happened to their predecessors.

The fourth one, though, another civilized worlds standard like the others and equally nondescript, was different at the end. He finally smiled when we finished the interminable wonderment conversation and sighed. "All right, that's it. Enough fun and games. I'm convinced." He turned, gestured, and we followed nervously, avoiding the puddles and eyeing those cannon suspiciously. But, this time, we all walked out of the lab.

Bogen awaited us, and bowed. "Did all go well, my lord?"

"Perfectly. Hard as it is for me to believe, it seems as if our friends here really delivered. Take good care of them, Bogen. Give them anything they want—except communication with the outside world. Understand?"

"As you wish, my lord," he responded respectfully.

We all began walking down the corridor and I started singing, softly and lightly, a ditty I neither understood nor had known before, but one I knew the function of quite well.

> " 'Twas brillig, and the slithy toves
> Did gyre and gimble in the wabe;
> All mimsy were the borogoves,
> And mome raths outgrabe . . ."

Laroo stopped and turned, curious. "What's that?"

"Just a little light song from my childhood," I told him. "I've been under a hell of a lot of tension the past few weeks, remember, and it's gone now."

He shook his head in wonder. "Umph. Crazy business."

"We'll see you again, won't we?" Dylan asked him innocently.

"Oh, yes, certainly. I have no intention of leaving just yet."

"Maybe a month from now," I suggested helpfully. "At least then we could talk about our lives here."

"Why, yes, certainly. In a month." And with that we went up to the quarters level while he and Bogen went elsewhere.

Freed at last of the constant guard, we walked out onto the lawn and sat in the middle of it, basking in the sunlight and warmth, stripping down and lying next to each other. For a while we said nothing. Finally Dylan spoke. "Did we actually just take control of the Lord of Cerberus?" she asked, wonderingly.

"I'm not sure. We'll know in a month, certainly," I replied. "If he lives to get off this island, he's the real one. If not, we'll just do it again and again until we get it right. But I think he was the right one."

She giggled. "In a month. We have a whole month. Just us, here, with every wish catered to. It'll be a relief. And then . . ."

"It's all ours, honey. All Cerberus is ours. Good old Dr. Dumonia."

She looked startled. "Who?"

"Dr. Du—now why did I bring *him* up?"

She shrugged. "I don't know. We sure won't be needing a psych any more. Except maybe to get that implant to report out of your head."

"Yeah, but I suppose that Dr. Merton could do that as well. I hope so."

She turned to me. "You know why I love you? You did it all yourself! Without *any* outside help! You're incredible!"

"Well, the Confederacy had to go along with the plan, you know."

"Pooh. You knew it all along. Every single one of your crazy, mad, nonsensical schemes worked. In a little more than a year you went from exile to true Lord of the Diamond."

"And you're the Lady of the Diamond, remember."

She lay idly for a moment, then said, "I wonder if we'd shock anybody if we made love out here?"

"Only robots, probably," I responded, "and we know what they're worth."

She laughed. "Shocking. You know, though—remember when they suggested we put ourselves in each other's minds? Who was that, anyway?"

I shook my head. "Too long ago. I can't remember. Not important, anyway. But why do you bring *that* up?"

She laughed. "It wasn't necessary. I'm a part of you anyway now. And you, me, I believe. At least I can't get you out of my head."

END REPORT. REFER TO EVALUATION. STOP TRANSMISSION STOP STOP.

Epilogue

The observer leaned back, removed the helmet, and sighed. He looked weary, worn, and even a little old beyond his years, and he knew it.

"You are still disturbed," the computer noted. "I fail to see why you should be upset. It was a splendid victory, perhaps a key one for us. We will henceforth have our own spy in the ranks of the Four Lords."

He didn't reply immediately. The computer irritated him, and he couldn't quite explain that either. Computers and agents were well matched to each other, and before he had always somewhat identified with the machine. Two of a kind. Cold, emotionless, logical, a perfect analytical working team. Was he in fact irritated at the computer, he wondered, or was it that the machine was such a reflection of his own previous ego and self-image that he couldn't bear the mirror it presented? He wasn't sure, but his mind did seize for a moment on the word *previous*. A curious word. Why had he used it? Had he changed that much?

I haven't changed! he told himself, banging a clenched fist down on the armrest. *They changed. Not me!*

But they are *you*, his mind accused.

What was so different about their missions, anyway? The planets, to be sure, were far more exotic than the majority of plastic and steel worlds he was used to, but not as different as a few on the frontier. Never before had that changed him. What had—down there?

Perhaps it was the fact that they—his other selves— knew that they were down there for life. No check back in, debrief, and lay off until the next mission. No return to the good life and the best the Confederacy could offer. A last mission. No more responsibilities to the Confedacy, no more working for anyone except yourself.

All his life he'd been trained to think in the collective sense. The greatest good for the greatest number. The preservation of the civilized worlds from internal forces that threatened it. As long as humanity in the mass was bettered, they'd taught him, it hardly mattered that a few had to die, innocent or not, or even an entire planet. Bettered. Protected. Saved.

Did he really believe that any more? he asked himself.

Plastic worlds. Did they, then, breed plastic people? Was Dumonia right? Was the alien threat more of a threat because of the way we'd remade ourselves?

And yet the civilized worlds were happy places. There was no poverty, few diseases, no hunger or other forms of human misery that had plagued man through the ages. Not even the frontier, with its vast technological support, was as miserable or threatening as past frontiers had been. He was raised in that culture and, seeing the historical record, believed in it. It *was* better than anything man had ever had before. That was the trouble. The basic puzzle that haunted him. It was neither bad nor evil. It was a *good* society full of happy, healthy, well-adjusted people, on the whole.

That thought cheered him slightly. Dumonia was wrong, too, in believing that the sparks of human greatness were extinguished in such a system. They hadn't been extinguished—they merely lay dormant until needed. The Warden Diamond proved that.

Humanity's strength and hope lay in that dormancy. In the fact that under trial the reserve was there to adapt, to change, to meet new challenges. Dormant but not extinct.

That thought brightened his mood somewhat, although not completely. That was fine for the collective, but not for the individual. Not for one particular individual in five bodies.

Twice now he'd followed himself on dangerous ground. Twice he had seen himself change, in some ways radically, putting aside his self-image, his devotion to duty and ideals—even the ideals themselves. In all cases he'd violated, once and for all, his personal standards, his own sense of himself as a bedrock, the ultimate loner who uses but does not need. These, too, were dormant inside him and came out when—well, when the leash was cut. The leash that bound him to the Confederacy, its authority, principles, and ideals. He had willingly been leashed, and the cut had not been of his own making, but still it was there.

What disturbed him most of all was that he was still on that leash. That very thought was horrible, a violation of all he'd ever stood for or believed in, but it was a truth that had to be faced. Those men down there—they thought themselves trapped, and him the free man. They were wrong. And as they envied him, so he too was envying them.

But, still, there was a mission, a problem. One that even *they* had continued to serve. He could at least address that.

"Evaluation?"

"Correlations with Lilith are fascinating," the computer told him. "There are certain totally irrational common grounds."

He nodded. "I saw them."

"We'll need to get someone out to Momrath, of course, but that may have been done for us from the data sifting in. We will also have to intensify patrols throughout the Warden system, since there *are* points of contact between alien and human here somewhere."

"We should tighten up on vacation resorts back in the civilized worlds, too," he noted. "Obviously that's the key place from which they kidnap their targets. They would have to be missing for at least a week to ten days."

"That can be done only to a point," the computer pointed out. "It would be helpful to know who selects those targets. So far the grand design, the pattern, eludes me, mostly because we do not have enough identified robot agents to correlate their positions. It seems obvious, though, that the aliens are quite subtle."

"We knew that from the start. Who the hell would ever

imagine an enemy alien force hiring the chief criminal elements to do all its advance work?"

"I worry that it is more than advance work. Let us postulate one or two conditions that seem reasonable from the facts, bearing in mind that we are dealing with alien minds developed in an unknown evolutionary pattern that might not follow our logic."

"Go on."

"We assume that they are either numerically inferior to our own forces or unwilling to take the casualty rates a direct attack might bring."

"That may be a wrong assumption," he pointed out. "After all, if they can make super-robots like this, they could do their fighting entirely with surrogates."

"Perhaps. But I tend to believe that the processes involved in perfecting these devices is too long, involved, laborious, and costly for such mass production. Instead, I suggest that their plot may be *entirely* on the subtle side. We have been looking too hard at the direct military option."

"Huh? What do you mean?"

"Suppose their plot is to bore from within? To weaken and disrupt key services, key facilities, the bedrock of our economic and social system? A carefully chosen and placed organic robot could do more harm for longer periods than any direct attack by planet killers. I need only look at your own psychological reactions to the Warden to see how easily and subtly we can be turned. The human race and its culture is such that it would destroy itself rather than be conquered from outside. There are parallels among the early independent planets and even earlier, in the age of nations on a single planet. We have often come very, very close to self-destruction rather than total capitulation. A direct attacker, then, would have nothing to win."

"So you think the choice of the Four Lords was more than just a clever expediency? Hmmm . . . Laroo indicated that Kreegan was the original mastermind; and Kreegan, to be sure, had a penchant for nasty and sneaky plots and behavior." He sat back. "Now, let me get this straight. You're suggesting that the aliens never intend to attack us directly. That the war they chose is the war they are now fighting. That they aim for internal disruption and collapse by exploiting our weaknesses, rather than conquest."

"It makes the most sense."

He nodded. "And it's the least costly of the alternatives. None of *their* people are exposed or jeopardized. The Diamond, and through it the robots, do the dirty work. It's even cost-effective. Assuming you're right—analysis?"

"If the Four Lords are directing things in this manner, and choose properly and correctly, it will work. Not quickly. We might not even *know* or *realize* the extent of their success until it's too late. And with the promise of those robot bodies and the chance to escape, the end could come not by kidnapping key people and replacing them but by mobilizing the best criminal minds of the last seventy years in such bodies and loosing them on an already weakened and infiltrated Confederacy."

The prospect appalled him. "But wait a moment. Only Cerberan criminals could be used. Those on the other three worlds have other Warden variants that won't step aside to allow a Cerberan mind-switch."

"Have you forgotten the Merton Process?"

He whistled and shook his head. "Then finding the aliens, bringing them out into the open, is our only hope. And we have no guarantees that there are any of them anywhere near the Warden system. It could all be handled by robots and third parties hired by the Four Lords."

"Perhaps one of the remaining two will tell us for sure," the computer suggested hopefully. "Or if not, perhaps our in-system patrols will get lucky."

"Correlate and transmit what we've got," he ordered. "We just have to wait and see."

"Done."

The man walked back to the living quarters of the module on the great picket ship, poured himself a drink, and sat down on his bed. All that the computer had suggested disturbed him, but still he couldn't bring his mind to focus for long on the larger problem and plot.

Cal Tremon ... Qwin Zhang ... Ti ... Dylan Kohl ...

Like some song that gets stuck in your mind and you keep hearing it over and over whether you want to or not.

I can't get you out of my head.

About the Author

JACK L. CHALKER was born in Norfolk, Virginia, on December 17, 1944, but was raised and has spent most of his life in Baltimore, Maryland. He learned to read almost from the moment of entering school, and by working odd jobs had amassed a large book collection by the time he was in junior high school, a collection now too large for containment in his house. Science fiction, history, and geography all fascinated him early on, interests that continue.

Chalker joined the Washington Science Fiction Association in 1958 and began publishing an amateur SF journal, *Mirage,* in 1960. After high school he decided to be a trial lawyer, but money problems and the lack of a firm caused him to switch to teaching. He holds bachelor degrees in history and English, and an M.L.A. from the Johns Hopkins University. He taught history and geography in the Baltimore public schools between 1966 and 1978, and now makes his living as a freelance writer. Additionally, out of the amateur journals he founded a publishing house, The Mirage Press, Ltd., devoted to nonfiction and bibliographic works on science fiction and fantasy. This company has produced more than twenty books in the last nine years. His hobbies include esoteric audio, travel, working on science-fiction convention committees, and guest lecturing on SF to institutions such as the Smithsonian. He is an active conservationist and National Parks supporter, and he has an intensive love of ferryboats, with the avowed goal of riding every ferry in the world. In fact, in 1978 he was married to Eva Whitley on an ancient ferryboat in mid-river They live in the Catoctin Mountain region of western Maryland.